I0653978

MAGIC REDEEMED

THE WITCHES OF SALT SPRING ISLAND
BOOK THREE

CORALIE MOSS

PINK MOON BOOKS

Published internationally by Pink Moon Books, British Columbia, Canada.

ISBN 978-1-989446-02-7

Editor: Michelle Meade

Cover Designer: Elizabeth Mackey

Proofreading: Beth Attwood

❀ Formatted with Vellum

ACKNOWLEDGMENTS

Love and rockets to #MrMoss

My gratitude to cover designer, Elizabeth Mackey.

My gratitude to editor, Michelle Meade.

My gratitude to proofreader, Beth Attwood.

My gratitude to Accountability Maven, Michelle McCraw, and to the gals who keep me afloat: Jess, Lily, Marit, Meka, and Tara.

The Beta Belles—Diane Castro, Kim Kennard, Leslie Mart, and Michelle McCraw. Thank you for reading MAGIC REDEEMED and sharing your thoughtful feedback.

The ARC readers. Your time is valuable and I am so grateful you read and reviewed. Thank you.

GLOSSARY OF CHARACTERS

(IN ORDER OF APPEARANCE)

Calliope Jones: Earth witch, 41-years-old, divorced mother of 2 sons.

Salt Spring Island: Located in the Salish Sea, SSI is sandwiched between Vancouver Island and mainland British Columbia.

River de Benauge: Druid. Can shift into a river otter.

Noémi: Earth witch. Sister to Calliope's mother. Former owner of the house & property now owned by Calliope.

Bear: Noémi's animal familiar. Able to manifest only partially.

Rose de Benauge: Plant witch. Healer. Sister to River. Maven of the Pacific Northwest Covens.

Kerry Pippin: Possibly a Magical. Assistant to Calliope at the Agricultural Commission's office.

Christoph Courant: Gyrfalcon shifter. Calliope's paternal grandfather. Also known as, 'Gramps'.

Harper: Gyrfalcon shifter. 18-years-old son of Calliope. Dating Leilani Brodeur.

Thatcher: Empath and Raccoon Whisperer. 16-and-a-half-years-old son of Calliope.

Benôit Courant: Gyrfalcon shifter. Calliope's father.

Airlie Redflesh: Water witch.

Leilani Brodeur: Witch. 18-years-old. Dating Harper.

Tanner Marechal: Druid. Can shift into a ghost wolf.

Ni'eve du Blanc: Druidess. Head of the Keepers. Tanner's teacher. Mother of Jessamyne.

Idunn: Norse Goddess. Holder of the Apples of Immortality.

Jessamyne du Blanc, aka the Apple Witch: Druidess, Keeper, Tree shifter. Former love interest of Tanner Marechal.

The Keepers: Women who tend to the trees that bear the Apples of Immortality.

Sallie Flechette: Fae. Magical talents as yet unknown.

Josiah & Garnet Flechette: Fae. Currently remanded to an underground prison for Magicals outside of Vancouver, BC.

Jasper: Maine coon cat. Service animal to Magicals. His magic mitigates the effects of Fae magic.

Wes (Wessel Foxwhelp): Druid. Can shift into a river otter.

Kaz (Kazimir Wickson): Druid. Can shift into a river otter. Love interest of Belle de Boskoop.

Meribah Flechette: Fae. Calliope's ex-mother-in-law. Mother of Doug and Roger.

James Brodeur: Half-witch, half-human. Botanist. Married to Malvyn. Father to Leilani.

Malvyn Brodeur: Sorcerer. Enforcer for the Board of Magical Governance. Jeweler. Father to Leilani.

Pokey: Raccoon. Thatcher is his favorite human.

Rowan Renard: Witch. Healer. Ob/gyn. Follower of Airmid. Calliope's best friend.

Genevieve (deceased): Witch. Calliope's mother.

House: The house where Calliope lives. Grows more sentient as times passes and as Calli's magic strengthens.

Roger Flechette: Fae. Son of Meribah. Twin brother to Doug.

Belle de Boskoop: Plant witch. Healer. Love interest of Kazimir Wickson.

Clifford & Abigail Pearmain: Druid and human. In their eighties. Owners of Pearmain Orchards.

Hyslop & Peasgood Pearmain: Cliff and Abi's grandsons. Have completed a 10-year training to become druids.

Doug Flechette: Fae. Calliope's ex-husband.

L'Runa: Witch. Fetish-maker. Specializes in blood magic.

The Witchling Way: Similar to the Girl Scouts (USA) and Girl Guides (Canada). For young witches.

Maritza Brodeur: Witch. Necromancer (acquired). Professor of Necromantic Studies. In her forties. Sister to Malvyn. Aunt to Leilani.

Alabastair Nekrosine: Necromancer (born). 32-years-old.

The Old One: The crabapple tree that grows next to Calliope's herb and vegetable garden. Anchors four portals. One is known.

Brooks Family Farm: The large farm where both Harper and Thatcher work in the summer, and on Saturdays.

Faebook: A social media network for the Fae.

Clyde: Son of Noemi. Cousin to Calliope. Has one sister.

Jack Kaukonen: Wolf shifter and officer of the RCMP (Royal Canadian Mounted Police).

Wolf: Tanner.

CONTENTS

MAGIC REDEEMED

INTRODUCTION

I was finished with the Apple Witch. My oldest son was in the Northwest Territories, healing from his wounds. His brother was at home, anxiously awaiting the arrival of his own magic. And Tanner? The druid was in the French Alps, finalizing his commitment to his teacher.

My discomfort was growing. I didn't trust the quiet that had settled over the island. Nor did I like the instability I was feeling as my earth magic was challenged by a stronger force.

Funny, how everything can change by being in the right place, at the wrong time. Or maybe, it was the wrong place, at the right time.

CHAPTER 1

I had never again wanted to go through the agony of having an enchanted tattoo removed. But here I was, on a sunny day in the middle of September, facedown on a padded chair at Salt Spring Island's only tattoo parlor, getting inked.

"Ready?" River, a druid of indeterminate age, settled onto the rolling stool and donned a pair of bright blue non-latex gloves. His cohort, Tanner, had been the one to excise the old tattoo by means of a chant, which had lifted the ink along with a layer or two of my skin.

"Ready as I'll ever be," I said, giving a relaxed thumbs-up. A local plant witch assured me I could use a heavy hand with her proprietary blend of pain-relieving herbs. The drops tasted of crushed grass and they worked wonders. I was in no discomfort, physical or emotional.

Once I was certain I wanted this tattoo, I tasked River with creating a design that would honor my aunt Noémi and her animal familiar, a towering Kodiak I knew as Bear. Noémi, who had raised me from age six on, died from complications of her dementia over the recent Labor Day weekend.

The stories I told myself about my aunt and her hands-off

parenting methods were based on a series of profound misconceptions. I had thought she didn't care about me or resented that my mother's death left her with a third child to raise.

The truth came to light in August. In a moment of lucidity from the depths of her dementia, Noémi had shed a hazy beam of light on my childhood. It wasn't that she didn't love or care about me, it was that she had promised her parents she would hide me and my mother after we were forced to flee the idyllic small town in Maine we called home.

Who Noémi was hiding us from, and why, were details she took to her death.

"I have to shave you, Calli."

The serious edge to River's voice made me laugh. "Is that you telling me politely I have a hairy back?" I asked, quieting the question that ran in a loop in my head.

"No, no, not at all," he said. "You've got peach fuzz. I didn't want you to be surprised at the sensation."

"So far, everything about this experience rates better than my first." I shivered as a droplet of cool water slid underneath my armpit. River patted my skin dry, sprayed a different liquid across my neck and upper back, and pressed on the transfer.

"Stay still." His fingers smoothed over the paper before he peeled it away. "Perfect."

I exhaled, sinking the front of my chest into the towel-covered padded support, only to jerk when he started the motor that powered his set up, and again when the needle bit into my skin.

"Steady, Calli. The first few minutes are the hardest." River set up a rhythm of applying gentle pressure with both hands, lowering the needle, then drawing a line. I wanted to say the movements were soothing, but the constant drone of the motor set my teeth on edge.

"I'm creating the outline first," he said. "Then I'll fill in the solid areas."

"How long did you say this was going to take?"

He chuckled. "As long as it needs, Ms. Jones."

I tuned out the noise, slipped one foot from its wedge-heeled flip-flop, and spread my toes against the flooring. Keeping my eyes open—which was something I had to make myself practice because accessing magic with eyes closed was not always going to be possible—I rooted straight down. Linseed oil, pine rosin, and cork, compressed to create the squares of linoleum flooring, warmed to the touch of my foot. Below that, a cellar gaped light-less and forgotten, its dirt floor mostly void of living things.

I wasn't fond of those kinds of spaces and quickly sent my inquiry in a more horizontal direction until I reached the weeds edging the alleyway and the trees lining the sidewalk. Sweet, green, rooty relief.

My mostly dormant magic had reawakened less than two months ago. As a forty-one-year-old witch, that meant I had to uncover and practice my gifts as much—and as quickly—as possible. And I had to study, as in books and lectures and labs and bouts of imbibing too much coffee. At the urging of River's sister, Rose, now the head witch of the Pacific Northwest Covens and a woman not to be questioned, I enrolled in a five-year Basics of Witchcraft program. I was a handful of sessions in and already itched to condense the time commitment to two or three years.

With that goal in mind I had taken a leave of absence from my position as an inspector with the local Agricultural Commission's office. My former assistant texted me frequently. Otter or cat gifs meant Kerry was having a good day. Terse messages describing my temporary replacement's antics meant she missed me. Today, I was on the receiving end of multiple images of kittens. I had to admit I missed Kerry, the regular contact with the farmers and orchardists, and the steadying presence of a forty-hour workweek.

Then again, upheaval had been the theme of my life since that first tattoo was removed and my magic had come back online. I kept telling myself that once my sons and my niece, Sallie, had settled into the routines of high school and work, I'd have more bandwidth for my magical education. I would join a coven, immerse myself in magical studies, and practice, practice, practice.

Or so I hoped. I nudged my sensitive foot and toes farther and felt my way into the tasty spots of magic lingering inside the nearby bakery. My mouth watered.

There was also the task of integrating my paternal grandfather into our lives. Christoph Courant had dropped from the sky —swooped, actually—onto my lawn barely six weeks ago, right at the end of a traumatic confrontation with my ex and his extended family.

Gramps, as my sons, Harper and Thatcher, had taken to calling Christoph, was a gyrfalcon shifter and a leader among the magical communities in the Northwest Territories. His white wings, speckled with black, were magnificent and permanent, and the genes he carried passed to his only son, Benôit.

Benôit was my father. I had no memories him as man or bird, yet at least one of my sons, Harper, had inherited the gyrfalcon traits. Within hours of me being released from the dampening spell inked into that first tattoo, Harper's air-based magic began to emerge in the form of feather tracts on his upper back.

The speed of his physical transformation, as one of his vertebrae began to enlarge and metamorphose into an anchor for wings, was wrenching, painful, and not entirely welcomed. Christoph had spirited the frightened eighteen-year-old to northern Canada to help him recover and to give him space to live among other winged shifters while he explored his options.

"What's the latest on your eldest?" River asked.

"You reading my mind again?"

"Mm-hmm." I couldn't see his shy grin, but I knew it was there.

"Seriously?"

He continued to puncture my skin with the needle and didn't answer.

"You know, you druids really have a lock on this whole enigmatic thing," I teased, keeping my body relaxed. "How're things going with Airlie?" Airlie Redflesh was another local witch. She had been one of thirteen at my initiation ceremony and assisted with the online lectures. Knowing I had a "thing" developing with one of River's friends, she'd confided she had a mild crush.

The druid took his time answering. "Airlie and I have a date scheduled for Friday night."

"Ooh, love is in the air." My toes tingled in anticipation of chatting with Airlie afterward.

"Calliope, this is our first date."

"Excited?"

"Terrified," he said, lifting both hands off my back and leaning away. "She's a water witch."

"But otter's one of your forms," I pointed out, unsure why a mutual connection to one of the natural elements would be problematic. Tanner's and my shared connection to earth made for compatible magic. And an intense physical attraction. I resisted the urge to push away from the chair and look over my shoulder. "It's the one you shift in and out of the most. Airlie's into water and you are, too, but in a different way—*ouch*. Isn't that like a perfect match?"

"That's what terrifies me." River again settled into his task. I breathed through the constant, grating buzz of his machine, focusing on the floor and on parsing the magical signatures in the surrounding buildings.

I tried picturing how my older son's recovery was going. The sparsely populated, physically spacious Northwest Territories were perfect for shifters and others like Christoph and Harper. The place was less supportive of Harper's girlfriend, Leilani. She was a witch and a natural imbuer whose magic—a blossoming combination of witchcraft and spellwork—was closer to her fathers'. She had lobbied hard to go along to lend emotional support and, if needed, to work in the kitchens of the shifters' compound. If she wanted to leave, home was only a few portal hops away.

"Oh, in answer to your question, Harper's doing well according to Christoph. Leilani's reports are a little less rosy, but I get the sense going north was a good decision for her, too."

River hmm'd, then said, "You can get up and stretch—take a break. I'll fill in the shaded areas next."

"Thanks." In the bathroom, I tried to peek at the design without success. The space was too tight to maneuver.

Back in the chair, I had to ask River *my* burning question. His friend—and my maybe-boyfriend—had been off the radar and completely incommunicado for weeks. Though I suspected the absent druid was behind the chunks of raw crystals I kept finding on my porch. "Have you heard anything from Tanner?"

"Sec," he answered. "Let me get this going."

Gaah. I had to close my eyes and concentrate on breathing in and out until my skin again acclimated to the sensation of the needle.

"You know Tanner's teacher is one of the oldest and most venerated druidesses, yes?" he said.

I went to shake my head, when River lifted the needle and reminded me to stay still.

"I didn't know that. But I don't know much about druids."

River exhaled through his nose. "Ni'eve du Blanc comes from a different time and she continues to live and teach at her own pace."

"Is that your way of saying you *have* heard from Tanner?"

"I've heard through the grapevine that negotiations between Ni'eve, Idunn, and what's left of the Keepers have reached a very delicate balance."

Oh. A Keeper of the sacred trees that bore the Norse

goddess's beloved Apples of Immortality had gone rogue. That rogue Keeper—Ni'eve's daughter, Jessamyne, aka the Apple Witch—had been involved with my maybe-boyfriend.

She had also set her sights on eliminating me from the competition for Tanner's attention.

"Calliope, druids become druids because they survive their training, not by an accident of birth. Tanner's a good man who takes his obligations seriously. He'll finish with Ni'eve, and then he'll be back." River lifted his inking gun and released the foot pedal. "I need to take five," he said. "My hand's cramping."

The druid's timing was perfect. Talk of Tanner agitated me, especially when I pictured him spending day after day in his ex's proximity. In France. I wasn't the jealous type, but something about Jessamyne had always irritated me.

Okay, a few things. No more than four.

I tried tracing the chipped edges of the patterned linoleum floor squares then closed my eyes and recalled the way Bear's paws had always—*always*—been a reassuring weight against my skin.

The stool squeaked and the cushion gave a funny sigh as River's weight settled. "Okay, where were we?" he asked.

"You were giving me the background on Tanner and Jessamyne."

The druid's *hmm* competed with the buzzing of the machine. "My understanding is Jessamyne wanted the status of being her mother's daughter and the arcane knowledge that came with being a Keeper. She made promises left and right regarding her fidelity—to Idunn, to the Keepers, and to Tanner—and she failed on all of them. She's got the biggest case of wanderlust I've ever come across."

I let River's assessment sink in. Tanner had yet to explain exactly when his association with Jessamyne had begun, and when their intimate relationship had ended. "Is that Wanderlust the yoga festival, Wanderlust with a capital *W*, or wanderlust with a small *w*?"

"That is wanderlust in all caps, Calli. And it's a very real condition, afflicting those who are constitutionally challenged to put down roots."

"From what I've seen of her," I said, muttering my opinion into the towel covering the face rest, "she could be wanderlust's poster child." And if the Apple Witch ever decided the cure to her condition was to settle on my island in her tree form, she had another think coming. I knew the best root ball specialists in all of Canada, and they owed me a job.

River stopped the motor again and laughed at my comments. "I would give a decade of my life to sit in on their negotiations. Far as I can put together, Idunn was *not* happy with either Ni'eve or Jessamyne."

I met Idunn in early August, in an encounter that I continued to pick apart and analyze.

The Norse goddess intimated she had much to say to the mother-daughter duo charged with protecting the lineage of trees that produced her magical apples. The words she saved for Tanner and me were the ones I treasured. According to Idunn— and evinced by her beloved apple seeds' enthusiastic awakening —Tanner and I might have a future. If he could get his butt out of France and back to British Columbia. Moving to Europe was not an option for me.

"And we're done," said River, quieting his machine. He blotted the design and held out a wide oval hand mirror. "Have a look."

I stood, clutched my T-shirt to the front of my chest, and shook out my legs. I turned my back to the big mirror running the full length of the wall and checked out River's work.

Even though I knew Aunt Noémi was dead, and Bear along with her, I wasn't prepared for seeing the likeness of her animal familiar's paw prints. River had positioned them precisely where I had often felt the ursine presence guarding and guiding me. The ink was stark, matte black, rimmed in reddish pink where my skin was irritated.

The emotional impact of Bear's permanent departure took my breath away. My sinuses tingled, a warning that tears would come whether I welcomed them or not. I returned the mirror before my shaking hand dropped it and sat on the stool. "It's beautiful," I said, pressing my T-shirt to my cheeks. "It's perfect."

River's smile was genuine and pleased. "Let me get you cleaned and bandaged. Then you can head out."

"Hey, Aunt Calliope!" My almost-nineteen-year-old niece, Sallie, waved from across the street. She waited for a break in the traffic before dashing to join me. "Can I see it?"

"River says I have to keep my skin covered for at least twenty-four hours."

"Okay." She gave a half-hearted pout and slipped her arms around my waist.

"How are you doing?" I asked, happy to see she had ventured beyond the protective wards surrounding my property.

"I'm trying to be out in public more. But it's really hard." She and I paused in the parking lot, close to my car, my arms circling her shoulders. I hadn't known this reserved young woman all that well prior to the summer's cataclysmic events. Her side of the family frowned on rubbing elbows with the Joneses. Sallie was revealing herself to me and her cousins—to all of us—in fits and starts while she processed overwhelming, and at times incapacitating, feelings of shame.

Her parents, Josiah and Garnet Flechette, were in jail for murdering at least two hidden folk, the race of Magicals who tended to apple orchards throughout the Pacific Northwest. The work of the hidden folk went unseen by most human eyes, and their direct contact with sacred apple trees put them under Idunn's protection as well as that of the Keepers.

The Flechettes were fae—a major detail I had learned over the summer and one my ex-husband never saw fit to disclose during the fifteen-plus years we were together.

"Are you ready for this weekend?" I asked. The coming Friday marked the first mentoring weekend of the academic year for magical teens. Sallie and Thatcher planned to go. Harper and Leilani would attend if they made it home from the Northwest Territories in time.

"Yeah. No… Maybe?" she said, staring worriedly out at the street. The six blocks to either side of the main thoroughfare, though bustling, were quieter than during the summer rush. I doubted Sallie saw any of it. "I wish I could bring Jasper."

Jasper was her therapy cat, a Maine coon on extended loan from yet another witch. The presence of the imperious feline helped mitigate the effects of withdrawal Sallie had been experiencing. Josiah and Garnet had collared their only daughter starting when she was on the cusp of puberty, using spelled ribbons and jewelry to mute her magic and hide her unusual features from human eyes.

With her parents remanded to a subterranean holding cell, there was nothing external prohibiting Sallie from expressing her magic. She was just now coming to grips with who she was, what her nascent magical skills might be, and where she belonged. The problem was she—like me—had to take toddler steps.

"Have you asked Wes and Kaz about taking the cat along? I'm sure you're not the only one who wants to bring a support animal."

"No," she responded, biting one of her already stubby nails. "Should I?"

"Yes. Absolutely. But I would ask Jasper's owner first." Steering us both toward my car, I clicked the key fob just as an oily, viscous sensation hit the bottoms of both feet. I sucked in a quick breath and tamped down the desire to stuff my niece into the vehicle and make a run for the safety of the heavily warded grounds surrounding my house.

"Sallie," I said, assessing our immediate area for visible threats, "do you feel that?"

She hugged me awkwardly, the bones of her forearms bruising my lower ribs. "I do, and I don't like it. It's making me feel sick to my stomach."

The magical signature echoed one I'd encountered the same day I met Tanner and began this whirlwind odyssey into the concealed world of magic and magical beings. Once again, the signal blinked in and out from the vicinity of the marina, a mere three blocks away. There, float planes, fishing boats, and yachts docked alongside one another. One of the more ostentatious yachts, the *Merry Widow*, belonged to my ex-mother-in-law.

Intellectually, I knew she was under house arrest at her estate in Victoria. Emotionally, my gut roiled at the thought of encountering Meribah Flechette anytime soon.

Sallie's battered fingernails contracted and elongated, switching erratically between her chewed-at human version and the claws Fae trained themselves to use as weapons. I swept away the shoulder-length hair she kept deliberately shaggy. Her ears were turning, too.

"Get in the car," I said, sliding one hand between her arms and my torso and keeping my voice steady. "Lock the doors and lie down. Now."

Sallie had been schooled into round-the-clock obedience by the succession of collars her parents forced her to wear. Though now free of the magic-imbued restraints, she released her grip and reacted without question. The speed of her acquiescence pained me.

I pointed to a strip of bushes and trees dividing the public parking area from the section reserved for business employees. I could dig my toes into the soil and keep my niece in sight. "I'll be right over there."

Sallie's face was streaked with splotches of red and white. She silently mouthed, *Okay.*

The sickening sensation heralding the Magical's presence grew stronger. I ducked beside a scraggly maple tree and pressed my hand into the deep grooves of the bark. Scuffing away leaves and a crushed can, I slipped one foot out of its flip-flop. Toes in the soil, I kept glancing at my car as I attempted to pinpoint the oddly colored spot.

Hating that Sallie would be out of sight, but not knowing how else to do what I needed to do, I closed both eyes and settled all ten toes into the soil. A circuit board of familiar magical signatures spread and multiplied across the insides of my eyelids and through my brain. The surface of the blackish area swirled with a rainbow of colors, like a shallow puddle on an oil-slicked bit of road. Added now were a handful of whorls—five maybe, or six— tightly joined and moving together. My eyelids flew open. The group was approaching a building that backed onto the parking lot. The building belonged to the Flechette Realty and Property Development Group.

I wiped my toes on my pants, forced my dirtied feet into the flip-flops, and hurried to my car. I didn't press the unlock button on my key fob until I made sure my niece saw me. "Sallie," I said, tossing my bag behind me and whispering, which was entirely unnecessary, "sit up slowly. I'm going to move us out of here and drive around the front of the real estate company's office."

"If you mean my family's business, just say it, Aunt Calli."

I nodded. "Yes, that one." I started the car, backed out of the slot, and stopped at the parking area's exit to let a gaggle of teens make their way along the crosswalk. The queasy feeling in my belly intensified.

"Do you feel that?" Sallie asked.

"I do. What do you think it is?"

Sallie pressed her lips together, grabbed the headrests of the front seats, and hauled herself forward. "It's not an *it*, it's a *who*, and I know who it is." She reached for the sunglasses I'd tossed on the dashboard. "Meribah and Adelaide share a lover and he's here. Complete with his faithful entourage."

Sallie flicked her thumb at the windshield and wiggled deeper into her seat.

The last pedestrian was safely on the sidewalk. I hit the blinker, signaling a right-hand turn, when two people stepped off the curb to my left. They were followed by a trio, then another couple. I watched, jaw agape at the precision with which the group maintained formation.

"Shut your mouth," Sallie hissed. "You're giving us away." I clamped my lips together, adjusted the rearview mirror, and pretended there was nothing more fascinating than whatever was going on with the blemish on my chin.

The man in the middle of the group demanded attention. Slightly shorter than the six others clustered to his back, sides, and front, he was the only one not wearing a Bluetooth device. Disconnected from technology, he was acutely connected to the swirling magical signature I could now see even with my eyes wide open.

The seven disappeared around the corner. I inched into traffic and glanced to my right in time to see the couple bringing up the rear step into the Flechette building. The reflection on the glass doors hid the interior, but a honk from behind hurried me along.

"That was *intense*," I said, bursting into a nervous giggle.

Sallie glared at me over the top of my sunglasses. "*That* was Odilon Vigne."

CHAPTER 2

"Hey, Mom. Hey, Sallie." My younger son, Thatcher, came barreling out the open screen door when we got home and enfolded his cousin in a hug. "Guess what?"

"You made dinner?" I asked. A mother could always hope.

"Close. I'm on kitchen cleanup tonight. Sallie's on dinner prep. And dessert's covered because—"

"Ta-da!" Leilani and Harper squeezed past Thatcher and tumbled down the porch stairs. Harper caught me up in a hug that forced me to exhale my breath. Lei-li brushed a kiss against my cheek and dodged the bumper of my car as her fathers, James and Malvyn Brodeur, drove through the wards and pulled onto the grass. "Daddy, Papa, we're back!" she yelled.

Harper whispered, "Missed you, Mom."

I didn't care one whit that Harper's tight embrace pulled at slightly raw skin at the base of my neck. "This is the best surprise," I said, overjoyed to have my son home. "Is Christoph with you?"

"Sure is." Harper exchanged a hug for placing his hands on my upper arms and turning me to face him. "I have something to show you. Don't freak out, okay?"

I laughed. I couldn't help myself. "Harper Jones, last time I heard that phrase, your brother was—"

"I know, I know, Thatch was letting you know I had sprouted feathers." Harp let go of me, grinned, and spun around. "Take a look."

I set my bag on the grass and took hold of the bottom of his baggy flannel shirt. I didn't know what to expect. I didn't know what I wanted or hoped to see, and I had no time to moderate my reactions. When Harper and Leilani left for the Northwest Territories with my grandfather, my firstborn had to be sedated and the awakening process of his forming wings artificially halted. Anything had to be better than that.

"Are you sure?" I asked.

"Positive."

His lower back was tanned, the skin healed from the injuries he'd sustained in August. I rolled the shirt higher and gasped. "Harp. You decided."

"I did." He hugged me again and waved at whomever was heading toward us. "I gotta go show Mal and James."

Harper walked away with a newfound confidence. I was dying to speak with Christoph about what had swayed my kid into accepting the winged part of his genetic heritage and all of that decision's potential repercussions.

Thatcher sidled next to me and shoved his hands into the front pockets of his shorts. "I want to make those kinds of choices, too, Mom." He bent to pick up the raccoon waddling down the stairs and let it perch on his shoulder. "I want to know what I am, besides a sixteen-and-a-half-year-old kid."

"Go look in the mirror," I said. Pokey reached for the finger I offered, sniffed, and determined I bore him no treats. "You're the Raccoon Whisperer."

"Yeah, but I want to be more." Thatch approached the Garry oak tree, extricated his four-legged companion's delicate paws from his hair, and lifted the animal onto a shaded branch.

Harper and Leilani, along with Malvyn and James, strolled toward the house. James clutched the handle of a picnic basket, its contents covered with a red-and-white-checked kitchen towel. He waved and quickened his pace.

"Calliope," he said, lifting the corner of the cloth and releasing the scent of fresh-baked lasagna. "I hope you don't mind the intrusion. We wanted to see everyone and thought a group catch-up made sense."

He was right, and it did. "I'm thrilled when anyone shows up with food." I accepted his right cheek, left cheek kisses. Mal delivered the same, and Leilani gave me another tight squeeze.

"Malvyn, could I speak with you for a moment?" I asked.

James offered Leilani his elbow and said, "You two can have as long as it takes us to make garlic bread." He planted a kiss on Malvyn's lips and escorted their daughter up the stairs.

I tugged on Mal's shirtsleeve and tilted my head away from the house. He followed me onto the grass and away from anyone overhearing. "Did something happen, Calliope?"

"I was in town this afternoon with Sallie. We saw a group of Fae walk into the Flechette building, the one Meribah owns that houses the real estate offices. I felt the group's magical signature before I saw them—Sallie did, too. Weird thing is, I felt the same signature once before, earlier in the summer, when Meribah's yacht was moored in the harbor.

"There was almost a military feel to the way they walked," I added. Mal fisted his chin and nodded as I spoke. The complicated watch on his wrist kept catching the sun and flashing my eyes. "Six Fae, all about the same height, walking in step. Two males in front, two males in back, one female to either side of the guy in the middle. All of them dressed in dark blue or black. Oh, and the guy in the middle was shorter. He was definitely the one in control. His hold was invisible, but I could feel it, and I think the blues, deep purples, and pinks sitting atop the signatures I'm more familiar with were his personal stamp." The more I relayed to Mal, the more details I remembered.

The multitalented sorcerer, jeweler, and enforcer for the province's Board of Magical Governance rested his hands on his hips. His pressed khaki slacks were more pristine than anything I would ever wear. "Anything else stand out?"

I brought my hand to my throat. Even now, the sensation of the Fae's magic triggered my gag reflex. "At first, everything came in through my feet. Then I could see the points and connecting strands whether my eyes were closed or open. The ickiest part was the sensation of being choked." I swallowed hard. "Sallie said the one in the middle was personally involved with both Meribah and Adelaide."

Malvyn stared at his tasseled loafers. "Calliope, you caught yourself a very rare glimpse of the scion of Clan Vigne. His father never leaves the lands they own in France. If there is a matter that requires his attention outside of his borders, he sends his son, and if Odilon Vigne is here in the flesh, we may have a problem."

He sighed heavily and held up one finger, with its perfectly buffed nail. "Let me clarify. Chances are one hundred percent that we *will* have a problem. That man does not show up to fix things. His role is to instigate chaos and control its inevitable fallout. He will stay until his creation has taken root, then he will extract whatever it is he has come for by whatever means are necessary."

"That sounds so creepy."

"*Creepy* doesn't begin to describe his methodology, Calliope. The family's logo is a strangler fig." Mal spun on his heel to face me. "Have you ever seen what hemi-epiphytes left to satisfy their urges and appetites can do to otherwise healthy trees?"

I nodded. I was aware of the destructive capabilities of invasive vines and had pangs of guilt whenever I thought about how well they responded to my magical cues. Hemi-epiphytes were a whole other level of resource-sucking bad-assery once they reached a particular stage of development. "I've seen photographs of what occurs in the more tropical zones."

"Then you have glimpsed what he and his clan are capable of." Mal's phone buzzed. He slid it out of a back pocket and glanced at the screen. "The troops are famished, and our presence is required." His gaze bored into mine again. "This is *not* a positive development, Calliope. But now that we know he is here, we can create better defenses. I'll make a few inquiries." Mal turned to leave, then paused. "It can be no coincidence that Odilon has arrived so close to Meribah and her sister being put under house arrest."

"All the more reason for you and me to keep in touch," I said, thanking him. Digging up more information on the Flechettes and their connection to Clan Vigne was added to my burgeoning to-do list. It occurred to me that I might have to return to my old job one or two days a week. Though I could run searches from any computer, the Agricultural Commission's local office had the added bonus of housing decades' worth of paper files.

I had the added bonus of my assistant, Kerry Pippin, and her family's extensive connections to every aspect of the island's commercial life.

Lest I forget, I sent myself a text, hurried toward the house, and scraped the side of my foot on yet another mineral offering. This one, a chunky cluster of tangerine- and cream-colored ferrierite, sparkled at the base of the steps. I palmed the specimen, smiled to myself, and made my way to my house's small, outdated kitchen.

The area seemed to shrink in size when more than three people tried to simultaneously reach for dishes and utensils, pour drinks, and get whatever else was needed to set the table and serve the food. Harper, Leilani, and Thatcher, arms and hands filled, squeezed by. I skirted the center island, placed the chunk of crystal on the windowsill, and raised my voice. "Outside, everybody. Picnic time."

Christoph, Malvyn, and James were already headed toward the front door, their arms loaded with picnic supplies, including tablecloths they'd pulled from who-knows-where. A honk from the driveway announced another arrival. Lifting my heels off the floor, I peeked out the window over the sink. My friend Rowan, a witch and physician with a busy OB-GYN practice, emerged from a familiar sedan, followed by Wes. The druid hefted a wood case filled with bottles onto one shoulder, and Ro lifted a big wooden bowl above her head.

Laughter and the clanking of bottles trailed alongside the house and across the lawn. Harp and Thatch set up chairs and an old bench in the flat area near my herb and vegetable garden, and then spread an old quilt under the adjacent crabapple tree. That, plus a couple of the tablecloths layered over the prickly grass, would have to do.

Surveying the scene, I came up one body short. Sallie was missing. If my niece wasn't joining us for dinner, I had a feeling I knew why. I left the back deck, headed upstairs, and knocked on the bedroom's closed door. Pressing my ear to the wood, I barely heard Sallie's soft voice when she said, "Come in."

"Hey. Ro's here. She came with Wes. I know they'd both love to see you." I hoped mention of those two would prove more tempting than staying on her side of the room she shared with Thatcher.

Sallie shook her head, the uneven ends of her hair swishing around her jaw and neck. "No. It's hard for me to be around Leilani and her fathers."

"I bet it is," I said. The night of my post–Blood Ceremony party, Malvyn had invoked his authority and taken charge of restraining Sallie's parents in a dazzling show of magic. The sorcerer had then taken the two Fae into his custody, as mandated by his position as the Enforcer. Sallie witnessed the entire spectacle.

A cell phone chirped from inside the fringed bag by her knees. Her sad-eyed gaze lingered on me before she pawed through her purse and read the message. "My girlfriend's on Fortune's Folly Road and she can't get past the wards. She can't even see the house. Can I ask her in for dinner? Please?"

Sallie's brief flare of happiness lit up the room.

"What's her name?" I asked.

"Azura."

"I would *love* to meet Azura." I extended my arm and wiggled my fingers. Earlier in the summer, Wes and Kaz had added a layer of protective wards that allowed humans to see my house while keeping everything hidden from Magicals. Our newest visitor was—obviously—on the magical spectrum. "C'mon. There's food enough for everybody."

Sallie linked her fingers through mine and hefted her feline shadow onto her hip. "I'm sorry I didn't tell you about Zura," she said. "I didn't know how to ask if she could come for a visit."

I kissed the side of Sallie's head and accompanied her to where an irritated young Black woman in a retro dress and heels paced at the end of the driveway. "Let me hold Jasper while you reach for her," I suggested, eying the two vintage suitcases standing next to the girl and wondering where we might find a mattress for yet another visitor. "I assume she'll recognize your hand?"

Sallie nodded and swallowed. "My nails look like shit, but she knows my rings." She transferred the furry Maine coon cat to my arms, grabbed my hand, and beckoned through the shimmering wards.

Azura screamed and slapped at Sallie's fingers. Taking a step back, she darted looks to her left and right and up to the sky, then peered at a spot right beyond Sallie's shoulder.

"Do that again, Flechette," she said, tentatively extending her arm. Sallie reached into the curtain of green light, grabbed Azura's wrist, and tugged.

"Hey," she said. "You look so pretty."

Azura shook off the compliment and kissed Sallie. The two pressed their foreheads together, whispered *I missed you* at the same time, and then broke apart giggling.

"Hi, I'm Calliope, and welcome to our home. You hungry?"

The young woman blinked at me and nodded. "Sorry for crashing the party, but it's taken me so long to find Sallie and once I had your address I couldn't wait and also, your cell phone reception bites."

"Yes, it does," I agreed, bending forward and searching the road to either side for a parked vehicle. "Did you drive?"

"Ferried from Swartz Bay, bussed into town from the terminal, then hitched a ride with a random dude. I could really use a bathroom."

"C'mon, then. You're just in time for lasagna and garlic bread. And don't forget your luggage."

Sallie hefted both suitcases and led Azura toward the house. I waved them off and headed to the feast. Jasper pressed his hind paws against me. When I let him go, he bounded straight for Rowan.

"What are the chances we can have one uninterrupted meal?" I directed my question to the assembled guests and family members within earshot while helping myself to a slab of James's casserole. Melted cheese oozed between layers of noodles, grilled red peppers and onions, and other ingredients.

"I think the odds are eighty-seven percent in our favor that Sallie's friend is the last surprise Magical to cross the wards onto the property tonight," said Wes. The druid was Tanner's best friend and appeared to be getting very cozy with Rowan. He balanced his plate in his lap while he leaned against the red-haired doctor. "River said he finished your tattoo. Care to let us see it, Calli?"

I swallowed and wiped my mouth. "Soon, I promise."

Thatcher made a show of clearing his throat and tapping his fork against the side of his glass of lemonade. He raised his arm and acknowledged the gathering of adults, teenagers, and one special feline. "I would like to propose a toast," he began.

"Wait for us!" Sallie waved, her other hand entwined with Azura's as they ran down the incline to join us. "Thank you, Thatch," she said, catching her breath and accepting the two glasses Christoph offered. I gave silent thanks for the timing of her girlfriend's arrival.

"I would like to acknowledge my great-aunt, Noémi." Thatcher closed his eyes for a moment and pointed in the direction of the house. When he opened his eyes, there was a clarity to the hazel coloring. "Noémi kept this house and this land intact against one of the greatest odds imaginable." He looked at me quickly. "Mom, I've been doing some research, and I wanted to tell you this when I knew more but tonight seems as good a time as any."

He cleared his throat. "Like my mom, Noémi was a witch. She also trained to become a shaman. When she was young, she became partially separated from her animal familiar. But her daemon—a bear—stuck around. I never told you, Mom," he said, tipping his glass toward me, "but I felt Bear's presence, too. That's how I knew which animal trails to follow and how I learned to communicate with raccoons and squirrels. Bear taught me all of that."

He wiped at the tears streaming down his face. "I miss her. Here's to Noémi and Bear, and to the spirits that watch over us."

I swallowed back my own tears, shared what little I remembered of my aunt, then finished with, "A toast, then, to Noémi Virginie du Sang." I spoke my aunt's complete name for the first time in memory. Every long-forgotten syllable resonated within my bones, from my bare feet up to the crown of my skull.

Du Sang. *Of the blood.*

I refrained from smacking my forehead in front of everyone.

Noémi Virginie *du Sang*.

Genevieve Valentina *du Sang*.

Calliope Viridis *du Sang*.

"So mote it be," Rowan and Wes said in unison. Christoph rose and spread his arms—and his magnificent wings—and took Thatcher into his embrace.

"So mote it be." The rest of our motley crew lifted their glasses to the house, to Noémi's memory, and to Thatcher, and drank.

"Where the hell did I get the name Jones?" Shocked, I muttered the question to myself, maybe in my head.

"Jones is such a common surname, at least along the Eastern seaboard, Calliope. Your mother's parents thought it would protect your identities when you moved west." Christoph's voice, booming in my ear, sent my head spinning. Literally spinning, as I looked left and right and left again at the concerned faces around me. I tossed back the sweetly delicious dessert wine and plunked my butt on the quilt.

"Why would Mom and I need protection?" I asked, posing the question for the second time that day as I stared up at my grandfather's winged form.

Christoph was poised to respond, when Thatcher interrupted. "Mom, Mom, wait a sec." He finished his lemonade and set the glass aside. Threading his fingers through his hair, he squeezed his scalp, then patted his palms at the air. "If your last name is really du Sang and Dad's last name is Flechette, then *technically* Harper and I could call ourselves Flechettes du Sang. *Blades of Blood.* Dude, that is so cool." He rolled to one side and fist-bumped his brother.

Malvyn interjected. "Mmm, technically Flechettes du Sang would be more like *blood darts.* I create them on occasion for clients, and if you two are interested I could show you what they look like and how they are used."

My face must have registered more than shock because Mal quickly amended his offer with, "But first you need training. Lots of intensive training."

"Mal!" James smacked his husband's forearm. "These are *children* we're talking about."

"Some of these *children* have seen a lot of bad things." Sallie rocked forward onto her knees and straightened her legs. She stepped closer to where Mal and James were sitting. The two men tensed, then eased up when she said, "I have a favor to ask."

"What is it, Sallie?"

"Could you make one of those for me?" She touched a fingertip to Malvyn's collar, the one I had never seen him without. The pounded gold pieces rested on his collarbones and circled the base of his throat. James wore a similar collar of delicate, overlapping leaves crafted in a different metal. Both examples of Mal's artistry shimmered with spellwork. "Could you make me something beautiful and unique that will help me find my magic—my *good* magic?" Sallie's fingers fluttered at her own throat and her voice dropped to a barely discernible whisper. "What my parents did to me was awful, but I miss my collar."

Mal took Sallie's hands in both of his and stared as though sizing her up. His eyes changed from deep, calm brown to a fiery orange-red as his power rose to a palpable level. "Sallie, I will do this for you. I will create a piece of jewelry uniquely yours. But first, I would like you to do something for yourself." He cleared his throat and looked to James for support. James gave a wordless nod and added his hand atop Mal's. "Go away this weekend with Harper, Leilani, and Thatcher. They are your friends, they are your *chosen* family. Go and see what you can discover about your magic and we will meet when you return."

"Thank you," Sallie said, her voice a whisper. She glanced at Rowan and Wes. "Can Jasper come this weekend, too? And Azura?"

The druid and the witch leaned in and came to a quick and

unanimous decision. "Yes," said Rowan, standing to pull Sallie into an embrace. "Jasper knows he's your helper and guide and buddy for as long as you need."

Wes directed a comment to Azura. "Would you care to share your magic with us?"

The young woman adjusted her dress's skirt, dusted bits of grass off her hands, and patted the intricate braiding to either side of her head. Closing her eyes, she hummed. The tops of her ears elongated into the characteristic Fae shape. Her facial features changed slightly. I wasn't well-versed enough yet to know if there were cues that distinguished one kind of Fae from the other. To me, her changes resembled Sallie's, though I had only seen my niece's Fae features when she was distressed. Even then, they shifted constantly and non-symmetrically.

Azura bent her arms at the elbows and cupped one hand over the other, slowly lifting the top hand about four inches away from the bottom. She made clockwise circles with both, mimicking the movements of someone rolling a ball of dough or clay. Bluish light lit up the space between her palms. Crystalline particles began to appear, thickening until the blue light lightened to white, then disappeared.

Azura compressed the crystals and produced a snowball. Opening her eyes, she spotted Thatcher, grinned, and beaned him in the forehead.

"Ice meets wood, baby," she said, and laughed. "And that is the full extent of my magic. I can make snow, if I'm standing still, with my eyes closed, and there are no interruptions." She shrugged and tucked her hands under her armpits. "I would really appreciate it if someone could show me how to do that without freezing my fingers."

ONCE THE REMAINS OF THE PICNIC DINNER WERE SORTED AND

those not sleeping at the house had left, I closed my bedroom door and changed into a stretchy cotton nightgown.

House gave a contented sigh on the heels of my energetic exhale. I grinned and patted the aged tongue-and-groove paneling adorning the room's walls. At some point—likely as my magic awoke—the house I grew up in had become a name-worthy animate object, sharing its memories and opinions with increasing frequency. All I could do was take it in stride.

I went to adjust the window. Sliding the curtains to the side, I pushed the bottom sash higher and inhaled the changing scent of the night's air. My bedroom faced north, onto densely packed woods and fern-filled underbrush just starting to transition into autumn's decay.

Taking in and letting out another breath, I became acutely aware of Bear's absence. The sting radiating across my upper back and the crinkle of the bandage reminded me I had at least one token of her magnificent presence. Though I missed the sensation of fur and the comforting weight of her paws.

Suddenly, someone—or some*thing*—rounded the house to my right. Instinct whispered I should pull down the window sash and duck. The natural barrier of fir and arbutus trees hid my ex-husband's property, and although I knew Doug was miles away in the psychiatric wing of a hospital for Magicals, his twin brother, Roger, was missing and unaccounted for.

I moved to the side of the window. I wouldn't put it past Roger to reconnoiter my house on his own. No outdoor lighting on this side left the thin strip of yard draped in shadows. What-ever was out there paused, then turned. The hair on my arms and the back of my neck lowered to half-mast, House stayed mute, and I convinced myself the nighttime visitation was nothing to worry about. Thatcher's raccoons could have been on a post-prandial stroll, as could any number of wild things, including Jasper.

Not everything that moved in and out of the shadows was a threat.

But given the excitement of the summer, I was heeding all warnings, including the little bell set off by the scratching on the outside of my bedroom door. I tiptoed closer. The pebbled skin on my arms smoothed. I opened the door a crack, expecting Jasper the fur ball to let me know he wanted to go out, or that he was hungry.

Instead, I got a different kind of beast, with an altogether different kind of hunger.

CHAPTER 3

"Hey, Calli. May I come in?"

Tanner Marechal slipped into my room at my startled invitation. His dark-brown hair, unbound, long, and luxurious, fell over the collar of his jacket. He had nothing on his feet, snug jeans on the bottom half of his body, a navy T-shirt on the top half, and a ravenous look on his face. He pressed one elegant, deeply tanned finger to his lips, eased the door closed, and turned the lock. Not a creak from the floorboards or a squeak from metal on metal belied his presence.

A jumble of questions crowded the tip of my tongue. Tanner locked his gaze on me, shrugged off his backpack and jacket, and pressed that same finger against my lips as he walked me toward the bed.

Caught off guard by his unexpected arrival, I bumped into the short side of my desk, sent the chair spinning, and almost slipped to the floor when my butt missed the mattress. Tanner captured the backs of my thighs and drew me up his body until we saw eye to eye.

My druid was leaner and stronger than he'd been six weeks ago. Desire and anticipation fluttered through my belly. All thoughts of prowling ex-in-laws dissipated. I clasped the back of Tanner's neck, hooked my ankles behind his butt, and held tight as he lowered us to the bed.

Laying his chest on top of mine, never losing sight of my eyes, he tugged at my clothing until I was naked and exposed from the ribs down. "Arms up," he whispered. "I need to feel your skin."

"Hello to you, too," I said, taking hold of the stretchy fabric and wiggling it over my breasts and head. "And why do you get to keep your clothes on?"

"The hostess has to invite me to get naked." He planted his elbows near my upper arms and stroked the sides of my jaw with calloused thumbs. His eyes glowed and his smile gentled.

"Tanner, would you please take off your clothes?"

He kissed my cheeks. "No," he murmured, "I want you to." Firm lips and warm breath bestowed a double caress.

I slid both hands between my belly and his, undid the button at the top of his zipper, and very carefully lowered the pull. With his face hovering in the vicinity of my neck, I moved my hands over the defined sides of his butt. The familiar bumps of glass-encased seeds were in place, embedded under his skin within the branches of his tattoo. Satisfied, I hooked my thumbs over the waist of his jeans and tugged the fabric over the rounded muscles until my toes could grab the waistband and push it past his knees.

Tanner kicked his pants to the floor. I fumbled for the bottom of his T-shirt and pulled it up his back and over his shoulders and head. Rocking to one side, then the other, he finished stripping himself.

"Wait right here," he said, nipping a line down the center of my torso. He unzipped the top compartment of his backpack and extracted a box of condoms and a small, squarish box. He reached in again. This time, he withdrew an oversized black tube and uncapped the top half, revealing a bright gold crayon. "Would it be all right with you if I warded this room, so no sound passes out?"

I sat up, crossed my legs, and tapped the side of my jaw.

"Please?" Tanner added.

"I think that's a very good idea."

The druid dipped his head in for a brief kiss, then crossed to the bedroom door and crouched. I gripped the edge of the mattress and leaned forward for a better view. He drew a mark on the floor close to the wall, then moved up the side, across the top and down the other side of the door frame before repeating the glyph the other side of the floor. Setting the stick aside, he touched the first marks with his left hand, the last marks with his right, and began a low chant. Pale amber light infused the magic words, traveled up the sides, and met at the top. Tanner recapped the golden stick and wiped his hands on his discarded T-shirt.

"Is that a new toy?" I asked, curious to know what else he had tucked in his backpack.

"Mm-hmm," he said, settling between my legs. I wanted to rub myself all over his beautiful brown skin like a cat marking its territory, but Tanner had me pinned. "I did a little shopping in Paris on my way to you."

"How long can you stay?"

"Ni'eve and I managed to work everything out. Mostly. She gave me a four-day leave." Tanner explored my face, neck, and front with his hands. I had missed this, the way he never seemed to get enough of touching me when we were together. "I'm due back in France on Sunday night."

"Are you mine until then?"

"Totally," he said, making promises to the underside of my jaw. "You can keep me in the house. I'll be your houseboy. Better yet, keep me right here. I'll be your bed boy."

I ran my hands up his arms, enfolding his biceps and the leather bands he now sported. "Have you been intimate with anyone? Because I have not."

He paused and looked into my eyes. "There's been no one else but you, Calliope Jones, since I met you. You're the only woman I want to be intimate with."

Tanner had grown harder as we whispered back and forth. Neither of us mentioned what Jessamyne had taken from him the night he'd left my party in pursuit of her, and the elderly couple she'd absconded with. The Apple Witch had harbored the idea that the seeds Tanner carried required a sexual act in order to be released. The seeds did not, and to protect the secrets he carried, Tanner had allowed Jessamyne to have him one last time.

To me, that kind of sexual encounter didn't count within the parameters of my question.

A tingle of sensation between my shoulder blades reminded me I needed to be careful if I was going to spend much of the night on my back. "Um, there's something I have to show you." I pushed him away and sat up, my back to him. "Be gentle."

Warm breath brushed against my neck. A light touch settled near my shoulder blades as Tanner twisted my hair to the side and lifted the corner of the bandage. The fingertips of his other hand spanned one side of the tattoo. "This is incredible, Calliope," he murmured, planting featherlight kisses on the back of my neck.

"River dusted off his needles and helped me refine the design. He inked it on, too."

"Should I be jealous of one of my oldest friends?"

"Not at all. River, Kaz, and Wes are like the brothers I never had," I said. "Besides, not only am I spoken for, but River's got a date with a water witch."

"It's about time." He resecured the medical tape and guided me to face him.

"Why do you say that?" I asked.

He grinned slightly and blushed. "I want my friends to find the kind of happiness I feel when I'm around you."

Leaning back on my hands, I crossed my ankles and waggled my feet. My almost-naked druid had perched himself on the edge of my bed. The parched part of me, the adult woman whose body lit up when he was around, wanted to drink in his presence. "I missed you," I said. "A lot."

"I missed you, too." He ran his hands down the sides of my thighs and calves and cupped my heels. Uncrossing my legs, he shifted my body on the bed until the mattress accommodated us both, then rolled me onto his chest. "I'm sorry I couldn't get regular messages to you."

"The crystals were a nice touch."

"How did you figure out those were from me?"

"Mmm, I *hoped* they were from you," I answered, cataloging every part of the face I had missed more than I let myself admit.

I tried to secure the hank of hair that kept swinging in front of my mouth. Tanner grinned and tucked it behind my ear. "Kiss me."

I followed his request and brought my head closer. I found his mouth and familiarized myself with Tanner's lips and their ripe-cherry color. Firm, generous, willing to soften under my inquiry and let me explore with my tongue and fingertips.

It didn't take long for the rest of my body to soften, to grow receptive and imagine instead of my tongue exploring his mouth, that he was exploring the inside of me. I tilted my head, fitted my mouth to his for one more taste, then broke away.

"Is there anything you want to know before I ask permission to be inside of you?" he said, his voice deepening into the moment.

I shook my head. "Belle has me on birth control and Rowan gave me a clean bill of health."

Tanner's expression went serious. He found my free hand and interlaced our fingers. Sweeping our joined arms to the side and over my head, he flipped us both, so he was on top. He searched for my other hand and pinned my wrists.

"The Physik at the compound in France gave *me* a clean bill of health, and I brought condoms." He lifted one hip enough to slide his other hand between our bellies. His fingers found my sex and cupped the entirety of the area. "Druids are known for their stamina. I hope you had a good dinner."

We laughed softly, together. "There are vines at my disposal that would tie you to my bed so fast your pretty head would spin," I whispered, pressing into his hand and nipping at his chin.

Tanner stopped talking. My fantasies of finally—*finally*—having full-on sex with my druid involved hours of creative, sweaty foreplay, a multitude of unusual positions, and rolling rounds of orgasms. For both of us.

In reality, we barely moved. We kept our eyes open, watching the other. I could feel myself swelling into his hand, getting wetter, juicier, as we kissed. When he lifted away enough to roll a condom on and resettle between my thighs, he was exactly where I wanted him to be. And when warm fingers cupped the side of my neck, I opened my legs wider and took Tanner in, adjusting him inside me in a series of slow, protracted movements.

With a minimum of fanfare and negotiations, our bodies rocked as one. Wordless, where-have-you-been-all-my-life joining. I bundled the last of my fears and inhibitions and imagined tossing them through the half-open window. For tonight, Tanner was all mine and I was all his.

He filled me. I molded myself to his shape and held tight. The ground below the house fed us, the beams and walls held us, and whatever spirits haunted the place turned their backs.

"I might be having a religious experience," I whispered. Dancing along the edge of an orgasm, my lover's length responded to my words.

Tanner's mouth hovered above mine. "Come with me," he whispered. I arched my chest so I could heighten the friction of his skin against my nipples and lifted my head so our mouths could meet. In that moment, I experienced a side effect of mostly wordless sex. My awareness moved elsewhere, out of my head and down. When I crested, it was as if I had finally mustered the bravery to roll my body to the edge of a chasm and let go into the unknown.

Tanner filled me as I wrapped my arms behind his neck and fell into waves of sensation that had me screaming beneath my skin and moaning into his mouth. He swallowed every strangled thing I had to say until my jaw and throat relaxed. Eyes closed, I collapsed into the softness of the mattress and drifted.

Many long minutes later, I closed my eyes and spun against the front of Tanner's body. I was powerless to move any more than that. He got the message and spooned me, gathering my hair into a loose twist, and covered us with the blanket as best he could.

I think I fell asleep. I was aware of the moment my lover left the bed and when he returned, tucking us chest to chest for warmth and connection. Languid in my half-asleep state, I drew my inner thigh over his leg, wrapped my arms around his neck, and clung to him as he entered me again.

SUNLIGHT TAPPED AGAINST MY EYELIDS AND NUDGED AT MY LIMBS. I resisted moving at all, instead rolling with Tanner's movements as he plumped a pillow, tucked it against the headboard, and sat cross-legged. He pulled the sheet over his lap and adjusted it to cover my back.

"Good morning," he said, rubbing my scalp. I draped my arm across his lap and nuzzled his thigh.

"G'morning."

"How'd you sleep?"

I couldn't stop the corners of my mouth from turning up, or the ripple of reaction zipping through my entire body, or the giggle.

"Someone's going to need a nap today."

"Someone will happily take a nap, if you supervise," I said. I stretched, opened my eyes, and clumsily adopted Tanner's seated position. "What's on the agenda?"

He glanced away and reached for the box he'd taken out of his backpack the night before.

Palming the cube of burnished wood, he said, "I had a jeweler I know in France make something for you." He lifted the lid. Nestled on black velvet was a round button, or pin, enameled and decorated with the face of a white wolf. I ran my finger over the smooth surface and was greeted with a familiar tingling.

"Was this the same jeweler that customized your badge?" I asked.

"I wondered if you would remember." Tanner wiggled the pin out of the holder. "I know it looks delicate, but he reinforced the metal with spells." He slipped his fingernail into the edge of the pin. The two halves separated on a microscopic hinge. Inside, a quartz-like stone clouded with white flecks pulsed with a faint light.

"The jeweler made one for me, too." He handed me the wolf's head pin and slipped a finger between his skin and the leather band circling his muscled upper arm. Embedded on the inner surface of the band was another pin. This one was flat, larger in circumference, and sported a miniature representation of my conjoined wands, complete with intricate filigree.

I gasped. "That's exquisite."

"Do you like it?"

I nodded vigorously. "The detail is amazing. May I see it again?"

He leaned in closer and tilted the leather to better catch the light. "I chose the image of your wand because it symbolizes—for me, at least—the before and after of your magic." He tapped the pin. "It also reminds me we all have the capacity to grow and adapt. Choices I made years ago caused me to forget."

Offering me a shy smile, he continued, "The wolf pin has been imbued with magic, but it's up to you and the pin to decide how it will function."

"Really?"

"Really, Calli. It's generalized magic, like a...a consciousness."

"Can I deactivate it?"

"Absolutely."

"Are you going to tell me how?"

"Soon as you kiss me."

I pulled the druid against me, kissed him hard, and waited for his answer.

"Open the clasp, sing the stone a lullaby, and its magic goes dormant."

I shook my head and giggled. "So this is the important stuff you've been doing the past six weeks?"

"Magical baubles for my favorite witch? Absolutely."

"What about Cliff and Abi?"

Our playful mood dissipated to the perimeter of my bedroom. Tanner rested his hands on my hips and took a deep breath. "They're alive and doing very well."

"I'm *so* relieved to hear that." After everything the long-married couple had been through, I was afraid I would never see them again. "When are they coming home?"

"The plan was for their grandsons to return from their stay at the Seelie Court, then travel to France and escort Cliff and Abigail back to the island. Only, Idunn got along with them so well, she invited Abi to become an honorary Keeper."

"What does that mean for Abi?" I asked, leading Tanner back to bed. "I thought Keepers had to start their training when they were very young."

"Normally, yes. But the tradition is again going through a major change and Idunn's rationale was that Abigail could choose to turn into her tree form just the once, when she is ready to pass over to the other side. Idunn's also given her blessing for Abi to take her final form here on the island."

"That sounds like no small thing."

"It's not. But the Pearmains have a thriving orchard, and their legacy will live on with their grandsons and, in turn, with *their* offspring. They've got the burial mounds, the portal trees, the tunnels, and the underland. It's the perfect spot, really, for a magical hub in this section of North America."

My mind reeled with the implications. Cliff and Abi's grandsons were descended from hidden folk who had intermarried with Cliff's ancestors. Near the end of their training to become druids, Hyslop and Peasgood Pearmain had become enamored of two Fae sisters. The young women were practically royalty in the Fae's Seelie Court. My ex, Doug, and his entire family were Fae of the Unseelie Court and evidently the two courts had differing opinions about—everything.

But I had a naked man in my bed and now was not the time to be sorting out political machinations among the varied contingents of Magicals.

I snuggled against Tanner's side and drew the sheet up and over my shoulder. "Both boys are home. Sallie's girlfriend showed up yesterday. And they're all leaving tomorrow morning for their first weekend with the mentors. Wes and Christoph are accompanying the Fearsome Foursome. Oops, Fivesome. Leilani's going, too."

"What you're really saying is you have a houseful."

I pressed my forehead into the side of his hip and spoke to my ongoing concern. "Four teenagers and my grandfather and I know at least three of them will notice the spring in my step."

"How about I casually stroll into the kitchen and you act surprised."

"Oh, that'll really fake everyone out." I couldn't help the laugh. Or the eye roll.

Tanner craned his neck, glanced out my window, and gestured. "Or I could get dressed, drop from there, and make a lot of noise at the front door to announce I've come for a visit."

"Deal," I said, starting to crawl over my bedmate. He palmed my shoulder, stroked his hand down my spine and over my butt.

"Wait. I brought you more gifts." Gripping my side, Tanner leaned over and lifted his backpack off the desk chair. He unzipped a padded side compartment and withdrew a long object wrapped in leather. Untying the cord, he opened the package to reveal a layer of oiled cloth.

He placed the object on my waiting palms and tucked his hands under his armpits. "I don't know how you're going to feel about this gift, Calli, but—"

"May I see it, then decide?" I asked. The shape and weight had me guessing Tanner had given me a knife. A *real* knife. Unrolling the cloth, I saw I was right.

"There's a sheath for it in my bag."

I curled my fingers around the handle and lifted the blade to the light. "It's a dagger," I said, marveling at the whorls of Damascus steel.

"Mm-hmm. Is it your first?"

"Yes. I love it," I whispered, tracing my lifeline with the tip of the blade, "and I hope I never have to use it."

The beauty and meaning of the gift required a long kiss of thanks that led to a round of fast, silent sex—after Tanner rerolled the blade in the cloth and leather and set the dagger on my desk.

"There's one more thing." Tanner withdrew a somewhat crushed pale blue bag with a black-ribbon handle, then leaned in and brushed his lips across mine. "Close your eyes," he whispered. His words were followed by little bites where my lips were plumpest. I bit him back.

He took my hand and guided it to the bag's opening. "Think you can guess what's in here?"

I rifled through tissue paper. One fingertip found something silky. Another fingertip slid over a bit of lace. I pinched the fabric and lifted. There wasn't much there to explore.

"Can I open my eyes?" When Tanner answered with a throaty purr, I peeked.

Black. Silk and lace and ribbons. This was *lingerie.* Everything in my drawer was underwear. Cotton, plain, and simple.

"Do you like this?" I asked, rubbing the silk between my thumb and forefinger.

"I like you," Tanner answered, "and when I saw this in a shop window on my way to the portal, I realized I wanted to see you in it."

I rubbed the silk against my cheek, then held the delicate garment at eye level. Something about the way it laced up the back had me wishing Tanner and I could spend the entire day ensconced in the sanctuary of my bedroom with the noise-damp-ening wards doubly reinforced. "Well," I said, not sure what to say beyond thank you and ask how soon we could have sex again.

"Do *you* like it?" Tanner's hand went from my knee to the inside of the other thigh until he found how ready I was to have him inside of me. Again. All I could manage was a nod, which encouraged his next question, "Would you like another gift?"

"Yes," I whispered, slowly curling onto my back. Tanner cupped my knees, unfolded my legs, and draped them across his shoulders. Sliding one palm up my belly, he exposed my sex and nipped down the inside of one thigh until his tongue found me. He stayed right there, licking and sucking, until I came, silk panties in one fist, top sheet in the other, walls glimmering gold.

CHAPTER 4

I managed to grab a one-minute shower before Tanner knocked at the front door as planned and hollered hello. I waited until I heard feet thundering down the stairs and voices raised in greeting before I ducked out of my bedroom, hair damp at the ends, and headed for the kitchen. The blushing druid and I pretended to be delighted at seeing each other for the first time in weeks.

"Who's here?" he asked, extricating himself from my embrace and kissing my forehead.

"Harper's in the backyard, training with Christoph," Thatcher piped in. "Sallie and her girlfriend, Azura, are still in the bunkhouse. I think." Jasper positioned himself between Thatch's legs and *mrowwl*ed to be picked up. "You hungry, big guy?"

My belly gurgled in response to his question and Thatcher laughed. "I gotta make breakfast and get to school, Mom. Harp said he'd drive. He wants to use the Jeep today."

"I'll cook," I said. "Feed the cat, then finish getting ready."

"Can you make me one of those breakfast sandwich things?"

I looked to Tanner. After last night, and this morning, he had to be hungry. "Would you like one, too?"

"I'm starved. Need help?"

"Go see if Christoph and Harper want anything to eat."

THE BOYS LEFT FOR TOWN IN A SPRAY OF GRAVEL, MUSIC BLASTING out the open windows of the Jeep. Thatcher had missed Harper. The mentoring weekend, with its promise of brotherly bonding, was coming at the perfect time. Thatch would turn seventeen in January and his insecurity about his magic being slow to manifest gnawed at me. I was still too new at all of this to make any predictions, other than suspecting whatever hidden skills my younger son possessed, his empathy toward humans and animals would play a part.

"Did you ever figure out who killed the two hidden folk you found on the mainland?" I asked Tanner. He was at the table slathering crabapple jelly from last year's crop across another piece of toast and didn't appear at all startled by my out-of-the-blue question.

"Sallie's parents, Josiah and Garnet. They admitted to chafing at Meribah's authority and the perceived perks she enjoyed as a friend to both the scion of Clan Vigne and his father. Josiah and Garnet decided they would try to curry the scion's favor—and attention—using aggressive tactics."

The more I learned about Odilon Vigne, the more I wanted to dig into his background and see what I could uncover about his local associates. My gut said Malvyn was right, that the man was not interested in yacht rides or the annual apple festival. "Odilon's here, you know. On the island."

Tanner's next bite stopped halfway to his mouth. He returned the toast back to his plate and flicked crumbs from his fingertips. "I did not know that, Calliope. When did you meet him?"

"I didn't meet him. I only first heard of him on Wednesday, after I got the tattoo, when I saw him walking downtown with his retinue. Sallie was with me." I crossed my arms and shuddered at the memory. "I felt that same oily magical signature you and I both sensed the day we met."

"Calli, this is not good news." Tanner set his knife across his plate. "This could indicate that he—and possibly his inner circle —have been here since at least mid-July."

"That's pretty much what Malvyn said." I pondered the countertop. "After you left and Christoph took Harper to the Northwest Territories, I took a leave of absence from my job in order to catch up on my studies. I'm starting to think I should go back."

"Why's that?"

My gaze met his. "I've gotten the sense from my assistant, Kerry—who still works there—that my temporary replacement has lopsided ideas about what an employee of the Agricultural Commission should be doing."

"Meaning?"

"Meaning he's acting as though he's more interested in mass enforcement of obscure regulations than dealing with the farmers and orchardists on a case-by-case basis."

"Do you have any reason to believe he has a connection to Odilon?"

I shook my head. "No. He seemed reasonable the day I met him. But I hate not having my finger on the pulse, you know?"

Tanner nodded. I continued, "Now that I'm aware there's a much larger population of Magicals on the island—and that there's more to our orchards and farmlands than apple trees and greenhouses—I feel that much more responsible for keeping my eyes on everything and everybody."

"It's hard for me to believe that Odilon traveled here from France for anything *but* business."

I agreed, adding, "Sallie mentioned Meribah and Adelaide were involved with him."

"Involved, as in doing business together?"

I shook my head. "Involved, as in a sexual relationship."

"That puts a different spin on things." Tanner moved crumbs

around his plate while he chewed his toast. "Meribah and Adelaide are confined to their property in Victoria. Where's your ex-husband? And his brother?"

"Doug's in Vancouver, receiving psychiatric care. And no one seems to know where Roger is."

"That he's missing worries me," Tanner said, moving to clear the table. I took the seat vacated earlier by one of the kids, interlaced my fingers in front of me, and pressed the pads of my thumbs together. The druid wiped the wood with a damp rag and settled into his chair. "I'm listening," he said.

"You and I met because we had both received anonymous complaints at our offices about the Pearmains and their supposedly nonorganic practices. We showed up to investigate those claims on the same day."

"That's correct. Best complaint I ever followed up on." Tanner leaned over and kissed my cheek. "But that's not why you're bringing this up."

I darted a sideways glance, returned to studying my thumbs, and said, half-jokingly, "Stop distracting me before I lose my train of thought. We know there are active and dormant portals on the island, and other elements related to transportation. I think we should go to my office. After hours." My thumbs agreed. I looked up to see what Tanner thought of my plan. "No one asked me to turn in my keys and I didn't volunteer."

"You pretty much read my mind."

"Does this mean you're up to a little breaking and entering?" I asked, taking in the eager expression on his face.

"Between the arrival of Clan Vigne, the actions of Clan Flechette, the deaths of the hidden folk across the Pacific Northwest and—" he thumped the table for emphasis "—and a temporary employee of the province making noise about properties known to have magic? The implications are too big to ignore. I suspect the Fae have caught wind of the natural resources here on the island—and maybe across British Columbia—and they're readying themselves for a campaign of acquisition. If Odilon makes it clear he is staying, it could mean that Clan Vigne is behind the murders or that they support the Flechettes' actions."

I pondered the long-term ramifications of that scenario and others. I didn't like any of them, not one iota.

Christoph stomped his boots on the porch and came in through the doorway, a faded denim shirt rolled to his elbows and his wings very much intact. He and Tanner hugged, thumping the other's back twice, before my grandfather asked, "Care to strap on a tool belt and give me a hand with a couple of home-improvement projects?"

"I'd be happy to put in a few hours of honest work."

"Good. I could use help framing up the area underneath the back deck. I have a mind to build a work space where the boys and I can mess around with magic." Christoph paused and pointed his finger at me. "You, too, Calli-lass. You'll be needing a proper laboratory, with benches and burners and distillation equipment. The kind of stuff that's best situated outside the house."

"Got any ideas for what we can do with the rest of that area?" I asked. The cellar, with its dirt floor and disturbing memories, hadn't been touched since August. "I mean, once L'Runa and I make another pass through and gather whatever else she needs."

Weeks ago, House had directed me to the old root cellar, where memories of blood and discord had been captured within clumps of dirt. L'Runa, a witch elder and instructor in the Basics of Witchcraft course, specialized in blood magic. She'd performed a cursory round of testing on the soil. We had yet to set a date to explore further.

Christoph rubbed at his chin and gazed out the sliding glass door to the deck. "We could expand the laboratory, create a workshop for multiple magical disciplines. Would take a lot of extra work. We'd have to remove a layer of soil, build a moisture barrier and pour concrete, but let me ponder." He headed down the hall toward his room. "Tanner, give me a few minutes and I'll be ready to show you around."

"What if you and L'Runa start to excavate and find there's more evidence in the soil?" Tanner leaned against the counter and voiced the very question nagging at me.

I rinsed the coffee carafe, deep in the memories of what I had felt in the space below the house when my cousins had locked me in there during a game of hide-and-go-seek that went sideways. That trauma had triggered my earth magic—or something akin to it. As the dirt around me erupted in whispers, what I had felt cascaded me beyond fear. I never mentioned the voices to either cousin, or to my aunt.

My hands were shaking enough that the glass carafe bounced against the side of the sink. "I think this is a sign I should call her today and get this over with while I have you and Christoph here in case anything gets stirred up. And I like Christoph's idea of starting fresh, making something useful of that space." Turning my back to the sink, I gripped the counter edge and looked into Tanner's eyes. "You're a druid. Can soil have or hold memories? Can it share those memories?"

I already knew the answer. I just wanted hear Tanner's reassuring voice spreading some science between layers of magic.

"Yes, and maybe," he said, lapsing into his instructional voice. The rich timbre worked its way into my sympathetic nervous system. "It's not the soil so much as what's growing in the soil, Calli. There's the whole mycelial layer, which druids and other Magicals—especially earth witches—experience as a communication conduit between living things with soil-based root systems.

"Then there's the stuff that gets mixed in with the soil due to location and usage. Around here, you'd find localized plant matter, blood, bones, decaying animal fur and feathers, sometimes human tissue." He crossed his arms, got a thoughtful look on his face. "Why do you ask?"

"Just something House showed me one day." A shiver rippled over my skin at the memory.

"Tanner! Got your belt ready." My grandfather's voice boomed through the house and put a welcome end to my musings.

Tanner nuzzled my cheek and brushed his lips behind my ear. "Think a man wearing a loaded tool belt might take your mind off things?"

I patted his cheek and grabbed a quick coffee-laced kiss. "Absolutely."

Once the druid's distracting backside was fully out the door, I reached for my cell phone, texted L'Runa to see if she was available to come to the house, and went to straighten my bedroom. The enameled pin with the wolf's face sat in its box, surrounded by crumpled black silk. I lifted the glorified thong to the light, then carefully folded it in thirds and placed it atop the stack of utilitarian cotton underwear in my drawer.

I loved that Tanner had gifted me something decadently sexy, but the dagger and the pin held more meaning. Propping my butt against the edge of the unmade bed, I lifted the stylized wolf and had a closer look at it in the sunlight. The circle was slightly larger than the Witchling Way pins my mother had collected for her achievements. My first thought was to utilize the wolf as I had the bear and apple pins, as a kind of a personal crest, or a conduit to a magical connection.

I found the seal pin that had yet to leave my bureau top. Tiny drops of black enamel gave the mammal soulful eyes. As I passed a fingertip over the smooth surface, it occurred to me I might need a symbolic reconciliation with my father before I could call upon the harbor seal as one of my allies. Benôit choosing a selkie over my mother was hard for me to accept. But then again, I had a pitiful lack of details about both my parents and their relationship.

Clearing a space on my desk, I set out the Witchling Way pins

I had first chosen—and the wolf I had been given—and mused on the words my mother had penned on the inside of an old book she had dedicated to me.

Nurture your Garden
Know your Roots
Watch for the White-Winged Man
Beware the...
...Water's Edge

What was my mother hoping to warn me away from? If I heeded the visions House shared of my mother, her sister, and my ex-mother-in-law arguing in the cellar, it behooved me to be wary of anything connected to the Flechettes. I included Odilon Vigne with my ex's extended family and excluded my innocent offspring and Sallie.

Then there was the last line of my mother's dedication, the one that ended with *water's edge*. Was it a reference to Benôit? Or a specific location? With most of my memories of my mother centered around being underwater, that last line felt weighted with portent.

I sighed, palmed the four pins off my desk and squinted at them, then darted my gaze to the shelf underneath my desk. The doll-sized trunk housed my mother's Witchling Way sash and the rest of the achievement pins she earned. Cursing at my crowded personal space, I moved the desk chair and lifted the rounded top of the trunk.

The basket of finely woven sweetgrass was right where I had tucked it. What I really wanted was something like a manual, or a booklet that explained each pin's requirements—anything that could offer more clues to my mother's magical abilities. What were her primary interests? Where did her magical strengths lie?

I opened my laptop, bookmarked the Encyclopedia Magicka page, and emailed Rose to inquire where I might get my hands on information related to the Witchling Way, its history and purpose, and why it was no longer an active organization.

"Mom?" Harper's knuckles hit my unlatched door twice.

"C'mon in, sweetie."

"Can we talk?" he asked. His broadening shoulders filled the doorway more than they had when he finished eleventh grade and wanted to have the safe-sex talk about him and Leilani.

I sent the desk chair rolling in his direction. He closed the door, settled into the seat, then scooted to the front edge. "Still feels weird when my back makes contact with solid surfaces."

"I bet. What else are you noticing?" I asked.

"I feel good about the decision I made. Most of the time." He rested his elbows on his knees. "What do you think, Mom? Should I have waited to let my wings develop until I finished high school? Or college?"

"This was your decision to make, Harper, and mine to support. The only advice I can give you comes from my own experiences." I settled on the far corner of my bed and folded my legs. "People older than me, and then someone I trusted, made all the decisions about the course of my magic. Here I am, at forty-one, having to learn and process things that most witches take for granted."

Harper nodded. "So for you, it's about having choices and making informed decisions."

"Yes. In an ideal world, Harp, we'd have all the details in front of us and all the time we needed to make the big decisions—the ones that inevitably show up as forks in the road where we have to choose one way or the other, and rarely, *rarely* get to experience both."

He nodded along as I spoke, then shook his head. "I'm not sure I can go to school here. And that makes me sad. Senior year is supposed to be..." He let his words trail off, but hunched shoulders finished his thought.

"Can the druids do something that would prevent your wings from being seen by humans?"

"Don't know." Harper rubbed the sides of his knees with his

palms. "But if I want to keep my human friends and live in the human world, I have to hide an essential part of who—of what—I am."

"Hiding your wings only hides the physical manifestation of the path you've chosen, Harper. If we can solve that problem, maybe there's way for you to exist as both grandson and great-grandson of men who have wings, and as Harper Flechette du Sang, master of the blood-blade."

That got a sharp laugh and some easing up. "I think I'm going to stick with Harper Jones for now, Mom, if that's okay with you. I have some shit to work out around Dad."

"I have some shit to work out around my dad, too," I said.

"Want to talk about it?" he asked.

I turned one of Benôit's thumb rings around and around while contemplating how much to share with my son. "Yeah, I do."

I decided to share as much as I knew. "I have no memories of my father, Harp. None. And my clearest memories of my mother take place underwater, in the ocean off the coast of Maine where I was born and where we lived with her parents.

"In some of those memories, my mother swims away from me, but there's no fear attached to watching her disappear. And I often see flippers beside her." I took a deep breath. "Christoph told me my father had wings, but he rejected the life offered by those wings and chose the sea. Benôit—my father—had a lover who was a selkie and she let him borrow her skin."

"Selkie?" Harper asked. "What's a selkie?"

"Another one of the mythical beings I'm sure we'll meet one of these days." A dry laugh caught in my throat. "A selkie can shed its skin and assume a human form when they're on land and become a seal when they're in the water. Anyway, Christoph hasn't seen my father, or heard from him, since the day he found these rings in a pile of clothes at the edge of the sea. He thought I would want them." I held out my thumbs. Harper's intense examination of the metal got me wondering if it would be better if he wore them. I was going to suggest we ask Christoph, when the final lines of the dedication scrolled across my vision.

Beware the...

...Water's Edge

Could my mother have been pointing to the selkie or some other aquatic magical creature? Could Odilon be connected to me through Benôit or even through my mother? Were the last two lines of her dedication warnings? Because *the White-Winged Man* had to mean Christoph. His arrival brought along with it a sliver of my father's story, and my father's story was starting to feel like a cautionary tale.

"It's a lot, isn't it, Mom?" Harper's voice brought me back to the moment.

"Sure is," I said, leaning back on my hands. "How do you want to handle your father?"

Doug had started falling apart at the seams around the time Tanner removed the rune tattoo from my belly. Then, on a Monday in early August when Harper and Thatcher were on their way to the farm where they worked, Doug waylaid the boys at one of their favorite bakeries and forced the two into his truck. I didn't have all the details about what happened in the hours after—I was waiting for Harper to share when he was ready.

What became clear was that Doug's deteriorating mental state was linked to his mother. He thought if he could somehow present Harper's wings as proof he had magic to pass on to his offspring, then Meribah would embrace Doug and invite him to rise to what he viewed as his rightful position within the Flechette Clan.

"I'm not even close to forgiving him, Mom. But I'm not as freaked out about what he did as I used to be."

"I will follow your lead. And you can let me know if you want updates on where he is and how he's doing." Malvyn was my point person on most things related to the Flechettes. He was the one who let me know Doug was at Grand St. Kitt's in Vancouver, for an as-yet-undetermined amount of time.

"Mal said the same thing, Mom. Thanks for wanting to protect me." Harper leaned forward and stood. "And thanks for the talk."

"Did it help?" I asked, unsure if we'd accomplished anything.

He grinned. "Yeah. I already know I'm not going to get everything figured out all at once, but maybe this weekend will help me decide on the school question. Gramps told me there are a few private schools for Magicals in Canada. He offered to take me around to visit them."

That was news to me, although I knew from Sallie there were schools for Fae children on Vancouver Island. "I'm excited for all of you. Selfishly, I want you nearby and I would bet Thatcher does, too."

"Yeah, I tried to feel him out about going away for school and he shut me down fast. So did Lei-li." He shoved his hands into his front pockets. "This family has had enough secrets, Mom. Be nice if it could stop here, now, with us."

"I agree." We hugged. "Think you can promise me that if I'm not available, or if you don't want to ask me about something specific, that you'll talk to Wes or Kaz or any of the other adults?"

"I promise," he said, nodding. "And while we're on the subject of honesty, what's the story with you and Tanner?" My face must have registered more than surprise. Harper threw up his palms and laughed. "I don't need all the details, Mom, just, y'know, are you guys—? Gah, this is so hard."

I tried to save my oldest child—and myself, and Tanner—from further embarrassment. "Tanner and I like each other a lot."

JUST AS HARPER LEFT TO PICK UP HIS BROTHER AT SCHOOL, L'Runa's response pinged on my phone. She was in town shopping for supplies for her coven's equinox celebration and could see me in twenty minutes. I swallowed hard. Debated if this was really how I wanted to spend the day. Figured since Tanner and Christoph were already engaged with renovations—and could assist if the witch and I ran into difficulties—today was as good a day as any to dig into my childhood trauma.

I shivered as I recalled what L'Runa said about the soil samples I collected in August. That some thirty-five years ago, a Fae female and two witches had shed their blood here at the same time. That the witches were related and one of them had shamanic training.

Thirty-five years ago, I was six. For part of that year, my mother was alive. How she died remained a void in my memory banks. Was I ready to have that blank space filled in?

Squaring my shoulders, I met L'Runa as she pulled into the driveway. She stashed her shopping bags in the house, returned to her car for her wood tackle box, and had me carry her satchel of supplies to the cellar's entrance.

Christoph and Tanner had finished their first project and were hauling a wheelbarrow filled with roofing supplies to the bunkhouse. Underneath the back deck, the pristine lumber framing out the walls of our future workroom gave me hope. I wanted to love and feel comfortable with every bit of House and the rest of the property. The root cellar was my final frontier. Christoph's proposition that we remove the soil and replace it with concrete was sounding better and better.

L'Runa rubbed my back. "Ready?" she asked.

"Ready as I'll ever be." I grabbed the tarnished handle, pressed the latch, and drew the tottery door toward me.

CHAPTER 5

After I propped the door open with a rock, I stepped aside and gave L'Runa the option to enter first. She paused at the threshold. "Hold this, please," she whispered. I set the satchel by my feet, accepted her giant tackle box, and cradled it against my chest.

Leaning into the space and sniffing the air, she then bent to secure the straps on her black cotton flats before placing her forward foot on the packed dirt, and her other foot on the concrete slab.

The witch raised her arms slightly, palms down, and stroked the air. "Fur over here," she mumbled. Her left arm jerked before resuming its tentative circling. "Just fur." She brought her other foot onto the dirt and continued to swipe horizontal circles, adding a rhythmic, shuffling step. I stayed glued to the newly poured walkway and its mute support.

"Here." L'Runa tapped the ground with one foot. "The trail of blood begins here."

Shaking my head, I reassembled what pieces I could remember, including Meribah's confession. There was bear fur here, because of Bear. There was blood here, because of a conflict between my mother, her sister, and my ex-mother-in-law, Meribah. Whatever happened, it was not the first time the three had come to blows. Meribah had also spoken of something dire that had occurred when she and Noémi were teenagers.

My mother would have been under six.

If I had known all of this earlier in my life, I might never had the misfortune of knowing the Flechettes.

Which would also mean I wouldn't have Harper or Thatcher.

I shook my head again to clear the emotions scudding in to cloud the moment, and hoped L'Runa could help me discern the truth, whatever it was, in the layers of dirt. I wanted to know, and I didn't want to know. I didn't need another reason to loathe my ex-mother-in-law. Nor did I want any reason to feel compassion for her.

"Calli?"

"Yes?"

"Is there something we can set my case on? I would rather my supplies not come in direct contact with the ground."

Christoph and Tanner had left a neat stack of cut up two-by-fours next to the inner wall. I grabbed an armful and handed them to L'Runa. She placed foot-long lengths side by side in the middle of the cellar.

"Is there anything else you need?" I asked, retrieving her case from outside. "Your satchel?"

"Give me a moment." She patted her chest and frowned. "There is so much sorrow in here, Calliope. When we're finished, I think performing burial rites would be the compassionate thing to do. It is time to appease the restless and put an end to their grief."

L'Runa allowed a handful of moments to pass before taking the tackle box from me and placing it on the boards. She undid the latches. The two sides fanned out and up like stadium seating, each row filled with vials and tins. Resting in the bottom were wrapped objects. The low light made it impossible to see any details. "Can you hand me the bag of salt? It's in the satchel."

I felt for a small bag within the bigger one. Its top was tied. "Would you like me to open this?" I asked.

"Yes." L'Runa stood and rolled the waistband of her skirt until her ankles were freed of the fabric. "Follow behind me," she said. "We'll have to draw a few circles. We'll include the corners of the room and take that little storage area into consideration."

She stepped to the sectioned-off area where Noémi had stored potatoes and onions and her homemade wines, and where I had come upon boxes of desiccated roots and plant bulbs I meant to pass on to Belle. L'Runa paused, palms out and facing down again. She shut her eyes and hummed to herself while making circling movements in the air. "This room has its own curiosities," she said, lowering her arms. "But I don't sense anything relevant to the story we want to extract today."

Closing the rickety door to the interior room, she reached into the bag I held open, felt for the wooden scoop and filled it salt, and began to describe the first circle. The L-shape of the room meant she would have to create three large circles—two in the front section and one in the back—and small circles in all of the corners. "Be careful to not step on the lines," L'Runa warned. "Once I have the circles drawn, we'll create openings where they overlap."

I assayed the area. The final small circle had been delineated and the white of the salt glowed as if with its own light source against the matte brown of the dirt. "This looks more like sacred geometry than witchcraft."

L'Runa brushed the last of the salt granules off the scoop and retied the bag's closure. "Can you leave those outside the door, please? And you're right, Calliope, about the geometry of what I've done here." She crossed her arms and drew her sweater snug to her chest. "When we teach witchcraft, we begin with the basics. We want our students to master drawing circles and casting within the circles, so that when the time comes—and the time will come, rest assured—you can cast with other materials and shapes. It is the *intent* behind the casting that is of supreme importance. You create a conduit to your intentions through good old rote, boring repetition." She laughed softly. "Hours and hours and hours of doing the same thing over and over again."

"What's the saying? Ten thousand hours to mastery?"

She nodded. "Since this is also a time for you to learn, we'll use candles when we call in the cardinal directions. And to bring a little light into the gloom." L'Runa ran her gaze over me. "I imagine this is hard enough for you without the added smell."

"I'm able to ignore most of it, but that's because you're here." Carrying incomplete stories of my mother, her sister, and Meribah was akin to wearing an article of clothing on my back that I could feel but never properly see. The weight of the invisible was becoming a burden I needed to share. "I'm looking forward to what you find."

"What *we* might find and together witness, Calliope. You'll be a part of this working right alongside me."

A shiver ghosted over my skin as the younger me crouched deeper inside adult me.

L'Runa moved inside the curves outlined by salt and wiped away small sections of the lines until no circle was cut off from the others. She occasionally bent to take a handful of dirt and sniff it or bring it to her ear and shake it in her fist.

"Calliope, would you please unwrap my dolls?" she asked, once she'd moved closer to the corner farthest from the entrance. "They're in my kit, wrapped in cloth."

I followed her instructions. "All of them?" I asked, once I'd lifted the top two and seen two more underneath.

"Yes, all four."

After untying the string around the first doll and unrolling the figure from its square of faded calico, I realized I had seen this doll before. The figure had been positioned on a shelf behind

L'Runa's desk during the video class where she delivered the first of her series of lectures on the uses of blood in spellwork.

I unwrapped the other three.

"Place one of those cloths at each direction and seat the doll on the cloth."

"Which one goes where?"

"Trust yourself to know," L'Runa said. She returned to dipping, feeling the dirt, and standing. She muttered at times, or held her hands close to her eyes, squinting in the dim light. By the time she finished a third circuit of the room, I had all four dolls in place.

L'Runa went to her satchel again and withdrew a thick bloodred candle. She handed the candle to me, then pulled out a blue glass apothecary bottle. Rolling the bottle between her palms, she turned in a circle, stopped in front of me, and unscrewed the black rubber top. "This is a combination of wormwood and valerian oils," she said, slowly emptying a dropperful over my fingers. "Rub the oil into the candle. It's fine if some of it drips onto the ground."

"Why these oils?" I asked. I flared my nostrils to take in more of the scents, careful to not drop the candle.

"Valerian is used to soothe anxiety—yours, and that of those who might communicate with us. Wormwood acts as a conduit, inviting the living and the dead to see one another and interact." L'Runa looked into my eyes, concern adding vertical lines between her eyebrows. I stopped turning the candle and cupped the bottom in my palm to hold it upright.

"I did not mean to infer this would be an opportunity for you to speak with your mother, Calliope." The witch wrapped her strong hands around my oil-slicked, shaking ones. "Memory will speak through the four dolls, one per person. Little Calliope, your mother, your aunt, and Meribah."

My throat thickened. I didn't realize how much I had hoped to commune with my mother until L'Runa spoke those words.

Tears rushed to flood my eyes. I held the waters back, forced myself to swallow.

L'Runa gathered an armful of smaller candles from her satchel and dropped a box of wooden matches into her pocket. "Let us begin."

She placed a red-and-orange-striped candle behind the doll I'd seated in the center of the wall facing east, and a blue candle behind the doll at the southern side of the storage room, where the two interior walls jutted into the space to form a corner. Stepping to the section of the cellar farthest from the door, she snugged a yellow-and-white-striped candle into the dirt behind the doll at the west wall, and a candle of swirling browns and greens in front of the one at the north.

She scraped a match along the striker and cupped her hands around the bright flame. When the red candle's wick accepted the light, she took it from me and began her invocation.

"Beings of the East, where the sun rises, bring light to the dark and warmth to our hearths. Help us illuminate the words." She crouched to light the waiting candle, then stood to address the next direction. "Beings of the South, where water flows. Smooth our path and soothe our wounds. Help us cleanse the words."

Another candle was lit, another quarter turn made. "Beings of the West, where air circulates and moves away stagnation. Help us find clarity in the words." The wick on this candle needed coaxing. L'Runa's waist-length braids swished across her back as she shook her head and murmured words of encouragement.

I had thought the dirt here was dead, or as near to dead as dirt got, and I startled at the tremor under my feet. L'Runa either didn't feel it, or ignored it, and went on to finish lighting the final candle. "Beings of the North, where earth provides the ground from which we rise and to which we fall. Help us release the words."

After, she planted the red candle roughly in the center of the cellar and straightened. She then began to stroll around the space, dropping her glance to one spot, then moving to another, as though contemplating what to plant where.

"Genevieve," she whispered, creating a singsong chant of the syllables.

"Noémi.

"Meribah.

"Calliope."

She reached into her tackle box, then bent to the ground again, this time in the corner of the room I most dreaded. When she stood, four tiny chairs more suited to a doll's house were positioned in a square.

L'Runa repeated the four names. I began to sense she and I were not the only ones present. Though I couldn't see the shapes of other beings, I didn't need to. I felt them. I felt the weight of my longing to know more of my mother. I felt the weight of Bear's sorrow in the dank air, and of Meribah's confession. I felt the weight of the suffocating events of the past.

While I adjusted to the heavy cloak of memory as it sagged against my chest, a ripple passed between the dolls. I shushed my inner jumble. Picked out overlapping voices. Aunt Noémi, coming from the doll occupying the north. My mother, from the doll at the south. And Meribah, resonating from the doll at the west.

You think you're so special.

I could cut you.

I could take her from you.

Meribah, no.

Go find your own.

She came to me.

She's mine.

From behind me, most unsettling of all, came the terrified whisperings of a six-year-old girl. L'Runa spun in place, stared at that doll and pointed. "Calliope, bring her here, please, closer to me. The others, leave where they are."

My legs required unfreezing before I could make myself take the few steps to the east-facing wall and take hold of the doll's clothbound torso. The center of my chest ached to embrace the childlike figure, yet my hands refused to take in any sensation that suggested the doll had a beating heart or working lungs.

I brought her to L'Runa. The witch cradled the hand-sewn creation in her arms, cooing, stroking the button-eyed face as she moved to the far corner. Rocking side to side in a familiar, maternal gesture, she pulled each voice's individual thread.

"Calliope. Bring your mother here and place her in a chair. Then bring Noémi, then Meribah."

I followed L'Runa's instructions. My bones turned into a gelatinous mess as I tuned in to the individual—and recognizable —voices as I neared each of the dolls. When I took hold of their stuffed torsos, a lifelike force pulsed through whatever L'Runa had used as stuffing.

The witch crouched near the circle of seated dolls and began to ask questions, listen for answers, at times nodding or inter-rupting. I stood apart. The responses tumbled around me like water over rocks. Unable to distinguish everything that was being said, I was half-grateful L'Runa wasn't asking me to partici-pate in a conversation I could barely follow and did not understand.

She's water. You're earth. You'll stifle her.
I can teach her. She's young. She'll learn.
Let me have her.
You can't do this alone. Let me help.
Let me have them.
They are mine.
There's a price to pay.
There is always a price to pay.
She is water.

You are earth.

She is mine.

"Calliope."

They are water. You are earth.

I can help. Please, let me help.

She is mine.

"Calli." L'Runa waved at me and spoke over her shoulder. She'd turned Little Calliope to face toward her chest. "Do you have any pieces of your mother's clothing, a scarf perhaps, or even a large scrap of fabric?"

I processed her question. Nodded. "Yes, in my bedroom."

"Please go and get it. Exit the circle facing inward, do not speak once you have left, and retrace your footsteps to me. I have paused the conversation and will wait until you've returned."

Again, I followed her instructions. Blinded by the bright sunshine, I hustled up the stairs and into the house, and finally exhaled when I kneeled in front of the trunk under my desk. A scarf that often fluttered at the periphery of my memories was folded and lying at the bottom. I took it and an abandoned quilting project and hightailed it back to L'Runa.

"Perfect," she said. Pointing to the quilt, she added, "Unfold this one first and hold it open."

I shook the sewn-together pieces and draped the squarish section over my palms. L'Runa placed Little Calliope into the fabric, folding and tucking until the figure was swaddled like a newborn. "Give me the other piece."

She picked up the doll that had spoken in my mother's voice, wrapped her in a similar fashion, and gave her to me. Standing, she picked up the bits of calico that had protected the dolls and rewrapped the remaining two. The look in her eyes when she finally stopped and faced me was grave. Candles sputtered around us. Distant birdcalls couldn't lighten the mood.

"I will take these two," she said, pointing to the Noémi and Meribah dolls. "These other two have need of a night together, preferably on your altar." She patted the bundles in my arms. "Create a place of beauty for them, Calliope. Bring in flowers and food. Light candles. They need to talk."

"Then what should I do?" I asked.

"We wait. But not for long." L'Runa worried at her lower lip. "I want to consult Maritza to confirm what was said here." Maritza Brodeur was a witch, and a professor of Necromantic Studies. I'd seen her raise two dead hidden folk after joining their severed heads to their exhumed bodies and get them to speak. If anyone could extract more from the dolls, it was her.

"Before Christoph arranges to have this soil removed," L'Runa continued, "I would like to perform a banishing."

"Why?" I asked, interrupting her extended pause.

"Because it is time to once and for all remove every physical and incorporeal trace of Meribah Flechette from your land. What she did to your aunt was unforgiveable."

"Can you help me understand what she did? I heard the words and I've always felt—"

"Meribah was precocious. Her Fae blades, the ones that form from living Fae bones, the blades they train themselves to release and retract at will, had formed early. Meribah decided to test her blades on Noémi's newly formed bond with the Kodiak bear that had become your aunt's familiar." L'Runa sliced the air with a downward stroke of her hand and swayed in place. Her pupils widened. "They were girls, coming into their gifts yet not ready for mentoring, unaware of their strengths and incapable of holding their emotions in check.

"Meribah was jealous of Noémi, jealous of Genevieve's innocent adoration. When the older girls came down here, they didn't know Genevieve was following them."

Take her.

Hide her.

Protect her.

Bury her.

"Meribah struck at Noémi, damaged her fledgling connection to her daemon, and turned her wrath on Genevieve when she saw the younger girl had tagged along."

L'Runa took in a long breath and blew it out. "Years later, when Genevieve showed up with you, the three of them returned here, to the scene of the first crime. Like your mother, you were curious and though you were told to not follow, you did.

"Your mother brought secrets with her—secrets she did not share fully, at least not down here for the soil to record. Meribah wanted whatever she was hiding, and Noémi tried to warn your mother against entrusting anything of value to the Fae."

L'Runa rubbed her upper arms and placed her right hand over heart. "I said this before, and it bears repeating and acknowledging. There is so much sorrow in here. So much."

"Will the banishing keep Meribah beyond the wards?"

"Yes," L'Runa said. "The ritual will prevent her and anyone else whose blood lies here from breaching the wards, whether they try above or below ground."

I gave a silent thanks to the skills and talents of my magical friends.

"My grandfather will be off-island all weekend with Wes and the teenagers," I said, holding the two dolls closer to my heart and cupping the backs of their heads. I couldn't bear to look at them, nor could I bear to not have them in my arms.

"Then we shall make arrangements for next week." L'Runa peeled her attention away from me and glanced around the cellar. "I think you should go and settle those two. I will close the ceremony and gather my things, once I have opened the circle." She bestowed a loving look at the dolls in my arms and sighed. "I didn't think I was going to have to part with these beauties so soon, but they are yours now, Calliope. May you find comfort in them."

"So mote it be," I whispered. "So mote it be."

CHAPTER 6

Stepping out of the cellar with the straw-stuffed dolls pressed to my chest, I was taken aback at the audacity of the cloud-less sky. I made it to my bedroom and cleared a space atop my bureau. By the time I'd washed my hands and face of the smell from underneath the house, everyone was inside. I darted to my bedroom to change my clothes. Tanner was lying on my bed, ankles crossed, reading a book.

"Hey," he said, his voice soft and concern in his gaze. "How are you? I got the sense you wanted to be alone."

"You're a smart man," I said, crossing to my closet.

"Want to talk?"

I shook my head. Stray water droplets from repeatedly splashing water on my face slid down the back of my neck. "Later. After dinner."

I was torn between joining Tanner on my bed or tending to the dolls. A little girl's longing for answers won out over lust. I hadn't done much more than set the handsewn figures atop my bureau. L'Runa had instructed me to take more care than that.

There was a worn but clean pair of handknit socks in a basket in my closet. I tucked one doll in each, and rolled down the tops, fashioning makeshift sleeping bags. The dolls didn't really bend at the waist. I propped them standing side by side, with their backs to the mirror, and attached the seal pin to my mother's doll and the bear pin to Little Calliope.

"I'll be right back," I said, reaching for the door handle. I slipped out before Tanner could ask me where I was going or what I was doing.

In the kitchen, I found a bud vase, a half-eaten bar of expensive chocolate, and two juice glasses. I poured two fingers of Aunt Noémi's dessert wine into one and apple cider into the other and left all that on the counter.

The garden hadn't produced many flowers. My attention had been elsewhere from mid-July on. A patch of perennial dahlias kept showing up, and this year the blooms were variegated and plentiful. I snipped two—one a deep burgundy and the other a fruity shade of orange—and pinched off the leaves in order to wedge the stems into the vase.

Back in my room, I rearranged the crowded bureau top as L'Runa suggested. The dolls seemed pleased with the treats. I was happy to surround them with meaningful objects, though my circlet, worn once at my ritual of initiation in August, needed attention. I straightened the stems of its delicate metal leaves, polished the tiny round mirrors, and lowered it over the dolls.

I so wanted them to speak to each other. And to me. My throat tightened. I had gone more than three decades without my mother and this was one of those moments when my allotment of memories felt woefully stingy.

"Are you okay?" Tanner swung his legs off the bed and sat up. His gaze met mine in between the spidery cracks blooming across the old mirror's crackled silver backing.

I gripped the corners of the bureau. Shook my head and closed my eyes, putting me in immediate contact with House and my land and our shared sense of waiting.

"What do you need me to do?" he asked.

"Help me find the missing links and pieces?" I ran my fingertips over the head of one doll, then the other. "Help me put the past to rest? Reassure me I'm doing the right thing by letting the boys go this weekend?" I shrugged. I was relieved the teens would be away from the island and away from danger for the next three days. Which wasn't much time to double down on Odilon and Clan Vigne.

Tanner settled himself behind me as I spoke. Leaning into the solid support of his torso, I sighed. Working investigations as a team was becoming a theme in our developing relationship. Adding Odilon to our ongoing search of the properties on the island wouldn't leave us much time for romance.

My druid gently guided me to face him. "I'm sorry I can't be with Harper and Thatcher this first time. I trust Wes with my own life, and I know he'll keep his eyes on your sons."

"I know there's no rational reason for me to worry. Christoph's going, too, and he's been mentoring teens for decades." I relinquished my stalwart spine and let Tanner pull me in closer. "The girls are excited. I almost wish I could go. Learning magic as an adult is hard," I added. I faked a pout.

"I've been doing this for so many years, Calliope, that I sometimes lose track of how new it is to you."

I snuggled my curves into Tanner, wrapped my arms around the back of his waist, and let myself accept his offer of support. He softened first and I followed, until the rhythm of our breathing matched. Leading me into a lazy box step, he danced us between the closet and the bureau until the sounds and smells of food preparation filtered in.

Suddenly, I had an appetite. "Let's go see what everyone's up to."

AFTER THE DINING TABLE HAD BEEN CLEARED, AFTER THE DISHES were cleaned, dried, and put away, a plate was piled high with fresh-baked cookies. I chose a treat for myself, waved the teenagers off, and settled onto the couch-sized swing on the back deck.

Strains of the theme music that introduced the boys' favorite video game floated out the open upstairs windows. I closed my eyes, let my toes skim the decking, and sent my awareness coiling around the bones of my house and along the periphery of the property. Feelers came back drowsy with a sated peacefulness, and I rocked the remains of the day out of my system.

I must have fallen asleep. An arm slipped under the backs of my knees, another behind my shoulders. The faint scent of mint told me the arms sliding beneath me belonged to Tanner. I was lifted up, carried through the house, and deposited on my bed.

"I need to brush my teeth," I mumbled, pushing up to sitting. I almost fell over to the other side. "Are you sleeping in here?"

"What's your preference?" Tanner sat beside me. "All five of the kids are in the bunkhouse right now, but I'm not sure who's sleeping where. Christoph's snoring on the futon in your office. I can sleep on the couch."

"I'm not ready for us to sleep together when the boys are home, now that they know you're here," I said, snuggling against his side. "Last night was a special exception."

Tanner slid a finger under my chin and lifted. I could barely open my eyes. His kiss assured me that, eyes open or closed, his lips would be on my mind all night long.

I SLEPT THE SLEEP OF THE EMOTIONALLY DRAINED, AND WHEN I unstuck my eyes, it felt like the house had come alive earlier than usual. Stumbling between my bedroom and the bathroom, I waved Wes in as he approached the front door. He toed off his boots and went right to my old office to speak with Christoph. Sallie and Azura were next, perky and chirpy as the morning's birdsong.

The teens hauled everything edible from the kitchen to the table. At least, it seemed that way. And after they'd devoured cereal and platters of toast and scrambled eggs, they raced to see who could pack fastest.

Christoph reminded his charges to clean up, and once everyone had used the bathrooms and washed their dishes, Tanner and I followed the sextet to the Old One for last-minute hugs and promises to have fun. This trip to Vancouver marked Thatcher's first time traveling via the portal system. I resisted voicing the evergreen maternal admonishment to be careful, bit my tongue rather than asked if the teens had packed everything they needed, and smiled hard instead.

The momentary change in air pressure at their departure through the portal situated within the crabapple tree set misshapen fruit to jangling at the ends of their stems.

I stared at the tree's scruffy bark, patched with greenish-gray lichen, seeing but not seeing. The ground around the Old One was supposed to be smooth and well-tended for when travelers departed, making it easier to pick up the stones that acted as tickets. My tree's multiple portals had been abandoned—or so Alabastair, my new friend and Portal Keeper, thought—and the stones had either never been replaced, or were buried under seasons of neglect.

Wes must have employed other means to get the gaggle of teens to the nexus in Vancouver.

Tanner touched the underside of my forearm with his finger-tips and traced a line to my wrist. I let him take hold of my hand and snug it against his chest.

"We could work outside until the office is closed."

A glance at the plants in my garden showed they were already in transition, with their brown-edged leaves and drying stalks. "I like that idea. I haven't done any gardening in weeks."

An apple dropped a timely reminder onto my shoulder. I bent to pick the ripe fruit off the ground. Shining it on my shirt, I offered it to Tanner and said, "I guess I should add apple-picking to the list."

He kissed my knuckles, let go of my hand, and palmed the crabapple. Turning, he looked over his shoulder to the back of my house. His gaze moved clockwise over my property: the slice of the driveway visible from here, the uneven border where untended lawn met the woods and undergrowth, the bunkhouse under construction at the far end, and all the way around to my garden area. As he lifted his arm and started to speak, a bright pink Volkswagen Bug paused at the end of the driveway, rolled forward, then reversed. A horn sounded.

"Hold that thought," I said.

"What's Maritza doing here?"

"I have no idea." I groaned. "Do you think if we ignore her, she'll go away?"

"Not likely." Tanner released my overall's straps. "If she's here without calling first, might be important."

I jogged across the yard, up the drive, and called, "Maritza!" She rolled down her window when I passed through the wards.

"Calliope. I'm normally not one to visit unannounced, but I felt it imperative that we use the threshold provided by the equinox to create an essential tool that you will use in some of your magical workings." She put the car in Park and lowered her black-rimmed sunglasses. Elongated ovals of Prussian blue twinkled from the end of each finger. "I brought most everything we need, and we should be done in under an hour. Perhaps two." She gripped the steering wheel and stared out the windshield. "Maybe three. Would you be amenable to an impromptu lesson?"

I was intrigued enough to not hesitate. Besides, L'Runa wanted to enlist Maritza's skill as a necromancer to decipher what information the dolls might share, and we needed her expertise for the banishing.

"Sure," I said, "the driveway's right here. Tanner's visiting, too."

"Delightful." Maritza raised one already perfectly arched eyebrow and permitted herself the hint of a grin. Readjusting her sunglasses, she said, "Always good to have a druid around should things get out of hand."

Tires rolling slowly over gravel sent me to the side of the driveway. I slid one hand behind the bib of my overalls and massaged the center of my chest. I was surprisingly not at all in the mood for things getting out of hand today.

Maritza parked her car, opened the driver's-side door, and stuck one leg out. She'd traded her signature platform sandals for orange Chucks with blinding white laces. Her skinny jeans and loose blouse were black, as was the oversized hobo bag she dragged across the gear shift into the driver's seat.

The work attire I'd grabbed off a hook in my closet looked even shabbier next to Maritza's ensemble. "May I carry that for you?" I asked.

"Please. Your dress is in there."

"My *dress*?" I shoved my hands into the overalls' deep front pockets. Every time I'd worn a dress this summer, my life had experienced a marked change. White cotton for the initiation ritual. Red silk for the Blood Ceremony. An embroidered party frock the night the Flechette Clan revealed their true faces and intentions.

It was no wonder I always reached for comfortable sweats or cargo pants or my gardening overalls first thing in the morning.

Maritza nodded and walked around her car, straight toward Tanner. He had tucked his shirt into his pants and drawn his hair into a ponytail. "Druid," she called, offering her hand. "Has Ni'eve released you from her tutelage?"

Tanner brought her fingers to his lips and bowed slightly. "The druidess and I will soon close this chapter of our relationship," he said. His voice carried to where I struggled with the weight of the witch's bag. "I was granted a three-day leave and chose to spend my time off with Calliope."

"Timing your visit to coincide with the equinox was fortuitous. This is a perfect opportunity for Calliope to create the particles she will need for casting living circles."

I had to heft the bag into my arms and hold it to my chest. "I thought witches used salt for their circles," I said, drawing closer. Then I remembered L'Runa's off-the-cuff lesson from the day before.

Maritza gave a patient sigh. "Do you recall the circle I cast in the burial mounds?"

My cheeks, already flushed from the sun, reddened at my lack of retention. I would never forget that circle she cast, nor would I ever forget my first sight of Maritza Brodeur. She had been walking toward the Pearmains' back porch, her silhouette hazy in the summer heat. A cluster of floating confetti accompanied her slow gait. Later, she explained she'd created those particles that very morning from plants and flowers growing on the property.

"Yes, I do."

"Making the components of your magic *in situ* makes them naturally more potent. Site-specific tools honor place over the application of more generic materials."

My fingers itched to take notes. Maritza continued. "Back to your question. Salt is not used for every magic circle. An excess of salt in the soil acts as a barrier to the cell walls of roots, causing them to eventually die from lack of hydration. Which is fine if that is your intent. Some rituals require a death.

"However, circles made from trees and plants that have a connection to where you are casting your magic make superior circles for the work you will do." She readjusted her glasses, adding, "Reduce, reuse, recycle. I believe it was an earth witch who first coined that phrase in the 1800s."

I almost giggled. Tanner saved me by offering to make Maritza a lemonade as he relieved me of the bag. I handed it over gratefully and added I would take a drink, too.

Maritza homed in on me the moment Tanner left. From our

first encounter at Cliff and Abi's orchard, the witch and necromancer had struck me as one of those Magicals who had one foot in the present and the other in a realm only she could see. "Allow me to explain the process, Calliope. First, we choose a place. We'll need a flat, circular area approximately—" she scanned me up and down "—eight to ten feet across."

She then assessed my property, tapping a deep blue nail against her chin and hmming to herself. "You said there were maps in your mother's books?"

I nodded. "Yes."

"Let us have a look. There may already be a sacred circle here."

"I think you're right," I said. I had shoveled matted grass off a handful of rocks during a burst of premenstrual energy. Their shape and spacing suggested their placement was deliberate. I reached into the chest pocket of my overalls for the map I had cobbled together out of pages I'd copied from one of my mother's *Good Housesweeping* books and showed it to Maritza. When I squinted, I could imagine where the rest of the rocks were located by following the hand-drawn design. "There are at least two stone pathways here, both large circles with smaller paths inside."

Maritza lifted the map and studied it against the array of uncovered rocks and clumps of dried grasses and moss. "Calliope, your land was once a place where witches gathered. Witches, and others. This map confirms what I sense." She handed it to me. "You may put this away for now and gather what flowers and herbs you can. Our color palette is somewhat limited this time of year, but there should be enough in your garden and among the wildflowers to start with."

The witch pointed to a fairly flat, clear area between where we were standing, and the bunkhouse snugged near the woods. "I will create the circle, and you will scatter everything you gather inside its circumference."

Witches, and others. What were my mother and her sister involved with?

I wanted to plant myself facedown on the ground, tap into the underlying magical, mycelial network, and tug and tug until I'd pulled distant memories to the surface.

Instead, I collected my gardening shears and an old canvas bag from the shed and plotted the route of my harvest.

CHAPTER 7

S tarting at the north, I walked along the cool side of the house and clipped a hank of untrimmed grass and a couple branches of salal, heavy with deep purple berries. I popped one in my mouth and pictured Bear happily rummaging in the bush for a late-summer treat. Rounding into the sunlight, I snipped crabapple leaves and a selection of herbs from my garden, including late-flowering rosemary and stems of dried coriander and dill seed. In the far corner, opposite the raspberry canes, the dahlias offered up more of their generously petaled blooms.

I continued around the periphery of the property, adding anything still green or flowering, including fern fronds with curling brown edges and little purple asters. When I finished, I went to where Tanner and Maritza were standing and gulped down the offered glass of lemonade.

"Let me wash first," I said, handing the empty glass to Tanner. I used the cold-water-only outdoor faucet to scrub my hands and rinse my face and neck. The bottom of my T-shirt served in lieu of a towel.

Back at the circle, Maritza distributed the plant matter throughout. She pointed to her heavy bag and motioned I should reach inside. Simple cotton muslin brushed against my dampened fingertips. When I went to lift the garment from the bag, its weight pulled me off balance and as I stood, I saw why.

"Be careful not to cut yourself, Calliope. Perhaps now would be a good time for Tanner to assist?"

I glanced over my shoulder. "Take this side," I said, indicating with my elbow. Both my hands were hooked under the wide straps of the sleeveless dress. Tanner wiped away sweat and bits of grass before offering me his hand and wrist. "Give me your other arm, too."

The muscles and tendons on his forearms strained as he adjusted to accept the full weight of the garment. I crouched and peered closer at the hundreds, maybe thousands of needles weighting the hem in tightly stacked rows. Curious, I tapped the tip of one with my finger. When the needle broke the skin at the barest touch, I quickly shoved my finger in my mouth and hoped Maritza didn't see the blood. "How am I supposed to get into this?" I asked. "The needles are—"

"Intimidating? I know. And deadly if provoked. I attached every single one of them and each tried to draw first blood." Pride coated Maritza's voice. "My brother is a master at his work."

"*Malvyn* made the needles?" The sorcerer presented himself as a doting father and husband. I knew him best as the Enforcer. Between his admission that he crafted flechettes for Magicals who preferred to carry darts, and now these thirsty needles, my early impressions of the man were changing.

"He did."

I was more curious than ever to see Malvyn's metalworking studio, though I had been hoping for something less deadly looking for my first piece of the jeweler's artistry. "What did you mean by first blood?"

"The one who feeds the first needle becomes the true owner of the dress." She hovered her fingertips over the fringe of metal and sighed. "I suspected this would be yours as I made it, Calliope. May it never draw more blood than is absolutely necessary."

I held up my pricked fingertip. "Guess this means I am the true owner," I said.

Maritza slipped a pair of reading glasses over her nose, reached for my hand, and assessed the cut. "Your saliva will help remove any blood that might stain the fabric." She peered at me; her eyes icy blue. "Only *your* blood, that is. Do try to keep the dress clean."

Oh, the charm of the magical world.

"Tanner, if you would please proceed to the circle of flowers and lower the dress directly into the center," Maritza said, waving him forward. "Calliope will step inside and stay absolutely still as you bring the straps over her arms."

Sounded simple enough. "Calliope, beforehand you will disrobe completely."

And there was the catch. I shuddered at the thought of the needles pricking the more sensitive areas of my body.

We walked to the circle of flowers and herbs as a trio. Tanner stepped inside and waited. My usually calm and steady druid was nervous. I paused to take a breath before undoing the side buttons and buckles on the straps to my overalls. The worn denim slid down my legs to the ground, followed by my T-shirt, then underwear.

I stepped over the low wall and steadied myself with a hand on Tanner's shoulder. The bottom of the dress pooled on the plant matter, while the top half was ready to receive its wearer.

Me.

My heart was beating against the backside of my rib cage. Pointing my toes and exaggerating my movements, I lowered one foot through the opening, then the other, and covered my breasts with my hands. Tanner drew the heavy muslin up the sides of my thighs and over my hips. "One arm at a time," he said. I drank in his reassuring presence. "You'll be fine," he whispered. "I'll be right here."

I lowered the shoulder he wanted first, then the other, and without further fanfare or bloodletting, I was adorned in a dress trimmed with thirsty needles. Tanner stepped out of the circle at Maritza's nod.

"Now, you twirl," she said, flicking her hand in an arc.

"Twirl?" I asked. I lifted my arms overhead, elbows bent, in an awkward approximation of a ballet dancer.

"Try this." Tanner's arms were outstretched but not stiff. He turned one palm to face the ground, raised the other toward the sky, and began to move his feet. Small steps sent his body into a counterclockwise movement. "Focus on your hand and you won't get dizzy."

Maritza tapped her cheek and added, "Relax your arms, Calliope. Start as Tanner showed you or just hold your arms away from your body. Let the land speak to you through your feet. Close your eyes when you feel ready. Your body will become a conduit."

I could do that, the listening through my feet part, and the moment I relaxed my gaze I understood what I needed to do.

Lifting my heels allowed the needles to brush over the scattered flower petals and other bits of nature's detritus without getting snagged on the grass. I began to step in a tight circle while using my arms for balance. The bottom of the ankle-length A-line dress swung out as I gained momentum.

It didn't take more than a dozen revolutions before the weight of those hundreds of slivers of sharpened metal created a perfect blade with which to shred the plant matter. Within minutes a growing susurration heralded the appearance of thousands of tiny flecks. They floated around my ankles and calves and headed upward. Instead of losing myself to the wonder, I figured out where to look, and when, to keep from getting nauseous or falling over.

Tanner and Maritza stood on opposite sides of the stone circle. Their mouths were moving, though I couldn't hear their words, and their gazes sought something only they could see.

Secure finally in my footing, I spread my arms wider, lifted my chin, and opened my eyes to the sky. The same fishing-net-like structure I had seen forming over the burial mounds at the Pearmains' now wavered overhead. This time, the strings encased only me. Squarish holes anchored translucent fields of light, shimmering the way the wards around my house did when they were activated.

The structure was breathtakingly beautiful. I continued spinning, the needles kept cutting, and more and more bits filled the air within the bubble until they stuck like confetti to its inner surface and even to my skin. When the overall effect passed from yellows into greens and the last strands of my hair unstuck from the back of my neck, I could have been suspended below the surface of the ocean.

Mama.

Had my mother danced her way into other circles, bare feet trampling this same ground?

At a tug from beneath my toes, I asked the question again.

Mama, did you dance here with Noémi and your sister-witches? Did you answer the call of the soil and the plants, or did the nearby ocean with her myriad creatures hold your allegiance?

Magical words flitted like tiny fish alongside the particles floating in the air. Sweat beaded on my upper lip. I licked at my skin, tasted salt on my tongue, relinquished earth for water as the salt triggered a change in sensation. I went from toes on grass to ankles tangled in seaweed.

Bubbles streamed from my mouth. Tanner and Maritza, still ensconced outside of my net, failed to notice I was suspended in water. The needle dress was weightless. The sea filled the space between my skin and the cotton. Metal tickled my ankles.

Lifting my chin, I searched the dome of the net. The sun

glowed within a hazy ring. Specks of glittery red joined the shredded plants. I shook one foot.

Wait.

Listen.

Tanner punched his arm through the magical bubble and grabbed my wrist. My dance came to a sudden stop. I stumbled, arms akimbo. The energy emanating off the interior surface of the bubble kept me upright and the little bits suspended. Tanner's eyes were open and glowing as he stared at me. Looking to my other side, Maritza's lips were still moving. Her eyes remained closed until Tanner's shout jolted her into action.

At Maritza's clap, the net dissolved. The last of the tiny dots and ragged flecks floated downward and the full weight of the dress pulled on my shoulders. The witch nodded at Tanner.

I couldn't hear very well.

Tanner stepped close, cupped my chin, turned my head to one side then the other, and asked me a question.

"I can't hear you," I said. My feet began to sting. Tanner said something to Maritza. She stepped in and took hold of the dress straps. Tanner covered my ears with his palms.

I grabbed his wrists as the pressure in my head increased, then popped. A sensation of warmth flooded the inside of my ear canals.

"Can you hear me?" he asked.

I nodded, mouthed, *Yes.*

"Calliope, we have to get you out of the dress. Now." Maritza's voice snapped me into action. I wiggled my arms, rolled the damp fabric over my chest and hips, and shimmied until I was surrounded by a pile of bloodied cotton and glinting, red-tipped needles. A rash banded the tops of my feet and each ankle.

Maybe I was allergic to the oils in some of the plants.

"What happened?" I shivered in the sunshine and showed Maritza my foot.

"Malvyn's magic has always exhibited a wild side. I'm afraid something in this batch of metal has developed a thirst for blood."

"Do I have to wear it again?" I asked, surveying the dress with greater respect. And trepidation.

Maritza shook her head. "I'll take it back. It's incumbent that my brother creates magical objects that are stable. We can't let our baubles and bits start thinking on their own."

She held my gaze and continued, "Well, most of us cannot."

Tanner took a step back and held the dress away from his front. "What would you like me to do with this?" he asked Maritza.

With a sweep of her hand, the witch took charge, directing the dress to float toward her. "I'll put it in my car and drive directly to my brother's. He'll want to have a look at the garment while residual traces of magic are still active. I will be in touch."

With that, the witch and necromancer shouldered her large leather bag, said goodbye, and walked toward her car.

"Calli? Would you like to put your clothes back on and let me tend to your feet?"

"I sure would." My limbs quivered from the sustained physical exertion of twirling in place and from the waves of magic that had danced through me, the ground, the dress, the flowers, all of it. The net overhead had served to contain all that magic, perhaps intensifying its effect. My feet throbbed; my cells hummed.

I was very thirsty, and lightheaded, and struggling to understand what had just happened. I got Maritza's teaching point about using locally sourced materials. What I didn't get—or like —was the needles wanting to shred my feet.

Tanner had a hand on my shoulder and was brushing particles off the backside of my body, shoulders to ankles. He finished, led me to the nearest flat rock, and went to get my clothes.

Dressed, I sat and rested my forearms on my knees and my forehead on my arms. Tanner rolled the bottoms of my pant legs so the fabric wouldn't touch the tops of my feet. I liked the sureness of his hands.

"Can you get me more lemonade?" I asked.

"Sure," he said, petting the top of my head. "Anything else?"

"Chocolate chip cookies fresh from the oven?"

"Coming right up."

CHAPTER 8

I'm not sure how long I sat on the rock in the sun. Shaky muscles suggested I had been in movement longer than an hour, but time had a way of warping during magical exercises.

Feet skimmed grass, footsteps came closer, and the smell of chocolate prompted me to lift my head. Tanner appeared, carrying a tray loaded with a pitcher of lemonade, a plate piled with cookies, and first aid supplies.

"How the heck did you do that?" I asked, reaching for the offered refill and downing half the glass in a series of swallows.

"Magic."

I rolled my eyes, held out my hand, and waggled my fingers. "May I?"

Tanner lowered the plate. I chose the thickest, most chip-laden cookie. The first bite had me closing my eyes and groaning aloud.

"Leilani made extra cookie dough and saved it in the freezer. All I had to do was cut slices and speed up the baking process."

"You can do that?" I caught a dollop of melted chocolate at the corner of my mouth and urged it back with my pinky.

Tanner grinned and set the tray on the rock beside me.

"You've been sitting here long enough for the oven to preheat. Maritza called and advised I let you come down at your own pace. She also said if you fell over, you'd probably been on your own long enough."

I crooked a finger and drew Tanner closer. "How long was she here?"

He brushed a kiss across my temple. "An hour and a half, maybe a little more. Have another cookie and finish your drink. I want to take a look at your skin."

I did as instructed. I wasn't the expert here and I needed the fluid and the hit of sugar to set me back on track. The alcohol-soaked wipes stung. The comfrey balm quickly soothed. I rested my other foot on Tanner's knee and looked around.

The ground inside the stone circle was carpeted by a thick layer of multicolored particles. I could smell the combined scents of leaves, stems, flowers, seeds, and herbs even over the melted chocolate coating my tongue.

"Maritza said to gather the particles and store them in the little bag she left." Tanner loaded everything back onto the tray. I stood on my own, shuffled side to side and declared my feet fine, and held the opened bag in both hands. Tanner steadied me with a light touch to my hip.

"How're we supposed to gather all this up?" I asked. There were more particles on the ground than could possibly fit into the bag dangling from my hand.

"A rake." Tanner went to the shed and returned with the one with finer teeth. He stepped inside the circle and ushered the particles into the center. I tossed him the bag and he managed to collect every bit.

Drawing the strings tight, I weighed the contents in my hands. "Kind of feels like there's some heavy magic in here."

"Blood magic always feels that way, Calli." Tanner flopped onto the grass and patted the ground beside his hip. "C'mere."

"I'm exhausted," I said, stretching out next to him and resting the pouch on my belly. He found my hand and interlaced our fingers. "And I suppose it's time to move on to the breaking-and-entering segment of our day."

"You're going to need more than cookies and lemonade after your adventure with the dress."

I grunted. My druid smiled in understanding and continued, "You shower. I'll make dinner. Then we'll go to your office."

TANNER DROVE US INTO TOWN. THE PARKING LOTS AND ROADSIDE spots were filled to capacity, typical for a Friday night, necessitating he maneuver his truck into a tight spot. "Come out the driver's side. I parked a little too close to the brambles." He pressed the pedal to engage the parking brake and reached for the handle of his laptop bag. "You ready?"

"Yes." I could have asked the brambles to make a path for us, which might have called attention to the next part of our night. Instead, I scooted across to the driver's seat. My dress rolled up and over my hips and I flashed Tanner a view of my underwear.

It was time for a new wardrobe and better accessories.

On the off chance that Kerry happened to turn the corner before Tanner and I were inside the building, I asked if he could grab a couple of leaves and do his cloaking thing.

"Good idea." Tanner plucked two massive volunteers from a bigleaf maple and chanted over them while we stayed close to the truck. By the time we mounted the stairs to the entrance, leaves floating above our heads and keys in hand, he assured me no one could see us.

Opening the vestibule door and then the one to my old office, I took issue with the changes made by my temporary replacement. My whiteboard was missing and there was no discernible order to the papers tacked to my beloved corkboard. All the work I'd done earlier in the summer to track the farms and orchards we knew, or suspected, had Magicals on staff or housed tunnels and portals, was wasted.

Unless he had taken research that was supposed to help the locals and was now using my research against them.

Ugh.

At least I had a few photos of my project walls on my cell phone. I shut the door on the man's chaos and my guilt, went to Kerry's desktop, and started up her computer. We knew each other's passwords. I had a search engine up in no time.

"Did you bring a thumb drive?" I asked Tanner.

He pulled a new one from his bag and set it beside Kerry's keyboard.

"Thanks. I know how the paper filing system's set up. I'll start pulling everything related to the properties that have been operating the longest." Kerry had already collated that information into a list, which she'd expanded to include every property that had more than five live, producing apple trees.

Tanner adjusted the desk chair and hovered his fingers over the keyboard. "Send me the list of orchard and farm employees, too. I want to focus on the apple growers. There's got to be some connection we're missing, between the dead hidden folk, Adelaide's bid on the orchard near Brooks Family Farm, and the Pearmain orchard.

"We know that Cliff's family has had a relationship with the hidden folk going back generations," he continued. "There's a tunnel system in place though we still don't know the full story behind who uses it and how.

"Then there's the big portal tree, and the trees transported here from Europe, the ones Cliff said they were hoping to make healthy again, and..."

A network of possible connections blossomed in front of my eyes, including the property where the Mother Tree grew. I still had no idea where that piece of land was situated. Maybe if I just—

"Tanner, give me that notepad," I said, waving my hand in his face. "The blank one—quick, before I forget."

I roughed out a map of the island, drawing circles in the approximate locations of the orchards I remembered off the top of my head. I added my property for good measure, and because of the Old One and its as-yet-unverified four separate portals. "Clifford trained to become a druid. And he wanted Abigail to train, too, but she couldn't handle the physical rigor, right?"

Tanner nodded. "But Ni'eve and Idunn treated her and you'll see, Calli, the change in her is remarkable. I think she'll be around for many more years."

I looked up from my scribbling. "When did you say they're due back here?"

"Monday."

"This *coming* Monday?" I glanced at him for affirmation the elderly couple would be home in three days. "And their property has all the potential and most of the infrastructure it needs to be a magical hub. Is that how you worded it?"

He nodded again.

"So who else would want to create a hub like that—or an even larger one?"

"The Fae," we answered as one.

"Odilon is Fae. All of the Flechettes are Fae, as far as we know." I showed Tanner the roughed-out map and pointed as I explained. "Here's the property Adelaide intends to purchase. It's close to the ferry that leaves out of Fulford Harbor. Beings can get to Vancouver Island in thirty minutes and to Victoria in another forty-five. Going by portal would be faster, but not if they're transporting goods.

"That property's situated in the most fertile part of the island, and our records show it was one of the earliest cultivated orchards on the island, though it's not as old as the Pearmains'.

"Here's my property," I said, pointing. Then I added the two squarish parcels owned by Doug sitting to the north and south of mine, and the two parcels to the east and west that were in a blind trust. The one to the east was a small triangle at the bottom of my land, and the one to the west, across Fortune's Folly Road, was considerably larger.

"I've got to find out who owns these two lots," I said, tapping the paper. "And we need to know more about the Pearmain tunnels, which properties they link to, and if they're even being used."

The longer I looked at the page, the more convinced I became we were missing something. I drew straight lines to connect all of the properties. Even with the help of L'Runa's comments about geometry and its use in magic, not a bit of what I'd drawn looked meaningful.

"What're you doing?" Tanner asked.

"When L'Runa was here yesterday, she drew salt circles in the dirt before we began the ritual in the cellar. Not one central circle, but three big ones and then five more in the corners.

"It's an oddly shaped space," I added. "She said a sacred space doesn't always have to be defined by a perfect circle. This..." I pondered the sketch some more. "This is bugging me. I feel like I'm missing something."

"Perhaps what's missing is simply more data. More confirmed magical sites."

"You could be right. The missing pieces could be right here." I looked over my shoulder and surveyed the office, with its stacked oak filing cabinets and cardboard storage boxes and went back to my sketch. I tried to make it more three-dimensional. "And then there's the underland."

I had stepped inside the underland on Cliff and Abi's property. From the outside, the structure appeared to be a very old, very abandoned grape arbor, its thickly intertwined vines dusky black and peeling with age, the leaves a deep purplish-green.

Maritza had acted as a kind of hostess that evening, as the druidess, Ni'eve, appeared, followed by the goddess, Idunn.

Maritza and her apprentice, Alabastair Nekrosine, had been there, too. The witch and the necromancer had eventually disappeared into the back of the tunnel-shaped structure, swallowed by the impenetrable blackness, on their way to who-knew-where.

Underlands and tunnels shared a similar shape. In my experiences, the resemblance ended there. Tunnels were defined. Underground and claustrophobic but defined.

What set me on edge about the underland was its potential vastness. I turned to Tanner. "I can wrap my head around the *idea* of the tunnel system, even though I know this island is comprised of massive rocks—the amount of excavation that had to be done to connect the tunnels is mind-blowing. And I've experienced the portal system. I don't get how that works, but..." I shrugged. "But the underland, that's a whole other level of magic. I mean, I met Idunn that night, Tanner, a *Norse. Goddess.* Who probably lives in another realm. And she touched me. She *spoke* to me."

"She gave us her blessing, Calli."

The golden glint was back, dancing across Tanner's eyes and around his head.

"She gave you and me her blessing, yes, Tanner, but she neglected to grant us the time to pursue what it means to have a —a—" I rubbed my sternum, remembering the delicate imprint of the tree that had appeared on my skin, then faded that same night.

"A Goddess-blessed relationship?" he interjected.

"Yes. That. A Goddess-blessed relationship. What does it even mean?" A drowning sensation filled me from the legs up. For an earth witch, I was developing quite the affinity with water, especially salt water and its habit of showing up at inopportune times was beginning to exasperate me.

I fought against what was happening to my legs. Clung to the thought I should be able to piece together all the data, follow all the maps and charts without getting pulled under the surface and being left to float, accompanied by memories and voices disconnected from shore.

I wiggled one bandaged foot out of the flip-flop, pressed into the carpet, and the wood below that, and searched for soil. It was time to ask someone about what kept happening to me, and soon. Tanner's voice reminded me we had a more pressing task at hand.

"It's all about rewards, Calliope. If we can solve this and put wrongs to right, our reward is time together." Tanner had set his elbows on the edge of Kerry's desk and rested the side of his face against his interlaced fingers. The look in his eyes as his gaze bore into mine was less about a sexual connection than it was about something I hadn't really experienced.

Read about, yes. Real life? Nope. I closed my eyes in an anxiety-fueled bid to remain connected with the ground underneath the building. I'd done it before, especially if it was a particularly long or difficult day. The earth acknowledged my call, drained the uncomfortable buoyancy from my body, and restored my equilibrium. I opened my eyes.

"You're holding something back," I said, certain I was reading Tanner correctly. "This isn't about a fated mates connection, is it? Because I don't know that I believe that. It's great in fiction, but nothing about my life has ever led me to imagine there was one person out there for me, if only we could just, I don't know, solve some great riddle or make it through a series of life-or-death situations."

Tanner had stood while I babbled and now stepped around the desk. He offered me both hands. I took them and wrapped his waist with my arms.

"When I was young and full of myself," he said, rubbing slow circles between my shoulder blades, "I might have ascribed to the notion of fated lovers, especially when Ni'eve chose me to study with her. I had been made to feel special within my family. I was chosen by a druidess at the pinnacle of her teaching years. Many things about being a Magical came easy to me, Calliope. Then I met Jessamyne. I stopped thinking with my head. I stopped listening to my intuition and I let myself be led around by a head-strong young woman with a plan I was never fully privy to. I got caught up in her crazy, and when I finally escaped her hold, I realized I had sacrificed parts of myself in the process."

"Can you get those parts back?"

"I'm working on it," he said, his voice and touch equally soft. "I'm working on it. Putting things to right on this island and protecting its portals and the sacred trees would go a long way toward helping me feel like I had earned back my druid blessing."

"I have a lot of work to do, too, Tanner. We can help each other."

He kissed the top of my head. The pulse of arousal that often arose when we were close thrummed through Tanner's body and swirled through mine. "Let's get back to getting what we came here for," he said, "and then go home."

CHAPTER 9

While Tanner drove the truck, I organized the messy pile of documents we had hurriedly photocopied. "I think what we're looking for is in here," I said, rifling through page after page of deeds. "I want to cross-reference this with those directories of Magicals from across Canada."

If only I could recall where I'd put them. I looked up and through the windshield and chuffed out a sigh, not really seeing the landscape in front of me.

"What's that all about?" Tanner asked, turning onto Fortune's Folly Road. He slowed down as he approached House's hidden driveway.

"This is a lot of work. On top of what I have to do for the Basics of Witchcraft courses. I'm one month in and I feel so behind." With Sallie to keep an eye on, and the distraction of Christoph's never-ending building and home-improvement projects, I had been getting increasingly scattered to the point of being inefficient. And it was frustrating.

He parked the truck and cut the engine. "Tell me how I can help."

I gently tapped at the edges of the papers, trying to get them more or less lined up. "I don't think there's anything you can do about my course work. That I have to fumble through on my own." I shook out an empty cloth bag and guided the papers inside. "Tomorrow's the equinox. I haven't joined a coven and I feel like I should at least make the attempt to mark the occasion."

"We can do a ritual together. It's every bit as valid as those performed by a full coven."

"I don't know what to do," I admitted. Surely, I could find instructions in one of the course manuals, or online.

"We can do something druid-style. No pressure, no performance anxiety, just you and me, naked on the grass."

That made me laugh. Some of the tension sloughed off my ever-tightening shoulders. "Hopefully you won't have to rescue me afterward or wipe off copious amounts of my blood."

I opened the truck's door, planted my feet on the gravel drive, and slid the heavy bag of papers toward me.

"But?" Tanner closed his door and walked around the truck to help with the other bag.

"How did you know there was a *but* in there?" I asked, swatting at his arm.

He held out his hand, palm up, and wiggled his fingers. I took that as an invitation and interlaced mine with his. "I'm getting to know you, Calliope Jo—Calliope du Sang. You have a maternal streak, in the best use of that word. You care for this place and somebody's messing with it. Cue the beast."

I couldn't help but laugh. "Yeah, that's me, the beast."

We headed toward the house, hand in hand, agreeing to table the next phase of the project for the morning. We left the cloth bags on the dining table, checked the windows and locked the doors, and then got ready for bed.

"Any word from Wes?" I asked Tanner. He curled up next to me, all long limbs and warm skin.

"No. The mentors have everyone turn in their cell phones as part of the arrival process. I wouldn't expect to hear from him—

or the kids—until Sunday afternoon at the earliest. Unless there was an emergency."

I placed one hand on my lower belly and the other on my ribs, feeling guilty I'd barely thought of Harper and Thatcher since they'd whooshed out of sight at the portal. Tanner placed a hand over my eyes and kissed my shoulder. "You've had an eventful day. Close your eyes. Try to sleep."

"I thought having the kids away meant we'd have wild monkey sex."

Tanner bit me and laughed. "We could, if you'd like."

I lifted his hand so I could see his face. He looked as tired as I felt. I rolled to my side and nestled into his warmth. "Tomorrow," I mumbled. "I promise."

Calliope.

Sweetheart.

Come here.

I woke, eyes wide open and glued to the textured surface of my ceiling. Tanner was giving off enough heat for two people and had flung off the duvet. No wonder I was sweating and dreaming of drowning in feathers. I sat up to readjust the covers.

Calliope.

Sweetheart.

Come here.

Chills marched down my arms and across my back. I crept to the end of the mattress, placed one tentative foot onto the floor, and waited. Tanner slept.

Mama? The tiny voice was coming from either my closet or the bureau.

Calli, come here.

The bureau. The dolls. I pulled Tanner's T-shirt over my head, opened the bottom drawer of the bureau, and fumbled to get my legs into a pair of sweatpants in the dark. The dolls were where I had left them, snug in the woolly socks. I tucked them into the crook of my elbow and left the room as silently as I could.

Go.

"Go where?" I whispered, passing the kitchen island on my way to the front door. I was on the top step of the porch before I thought to stop and question what I was doing. The dolls' button eyes—serious, bottomless, and black—reflected the diffused light of the cloud-shrouded moon. Rain was coming—if not tonight, then tomorrow or Sunday—and not a day too soon.

Find water. I glanced skyward again. Could they feel the rain?

Ground water. I scooted back up the stairs for my pull-on leather boots. The dolls resisted me setting them on the boards. Slipping my feet in one-handed, I snagged the bandage atop each foot and winced.

"Ouch."

Go.

There were no ponds or creeks on my land, not even a vernal pool or dried-up wetland. At least, not that I knew of. "Go where?"

My night sight sharpened as the moon disappeared. I was on my driveway, unsure which direction to take next, when the first droplets of rain landed on my upraised face.

High beams flashed as a vehicle turned onto Fortune's Folly Road. Tires smacked against the macadam. A flatbed truck passed. I didn't think the driver noticed me.

"Go where?" I asked again. Garbled words flew past my ears. Blurry-edged images filled my head and body.

The rain began to dampen the heads of the dolls and the socks I'd stuffed them into. The shoulders of Tanner's T-shirt were soaked, I was getting cold, and it dawned on me I might be losing my grip.

. . .

Tanner found me on the couch, under the crocheted afghan, my hair still damp and the dolls clutched in my arms. "You okay?" he asked, crouching next to me. Behind him, the sky had cleared.

"It rained last night," I said.

"And you needed to experience it firsthand?"

I glanced at the dolls. They remained mute, like whatever had animated them during the night had run out of power. "They wanted me to find water."

"Did you?"

"No. Only the rain." I made no motions to move. Tanner asked if I wanted something hot to drink, and when I thanked him and asked for tea, he covered my legs with an additional quilt.

I closed my eyes, heard him fill the kettle, set it on the stove, and light the burner. I opened my eyes when the druid placed a mug of tea and a plate of toast on the table. "Let me know if you want anything else," he said. "I'm going for a run."

Warming my hand over the steam rising from the mug, I gave him my thanks and a weak smile. "I'll be ready to start working by the time you get back."

With the dolls back on my bureau and more toast in our bellies, Tanner and I took the big jumble of papers we'd carted out of my office and created a dozen smaller stacks on the dining table, each stack devoted to a single property. "Off the top of your head, do you know which of these farms and orchards are owned by Magicals?" he asked, dropping one of the directories on a side chair.

"I'm certain of a couple, yes. The ones owned by humans probably employ one or more Magicals. Some, like the Pearmains for instance, might have longstanding relationships with

Magicals unlike themselves." I surveyed the piles and groaned. "So much work."

I made a first pass through each property and added names and statuses to our list: current owner, previous owner, and whether they were Magical.

"I'll also start a list of our questions," I said, shifting my focus at the clang of dishes and utensils meeting the countertop. "Clifford and his grandsons would be the ones most knowledgeable about the tunnels, right?"

Tanner suggested it was the two hidden folk who tended the tunnels—and who had died—who would have best known the details of the underground network. He voiced his uncertainty about how much Peasgood and Hyslop had been taught prior to the ten years they were away from the orchard, following in their grandfather's footsteps by training to become druids. "We can ask Cliff next week, once they've settled in."

I seconded that idea, adding how relieved I was to know he and Abigail were finally coming home. I desperately needed to see them in person. "I'd like to table this for tomorrow, after you've left. Let's go outside and celebrate the arrival of autumn."

"Good idea."

Another round of seasonal rains was hunkered on the horizon. The rain in the middle of the night was too fine to make a difference to the grassy areas of my yard, which were still bone dry. I suggested we put votive candles in canning jars as our fire element and for illumination, adding, "I think we should just use the circle Maritza made yesterday."

I moved to where I'd spun my dance, lowered myself onto my hands and knees, and listened through my skin.

You steward the land, Calliope.

Syllables rumbled against my kneecaps and finger bones. This was not the voice of my mother, or of the Apple Witch. I pressed my forehead and sternum to the ground, straightened one leg, then the other, and listened through the front of my body.

Tanner walked out of the house with a tray of jars filled with lit candles and paused when he saw me. "You okay?" he called.

I waved him over. "I heard a voice."

"Was it a kindly voice?" He set the tray on a flat rock and moved with studied efficiency to place the eight candles evenly around the periphery of the circle.

"Yes."

"Good. Can you stand to take off your clothes? Because we can start our ritual right now. And it'll be better with nothing between you and the earth."

"Okay. I think I'm ready." Lavender oil from shredded plants wafted into my nostrils. "Tanner? I really am okay. A little weirded out by the dolls, but okay."

"I'm worried about you and these episodes." He stroked my back. "Stay put. I want to enhance the wards around the property."

I lifted my head and watched Tanner stride, loose-limbed but purposeful, toward the edge of the woods. He pulled the same small black container he'd used two nights before out of a front pocket, drew in the air, and walked to another spot about ten feet away. It looked like he intended to encircle the entire property with yellow-gold markings. As much as I enjoyed watching him move, the tug from below my palms was growing.

I pushed myself up, sat back on my heels, and lowered the straps of my overalls. After shrugging out of my T-shirt I rolled onto my feet and finished disrobing. My clothes went to a rock outside the circle and I went back to the ground on my hands and knees.

Come closer.

The same gravelly voice extended an invitation. I patted the area, removed a few sharp bits of rocks and broken sticks then lowered myself belly down, legs apart, arms away from my sides. I needed a few breaths to adjust to the sensation of the grass against my naked breasts and the cooling air on my back. And then I was in.

Breathe with us.

A chorus of voices. I closed my eyes. Inhaled. Exhaled. Inhaled again. The ground below me expanded. I exhaled and sank.

Open your eyes.

Skin. Grass. Fingers. Rocks.

Jars. Little flames. Trees. Sky.

Open your skin.

The ear pressed to the ground picked up a faint crackling. Tiny fuzzy threads reached between my cells and into the outermost layer of skin. From there, the threads thinned, passed through the dermis to my connective tissue.

I inhaled and I exhaled. The vibrations from Tanner's feet hitting the ground came closer and were followed by the *swish* of clothing sliding off limbs. The warmth of his naked body neared. I lifted my head, opened my eyes, and swept my gaze over the wards. "They're glowing," I said, containing my awe to a whisper.

Tanner lowered himself to his hands and knees, his gaze on me. The golden light wavering across the wards that circled my land was reflected in the druid's eyes. He pressed his chest to the ground, adjusted his limbs, and let a lengthy exhale settle him. His fingertips rested on my shoulder. "Do you feel it?" he asked.

Yes.

I continued to breathe. Strands, translucent and white, emerged from the surface of the ground like a forest of pea shoots only much more delicate. Minute black spots appeared at the tips of the strands. No longer able to resist autumn's call, I had to close my eyes and breathe out.

"We call this going loamy," Tanner said. Now it was his voice sending vibrations through the ground to meet my bones. "Do you feel the Joining?"

Yes.

I felt the Joining, little messengers at the cellular level

coursing through my body once they found my fascial tissue and the walls of my arteries and veins. I closed my eyes to the golden glow and allowed the soil to know me.

TURN YOUR HEART SKYWARD.

I rose. Lay on my back. Adjusted to the sensation of my heels, calves, and buttocks resting on ground I had warmed. After a couple of minutes, Tanner pushed away, sat, then lay on his back, too. The fine white strands brushed against the sides of my arms and legs and torso, grew longer, covering more—but not all—of our exposed skin.

I opened my eyes to the star-filled sky. Inhaled. Each star found a corresponding spot on the front of my body. Each patch of darkness did, too. A shooting star tickled as it crossed my belly. The very top of the wards caught more stars in their netting and held them there like fireflies in a jar.

Listen.

One ear tuned in to Tanner's breath. The other ear sought and found leaves brushing against leaves, fir needles sliding against fir needles, as the wind began to stir.

Listen to what lies below.

I opened up my back.

Skin. Ribs. Heart chamber.

I ventured into my organs.

Kidneys, liver, and lower, to my womb.

Waters ran alongside my bones, flowed through my fallopian tubes and down my inner thighs. Salt water. Fresh water. The ends of my hair spread toward the trees, toward the stars, and down toward the shared layers where those little white strands had infiltrated.

What do you want to know?

Nothing, I thought. *Nothing. It's all right here.*

. . .

I might have fallen asleep. For all I knew, days might have passed. I might have come apart and been re-formed. The votive candles had burned out. The sky was clear black in areas, fuzzy-edged and dark gray in others.

"Tanner?"

"Yes?"

"What was that?"

"That was the Joining." Tanner rolled to his side and stood. I followed, heavy-limbed and slow, and reached for our clothes. He gathered the empty jars to the tray, and we walked toward the house without speaking.

"I want to shower. And I feel like I shouldn't shower," I said. I was standing in the middle of the ground floor of my house, naked, certain I could pass for a human mushroom.

"If we were near warmer waters or a stream, we'd bathe outdoors. I think it's okay to acknowledge we're modern Magicals and take showers."

"I also don't feel like talking," I admitted.

"Go shower first. I'll make hot chocolate."

Bundled into worn flannel pajamas, I warmed my belly with the richest cocoa I had ever tasted while Tanner had his shower. Once he'd dried and slipped between the sheets, he admitted he'd forgotten about the bag of cocoa powder he'd bought in Paris until tonight.

The scent of my land's underlayers clung to the insides of my nostrils. When I sniffed at Tanner's shoulder and in toward his armpit, I found the same scent.

I didn't want to pick apart the experience I had just shared, with Tanner and with my land. I finished my cocoa, set the mug on my desk, and promised my teeth a double brushing in the morning.

"Good night, Tanner."

"G'night, Calliope."

CHAPTER 10

Tanner left with Sunday's sunrise, the smell of coffee and a promise on his breath. We'd overslept, with no time for morning sex, leisurely or otherwise. I waved goodbye from the deck. The tremor from his departure sent more apples tumbling to the ground, a good reminder I really needed to get the ripened fruits picked and processed.

I dressed, wanting to preserve Tanner's lingering scent on my skin and my sheets as long as I could. Brunch was a bowl of yogurt and granola eaten at the table, where I once again sorted through the piles and sketches we'd made and read through our handwritten notes.

It was clear to me my temporary replacement was connected to Odilon Vigne—or the Flechettes—either directly or via a more circuitous, less easily traceable route. My musings on just how I was going to get my hands on that information was interrupted by Thatcher texting to let me know the five teens wanted to stay in Vancouver overnight to attend a concert. He reassured me the adults were on board and would be staying with them at the retreat center overnight. They would take the portal home early enough Monday to make it to school.

I sent an immediate yes, set my phone on the counter, and glanced beyond the kitchen and living room windows. The sun was shining. There wasn't a cloud in the sky. No one needed me for anything. The fingerprint-coated cabinet facings and lurking dust bunnies could wait another day or week to be cleaned.

What if I took today to venture out on my own? Maybe a short portal trip to test my ability to find my way there and back would make for a good start. If that went well, I could expand my range or return home and settle down to work on any number of projects.

Before I could overthink my idea or lose my bravado, I tucked my wand into the thigh pocket of my cargo pants and affixed the wolf pin to the lapel of my long-sleeved blouse. Back in the kitchen, my phone went into another pocket. I refilled my water bottle, added it to my cross-body bag along with a packet of dried fruit, and declared I was ready.

House suggested I leave a note. I pulled open a kitchen drawer, wrote "I'm going portaling" on a Post-it, and cocked my head. Was *portaling* even a word?

I left the note on the middle of the refrigerator door and grabbed my new shoes. A local leatherworker had made them to my specifications, the soft soles providing a supple barrier between my skin and the ground. My as-yet-untested theory was, the Mary Jane–style shoes would allow me to gather information through my feet without having to constantly remove my footwear.

I traced my gaze up the trunk of the Old One, trying to recall where Alabastair had placed his hand the night he escorted me to the Flechette estate on Vancouver Island. Pressing my hand against the same spot, I automatically closed my eyes. A gentle undulation under my fingers nudged my awareness to where bark and patches of lichen morphed under my palm. I slid my other hand into the pocket where I'd stashed my wand and gripped the applewood tight.

"I'm ready," I whispered.

Nothing happened. I cracked open my eyelids, cleared my throat and repeated the words louder and with conviction.

The air around me darkened. Flickers of sunlight danced at the tips of grasses and leaves, reminding me of the daytime solar eclipse the boys and I had witnessed the summer before. I held my breath as the sensation of entering a vacuum began, then stilled.

"Calliope? What are *you* doing here?"

I was in limbo. And Alabastair was here with me. Or at least it felt like he was. I couldn't see a thing and my belly didn't know whether to give up my breakfast or hold on.

"Bas?" I asked. "Is that you?"

"Of course it's me. Who else would it be?"

"But—"

"No buts, Calliope Viridis du Sang. I am the Portal Keeper. You touched your portal tree. Thus, I am at your service," he said, his voice clipped. "Even though you summoned me at a less than opportune moment."

"I was trying to do this on my own."

"Do what?"

"Take the portal to—" My mind went blank.

"To where?"

"I don't know."

My long-suffering necromancer friend heaved a sigh. "Calliope, unless you're heading on a magical walkabout, one does not simply place one's hand on a portal tree, give your red heels a click, and wish yourself back to Kansas."

I kept my hand on the tree and searched the ground. Two faint, deep red half circles glowed in the vicinity of my feet. "How did you know I was wearing red shoes?" I asked. They'd been dyed to match my gauntlets.

"I ventured a wild guess."

An uncomfortable minute passed.

"Alabastair? Am I supposed to ask you to accompany me, or could I try this on my own?"

"I suppose today is as good a day as any."

The brush of heavy drapery swooshed against the side of my leg. Bas appeared in front of me. This time, sans cape.

"Nice bathrobe," I said, admiring his sartorial elegance. He snorted.

"It's a housecoat, Calliope. A house. Coat. A garment designed to be worn indoors when one desires to affect a look of leisure."

"I apologize for interrupting whatever leisure activity you were pursuing."

"Apology accepted. Now, where would you like to go?"

"Seattle?" I said, realizing I should have put a little more thought into what soloing from portal to portal entailed.

"Been there, done that." He waved his hand to hurry me along. "Aim higher."

"France?"

Bas's eyebrows arched elegantly. "Planning a little tryst with your favorite druid?"

"Is that creepy?" I asked. It suddenly occurred to me Tanner might be otherwise engaged in druid-y things.

"I can't imagine that man would find a surprise visit from his favorite witch a hardship." He adjusted the belt on his housecoat and shifted his weight to his other leg. "Ready?"

"Wait," I said. "Can I really get to France and back before tomorrow morning?"

"Of course you can." He slid one hand into a pocket trimmed with a curlicue of braid, pulled out a pastille tin, and handed it to me. "Sublingual tablets for nausea. Pop four under your tongue, allow them to dissolve, then go. You'll be fine."

"Okay, tell me how to get there and how to get back."

"Do you have your wand?" he asked. I nodded. "Good. As you discovered that *terrifying* night in August, your wand was crafted of wood freely given from a portal tree. Ergo, your wand will function as a portal key and return you home."

Lesson duly noted. "Does the wand get me to *any* portal tree?"

"No, only this one."

I gulped. "Should I be doing this, Bas? Tell me the truth." The surge of excitement that had gotten me this far was cooling fast.

"Calliope, I will always tell you the truth. You're a witch. You will be tested. And some of those tests will come when there is no one familiar around to help. You will have to make decisions on the spot. Better to test your wings when there's no pressure, no life or death consequences." He gripped my shoulders. "Let me ask you again. Are you ready?"

"Yes." I squeezed my fists and fixed my posture.

"Lesson number one. Speak clearly." He lifted my chin. "E-nun-ci-ate. Lesson number two—have patience. There may be other travelers ahead of you in the queue, especially during rush hours. You will feel a slight tug in the vicinity of your navel as you get closer to the portal activating. Do not let your attention wander. Period."

"Can I specify any destination in the world?"

Alabastair paused. "Well, yes. But not every destination is a direct trip. And some trips are rather arduous." He looked me up and down. "For instance, you are not dressed for the desert, the tropics, or the more northerly stations. Do you know where in France you want to go?"

"Tanner's with his teacher on Mont Blanc."

There went those perfect eyebrows again. "You do know that's the French Alps, *n'est ce pas?*"

"*Oui?*" I answered. I knew very little French. This trip was doomed.

Bas tsk'd. "Don't give up so easily, Calliope du Sang. You will go to Paris first. Your ensemble verges on the overly casual but adopt the right attitude and no one will notice. Once you arrive, speak to a Portal Keeper. They're usually hired from the fairy realm—dryads, tree nymphs, and the like—and they will answer in whatever language the traveler uses. Tell them you wish to visit Chamonix and do not let them intimidate or distract you."

"Chamonix," I said. I repeated the name twice for good measure.

"*Es-tu prêt?*"

"*Oui.*"

"*Bon voyage, ma chère.*"

Alabastair squeezed my shoulders once more, took a step back, then another, and disappeared into the charcoal gloom. I gripped the tree, straightened my spine, and said, "Paris. Please."

I FORGOT TO TAKE THE TIME DIFFERENCE BETWEEN BRITISH Columbia and France into consideration. By the time I landed in a copse of unfamiliar trees in the Bois de Boulogne—I only knew my location because of the nameplate attached to the tree—the sky was dark, and the night air was heavy with the potential for rain. Somewhere along the way I'd lost my can-do attitude.

"Do you require assistance?" With the crackle of heavy feet landing on dried leaves, a barely dressed being appeared in front of me. I noticed its horns first. They gleamed like polished chestnuts in the lanterns' light and were set flush against the being's head. Tufts of slightly more reddish hair tumbled over the horns and its forehead.

"I might have made a mistake," I said. I stuck out my hand. "I'm Calliope. Earth witch."

He looked at my hand, then grasped it in both of his. "Gilles. Portal Keeper, tour guide, and companion for hire." He bent at the waist in a mock bow. "Once I am off duty, this faun could be all yours."

I dropped my gaze to the ground. Hooves to match the horns and ankles to envy. "That's very nice of you, Gilles, but I'm meeting a friend in Chamonix."

He feigned a broken heart, recovered, and pointed toward the narrow, curved pathway between the rows of trees. "Cross the path, count two trees in that direction. Jacques will assist you."

Other travelers arrived. The faun turned to answer their questions. I felt inside my bag for the tin Bas had pressed into my hands. Dropping four tablets under my tongue, I imagined I traveled this way all the time and presented myself to Jacques.

He wasn't nearly as flirtatious as Gilles. The older faun took my palm, slapped it against the tree, and sneezed.

The ride to Chamonix was bumpy, its portal tree situated in a section of hilly land overlooking a small city. I was the only one there. Waiting for the Portal Keeper to appear—assuming every tree had one—I squealed when a pair of arms wrapped me from behind and lifted me off the ground.

"It's you," Tanner said. He pressed his nose to the side of my head, inhaled, and lowered me to the ground. He spun me to face him and asked, "Where is everyone?"

"I came by myself," I said. This man had seen every inch of me, up close, personal, and naked. We'd bathed muck off each other. We'd grappled with each other's exes. We'd said our goodbyes only a few hours ago. And here I was standing on a hillside in the French Alps, enfolded in his arms, feeling giddy. I wanted Tanner to be proud of me. "Christoph and the kids decided to stay in Vancouver overnight and I—"

Tanner didn't let me finish my sentence. His lips, warm and firm and tasting faintly of wine, sought and found mine in the dark. He had my shirt unbuttoned, my back against the tree, and his hands on my breasts before I could register whether we had company. "How long can you stay?"

"Long enough?"

"Can you handle one more portal?"

He held me tight with one arm, reached for the branch overhead with the other, and said something in French. I recognized the word for *castle*, and then the world went dark. I opened my eyes to see the flutter of Tanner's pulse at his throat. He grabbed my wrist, suggested I duck, and led us out from under the lowest branches of an old—very old—spruce tree.

I clutched the sides of my shirt together as we jogged across a trimmed bit of grass to a stone walkway that ended at a tower. More of the same stone chilled the bottoms of my feet as I stepped onto a narrow set of stairs lit by wall torches. Real ones, with open flames. We circled for three floors until we came to a landing. Like the two before, this had one door. Tanner pushed it open, hauled me inside, and dropped the latch.

Walls of the same stone circled the main room. Tanner strode to an inner door and pointed. "That's the bathroom. Cold water only." He swiveled and pointed to the single mattress on a metal frame. "That's my bed. It's very warm. Or it will be."

I slid the strap of my bag over my head, dropped my jacket and blouse, and unbuttoned my pants. The look in Tanner's eyes said he appreciated I'd neglected to put on a bra. He looked lower. "Take those off."

I slid my hands between my cotton underwear and pebbled flesh and did an approximation of something just this side of sexy until I'd stepped out of pants and undies both.

"Get in bed."

I did, slipping between two sheets, crisp with cold. Tanner took his time with his zipper and his shirt and whatever else he was wearing. I stopped paying attention to what he was shedding and focused on what he was revealing.

As soon as he was fully naked, he dashed to the bed. I wiggled closer to his heat and claimed his leg with mine. Tanner rolled on top of me, rocking himself between my inner thighs until I spread my knees.

"You make me hungry." He kissed his way down the front of my torso. I took one of his wrists and brought his thumb to my mouth to suck. He returned the favor, only lower.

"I didn't come here to make you give me more orgasms," I said. "I was just curious. I wanted to have an adventure."

"I'll be your tour guide," he said. He lifted his head and nestled my knee over his shoulder.

"I think you should give me the tour in French. It's the only way I'm going to learn."

"I will teach you. And then I will test you."

I groaned and gave the language my best effort.

CHAPTER 11

Tanner escorted me to Paris on Monday morning and put himself squarely between me and the portal guide. "Calliope is my friend, Gilles."

The faun smiled at Tanner, winked at me, and said, "Bid her adieu, druid."

I was whisked away after a quick kiss and a burning gaze that never left mine. At home, nine hours behind Chamonix, I was greeted by two bats playing a looping game of chase across the starlit sky. I gave in to the heaviness of sated limbs and rested the back of my head against the Old One's rough trunk. Tanner had mismatched my blouse's buttons and buttonholes when he dressed me. No wonder the faun gave us both The Look. I undid the buttons and passed my hand over my breasts, my skin well-nibbled and tender.

I had done it, made a solo journey using magical portals—with assistance on both ends, yes—but no one was hurt, and nothing blew up. I wasn't naive enough to think this harkened the arrival of *my* new normal, but I would take the accomplishment.

House exuded quiet contentment and nudged me back to bed.

. . .

I WAS AT MY BEDSIDE DESK, RESEARCHING EUROPEAN-BASED FAE clans, when Christoph barreled in. The screen door slammed against the door frame, Jasper screeched, and my grandfather swore.

"Need a hand?" I asked, calling through my bedroom doorway.

"Good morning, Calli-lass, and no, nothing to see here. Just an old man and an ornery cat."

Jasper tore into my room, leaped on the bed, and stuck one leg in the air. He scratchily licked at himself, cleaning off an invisible layer and settling scattered tufts of fur. I stood and went to check on Christoph. "What happened? Jasper seems riled."

"I ran into an old friend at the portal station in Vancouver and we lost track of time. The cat is objecting to being left in his carryall too long. That's all," he said, waving me off. "Nothing more."

"Where are the kids?"

"They're not here yet?" he asked.

I shook my head and shot out of my chair. "Could they have gotten—" a loud pop sounded from the backyard, followed by laughter and a few whoops "—lost?" I asked, finishing my question as I hurried to the front door.

Behind me, I heard Christoph slide the largest frying pan we had onto the stove and light the burner. "I gave them explicit instructions, Calliope. And Wes promised he would stay with them until they were at the proper portal and had departed."

I exhaled my relief.

"Mom!" Harper, Leilani, Thatcher, Sallie, and Azura crowded through the doorway and spilled into the kitchen like a litter of mammoth puppies. "That was so awesome!"

I patted the air with my palms, and said, "Who needs to get to school and who needs breakfast?"

"We're all starving," Leilani answered, sliding between Harp and Thatch to join Christoph by the stove, "and it's me and the guys going to school. Zura's going to help Sallie at Brooks Farm. The new aquaculture ponds are getting filled soon and they need extra hands for planting the retaining walls."

"Then let's get your bellies filled and you can tell me everything tonight. How does that sound?"

"Good," was the unanimous answer, followed by, "Shower," "Scrambled eggs," and, "Just toast, please."

A few of Christoph's feathers stood out at odd angles. I reached across the kitchen island and ran my fingers between them, sliding them back into place. "You manage to keep your wings incredibly clean," I said, "even in the midst of meal prep."

"I've got a reputation to maintain."

"Ooh," said Leilani, nudging him with her elbow. "Are you going to tell Calli about that someone special you hung out with this weekend?"

My grandfather snorted. "No. And that flame's too high. You're going to dry out the eggs."

Tanner had left his truck at my house and given blanket permission for its use. Sallie and Azura claimed it theirs, and left after Harper, Thatcher, and Lei-li filled the Jeep.

"Harper reversed his decision about school," I observed.

"He wants to give it a try, Calli-lass."

"What are your plans?"

"A nap, then back to work on the bunkhouse. You?"

"I have errands to run in town." If I shared my real plans with my grandfather, he'd insist on accompanying me—which could never happen because of his wings—or cite a dozen reasons why me dropping in on Odilon Vigne was a bad idea.

Maybe I was developing a reckless side. Maybe I was riding high from my quick visit to see Tanner. Maybe I just wanted answers to the questions raised by Tanner's and my after-hours visit to the Agricultural Commission's office.

A few of those questions ran in a loop in my head as I showered and shaved my legs. I rolled my hair into a towel and wore the turban into my closet. The meeting I hoped to orchestrate required more than a fresh pair of cargo pants, a clean T-shirt, and a determination to get answers. If I could get myself to and from Chamonix, I could get myself in and out of the Flechette Realty and Development Group's local office.

Surrounded by clothing on hangers and in baskets, shoes in boxes and scattered over the floor, I felt like I was looking the old Calliope. There had to be something in here that would bolster my newfound confidence.

A knee-length dress in a muted floral pattern of greens and cream caught my eye: sleeves to the elbows, a zipper up the back, and most important, pockets. I shrugged it over my head, did what I could with my hair—my blow dryer had died a long time ago—and stuck my wand in the right-hand pocket. I was ready.

On the drive into town, I almost gave up. But Odilon Vigne was not going to go away, and I knew in my gut that if could confront my ex-husband and his family in a field at night, I could introduce myself to another of their ilk.

I had my wand and could draw on my talent for naming. I had my father's rings on my thumbs and my emergency stash of Christoph's feathers in my purse. I had the wolf pin affixed near the dress's collar. If Odilon tried to harm me, or take me away, I would be found. Satisfied with my logic, I added a swipe of lip gloss, locked my car, and murmured a spontaneous, *Goddess, keep me safe*.

I hadn't actually been inside the Flechette building since Doug and I signed our divorce papers. His lawyer's offices were in the smaller suite to one side of the entrance. If Odilon in reality was anything like his rumored persona, he would be in the second-floor suite of offices with their three-hundred-and-sixty-degree views of the entirety of Ganges Harbor and the hills to either side.

Climbing the stairs brought me to the landing where I was boxed in on three sides by clear glass walls and a set of doors. The reception desk—chest height and easily ten feet long—usually had two people at phones and computers. I stepped over the threshold, walked to the lone individual standing behind the burnished counter, and removed my sunglasses.

"May I help you?" Though I didn't recognize him from past visits, he had a Bluetooth device in one ear and a phone receiver in the opposite hand. He could have been one of the Fae Sallie and I had seen last week. He was dressed the part—crisp white shirt, navy trousers, and a muted tie. The only sign of flash was a gold tiepin.

"I'm here to see Odilon Vigne," I said.

"Is he expecting you?"

"He might be." I glanced at the empty chair to his left. When my ex worked out of this office, two people at the front desk meant there was always someone around to answer the phone and see to walk-ins. There was no sign of the receptionist or her collection of cartoon figurines that I remembered from prior visits. "Where's Patrice?"

"She's been—retired. What did you say your name was?"

"Calliope du Sang."

His eyes widened before he returned his face to neutral, set the phone in its cradle, and stood. "I will see if Mr. Vigne can see you now, Ms. du Sang. Please, have a seat. May I get you a water?"

I followed his gaze to the waiting area, declined his offer, and lowered myself onto a leather chair, one of those that felt like it could swallow you whole. I stayed perched on the edge, ankles crossed, knees pressed together, purse on my lap.

In my mind's eye, I radiated calm and collected—until I heard an office door snick open and the subtle tap of leather heels on the wood floor. A man's figure appeared at my side, with a cultured voice to match the impeccably tailored dress slacks, fitted shirt, and French cuffs. The family crest Malvyn mentioned —a strangler fig enveloping a tree—was engraved on gold cuff links.

"Calliope Viridis du Sang. I don't believe I have ever had the pleasure of meeting you in person." He extended his hand. I thought he meant to shake mine. Instead, he bent from the waist, lifted my hand to his lips, and insisted I meet his gaze.

There was serious magic—an unctuous marbling of purple, magenta, and cerulean blue—coursing through this man. And there was an equally serious backstory hidden behind his seemingly ordinary brown eyes.

"Odilon Vigne," I said, rising. "Thank you for seeing me without an appointment."

"Could I have my assistant serve us a coffee, or tea? Perhaps a glass of wine?"

I shook my head, tugged my hand from his grip, and debated asking to use the washroom. "I came here to talk."

He crossed his arms, the movement a graceful pause in what was going to become a dance. I had the fleeting thought I should have worn something floor-length for this meeting. That, or body armor.

"This does not feel like a social call."

"It's not."

He directed me toward the short hall, then spoke to the man who'd resumed his post behind the desk. "Raul, no interruptions, please."

Odilon's office overlooked the parking lot behind the building, not the more enticing harbor view. I eyed the room's setup and chose one of the chairs in the seating area near the windows for its vantage point.

"Sit. Please," he said, closing the door. His hands brushed my upper arms as he stepped around me and seated himself with practiced ease. "To what do I owe the honor of your company, Ms. du Sang?"

Dresses were tricky, especially when seated almost knee to knee with someone I had adversarial feelings toward. I shifted slightly and affected a legs-closed, spine-straight, do-not-mess-with-me posture. "I heard you were in town and, as an employee of the Agricultural Commission and steward of the island's orchards, it behooves me to know the faces behind those who appear to be actively purchasing—or trying to purchase—large plots of arable land."

I left out the part for now about actively harassing landowners in order to get their hands on that land.

Odilon eyed me with cool assessment, stopping his gaze at my feet and the footwear that wouldn't last five minutes on muddy, manure-soaked ground. "Although you are not currently active on the SSIAC's payroll, you are able to act as their representative?"

My spine froze and my brain went blank. Why would he have that information on the tip of his tongue? "I'm on a leave of absence," I said finally, and left my answer at that. "I'm here to ask you about properties the Flechette Group owns here on the island, as well as properties the Flechettes are rumored to be interested in."

"Fair enough. This is, after all, a realty and land development business."

I tilted my head to the side and feigned confusion. "Why are you doing business with the Flechettes in the first place?" I asked, gesturing around the room. "Isn't your home in Europe?"

"Who said I'm doing business with Meribah and her associates?" he asked, settling his back into the chair and crossing his legs.

"I assumed you must be involved with them in some capacity, seeing as how this is their office."

Placing his elbow on the curved arm of the chair, he rested his chin on his thumb and tapped at his temple with one finger. "I have been *involved* with Meribah and Adelaide Flechette on a

personal level for some time. The three of us are no longer a…"
He hesitated. "We are no longer an ongoing concern. There is
something about majority stakeholders being placed under house
arrest, with no relief in sight, that can have an immediate and
rather deleterious effect on the health and reputation of a
business."

"And on personal relationships?" I added.

"I purchased this company from them last week," he said,
ignoring my poking. "At their request, I would add. Raul ordered
new signs for the building. As soon as they're installed, we shall
announce the change in ownership."

My feet sweated in my shoes. My palms were next. I had no
snappy comeback. And there was no way I was going to let
Odilon know what it cost me to sit still in his presence and
remain polite.

"Would you like me to tell you more of this story, Calliope? I
have a feeling you will find it interesting."

I mimicked his relaxed posture—or tried to by shifting my
hips slightly and repositioning my knees to face him. "Please,
continue."

"When my father decided he wanted to increase our family's
real estate holdings, he—like many other forward-looking business people—looked to the West, to the United States. At my
urging, he then looked to the north. And what he—what *we*—saw
were lands ripe for our methods."

"Your methods of what?"

"Acquisition. We acquire land in order to ensure that our
expanding interests are maintained and to continue to secure the
future for our offspring."

"You have children?"

He trailed a gaze over my body, cataloguing every square inch
of my external real estate, performing an organ count on the
inside, and assessing my usefulness. The sweep might have
burned my clothes off if I felt any kind of a sexual attraction to

this man. I didn't. My dress stayed on, but I gave up all pretense of not sweating.

"I plan to have children when the time is right and when the suitable partner is found."

"Why farmland?" I asked, steering us back to the topic I had come to put on the table. "Why orchards?"

Odilon kept his lips together and offered me the smile of the long-suffering. "Calliope. You disappoint me. You know the answers to your own questions."

"I want to hear it from you, Odilon," I said.

"There is a wellspring of magic on this island, a liquid heart-beat, if you will indulge my poetic side. There are similar store-houses of magical energy throughout all of North America, from Mexico to the northernmost territories of Canada. Clan Vigne wants access to those raw materials."

"Why?"

"Still with the sophomoric questions?"

"Why, Odilon, when you and the rest of Clan Vigne already control villages and towns and entire mountains in France?"

"Because we are running out of magic." He pressed his elbows onto the arms of his chair and brought his fingertips together at his chin. His irises began to flicker and change color. "Century after century of inbreeding among the Fae and a focus on the accumulation of material wealth has depleted our resources. We need new blood."

"And soil." I bit my tongue so as not to add *portals, tunnels, and the underland*, all of which granted access to other places—and other realms.

He nodded. "Yes. And land. And the riches within those lands." A silence grew between us. "I can see why Meribah wanted you for one of her sons. You are smart, Calliope. Magically unedu-cated and completely underdeveloped, but you have fire."

Cue my exit strategy.

Odilon noted the discomfort I could no longer conceal, smiled tightly, and continued. "Rumors surrounding the du Sang lineage speak of those in the bloodline having talents and abilities we rarely see these days. Alas, you provided Meribah with grand-sons, not the females she hoped would carry on the Flechette name. She disposed of you without fully understanding what she was giving away."

I pressed my knees together. I wanted to bolt out of the office and never return—and I wanted to stay, no matter how uncom-fortable this conversation got, and wring every bit of information possible from this man.

Odilon continued. "I, however, have no such outdated ideas. A child is a child, and I would find any sex acceptable. You've proven your fertility, Calliope du Sang. Do you desire more?"

"More what?" I asked.

"More children. More wealth. More—" he spread his fingers wide and contemplated his upturned palms "—power?"

"Odilon, what I desire is not more power."

"Then by all means, let us explore what it is you do desire." The glamour he held in place wavered. His skin shared the same underlying cool, bluish hue as Meribah's, only now his eyes glinted with lustful curiosity.

Apparently, I was prey. I avoided getting pinned by his stare and shifted the direction of my questioning. "Are you aware that the hidden folk who tend the sacred trees here and elsewhere are being murdered? We know of four thus far and we're working to see if any missing have gone unreported."

"That which you profess to desire has a rather macabre ring to it." He shrugged his shoulders, smoothed his tie between his fingers, and straightened the tie clip. "In answer to your question, yes." He looked over at me. "Before you ask your next question, you should know that I did not have the hidden folk, or any other beings, magical or otherwise, killed."

He smiled to himself. "Well, not recently and certainly not on Canadian soil."

"You do know that Josiah and Garnet Flechette are in custody and that they have confessed to killing the two hidden folk we found in July?"

He nodded and recrossed his legs. "Josiah and Garnet are a perfectly matched pair of greed-filled Fae. I abhor the blatant show of their...appetites. I prefer my employees and potential business partners take a more refined approach. Those two took my musings as gospel, my interests as doctrine, and warped my vision to suit their own. Their actions were purely their choice, and I wipe my hands of the barbaric nature of their acts."

Odilon twirled one of his cuff links. "Would you care to have dinner with me, Calliope du Sang? Allow me to tell you tales of my home and my family, share with you my dreams and visions for the future?"

I wiped my palms on my dress and slid my hand into my pocket, discreetly palming my wand. "I don't think that would be a good idea."

"Then let me see if I might convince you otherwise." Odilon's full name coursed down the sides of my tongue. I was on the verge of pointing my wand and speaking three names when he moved to the desk and picked up the lone object on its surface—a large tablet. He turned it on, swiped twice, and handed it to me. The steel gray backing was cold to my touch. The front was a photo album.

The first images were of Sallie, by herself and then with Azura. Their surroundings weren't familiar, but as soon as I saw Christoph's wings in the next set of images, I knew the photographs had been taken during the mentoring weekend.

"Please, continue," Odilon said when I stopped at the first image of Harper without his shirt, his back a map of delicate bones and translucent skin. The next image was Thatcher, laughing. I turned off the tablet.

"Do you see anyone you know?"

"Maybe."

"Do not test my patience, Calliope."

I set the device on my lap and stared. Or glared. Odilon's glamour shifted again, revealing more of his face. This time, his skin took on an even darker bluish cast. Wavering panels of light smoothed his sharp edges, highlighting his cheekbones, then the aquiline curve of his nose, as though I was looking at him under the surface of the sea.

His eyes went from the icy color he showed me when our conversation began to turn, to the warm, trusting brown he had greeted me with. These eyes radiated compassion, longing, and the desire for connection. I came unmoored as the open window behind Odilon let in the breeze coming off the harbor.

Salt water.

Maine.

Mama.

Odilon slid cool hands under my overheated palms and squeezed. "You will dine with me, Calliope du Sang. This Thursday night. Seven o'clock. On the *Merry Widow.*"

"What if—" I stammered. I was caught in a net of my own making.

"I have neither the constitution to offer nor the inclination to accept what-ifs. We have much to discuss. You will be there. For the sake of this island and for the sake of your children's future. Or else."

CHAPTER 12

I regained my faculties from the front seat of my car. My clutch purse was on the passenger seat and my seat belt was engaged. I fumbled for the release, adjusted the strap so I could take deeper breaths, and pressed the door lock. Hands on the steering wheel and eyes straight ahead, I wondered how I had gotten here from Odilon's office. The last thing I remembered was—

The last thing I remembered was his threat. I show up to dine with him on the *Merry Widow*, or else. The *or else* was tied directly to my sons, to Sallie and Azura, and to the health of the very soil under our feet.

I was in a fine mettle by the time I turned right onto Fortune's Folly Road, drove over a random gardening tool, and jerked to a stop on the grass. I parked, ducked around the side of the house, and located Christoph. He was balanced on a ladder, hammering away at the roof of the bunkhouse. I called, waved once, stomped into the house, and kicked off my shoes. I didn't care where they landed.

Odilon Vigne had scared me, which in turn triggered all this —anger. This was new for me, especially the desire for retribution that came after the anger. I wanted to lash out, hurt someone Odilon cared about, take something of his and break it.

Goddess, I was frustrated. I had to either channel my anger or do something to haul my sense of self-worth back to where it normally resided right alongside my spine.

There had to be a way to outsmart his maneuverings and get him to withdraw his business interests from this island—and British Columbia, and maybe all of North America. Surely his father had a vineyard or a cheese-making concern that Odilon could take over and make his own. Or a slew of potential wombs to carry on the Vigne lineage.

I struggled with the zipper on the back of my dress. Adding insult to injury was the text Kerry sent while I was talking with the Frenchman. I hadn't remembered to check my phone once I was in my car.

"READ YOUR EMAIL THEN CALL ME." Kerry—or my replacement—must have figured out someone had been in their office over the weekend and they were pissed because they'd deduced it was me.

Guilt punched a hole in my ballooning anger. When I opened Kerry's email, I scanned through once, then made myself sit and give her lengthy rant proper attention. Orchards and farms all over the island were being cited for breaking laws and regulations. Every single one was an established, family-owned endeavor, and all were under intense scrutiny. The organic ones especially were being threatened with decertification.

Behind it all? The man brought in to replace me. Kerry was irate with him, terrified for what his unfounded accusations meant for local businesses, and ready to quit. I called her private number and was sent right to voicemail. "Kerry. It's Calli. Thanks for reaching out. We need to talk."

Odilon's arrival on the island at the same time as locals coming under threat could not be a coincidence. These locals held exactly the types of land Clan Vigne was intent on acquiring

—fertile, prepared by years of proper stewardship, and likely home to tunnels, portals, and other magical trees known and forgotten.

I had to do something. I tapped on my cell phone and scrolled through my contacts. Rose. She'd stare me down, though I was a good three or four inches taller, and make a comment about what a bumbling witch I was. Going into an emotional tailspin about all the choices that had been made *for* me—by my aunt, by Meribah, by Doug—just added fuel to the fire. Lashing out at the head witch was not good idea. Rose was a hard *no*.

Tanner. Another *no*. We were getting closer, but we weren't yet a team. Tanner, River, Wes, and Kaz were a team. The witches I'd been getting to know were a team. Even my sons were part of a team, as all five teenagers cheered each other through the challenges of finding and accepting their individual magics.

I shut my laptop and stripped out of my dress. I'd have to scrub extra hard to rid the garment of the stink of Odilon Vigne's cologne. I slipped my legs into the cleanest pants in my laundry basket and found a passable long-sleeved shirt.

Alabastair had said he would always tell me the truth. Right now, I needed someone who would do that for me, who wouldn't want something in exchange. And like he'd said, if I put my hand on the portal tree, he'd be there, even if he was practicing to be a necromancer at leisure, whatever that meant.

My hand hovered over my new dagger. I curled my fingers around the leather grip. Would I need it? I snorted softly, relaxed my fingers and released my hold, and chose my wand.

And the dagger. Something about holding a length of Damascus steel in my hand set my pulse to fluttering in anticipation. I strapped the leather sheath around my thigh the way Tanner had demonstrated. It took two tries to get it to sit parallel to my femur while not cutting off circulation.

Satisfied, I grabbed my cross-body bag. My water bottle was full, the dried fruit snacks were untouched. I was almost out the door when I doubled back for the tin of anti-nausea tablets, in case Bas had in mind to test me.

Propping my butt against the crabapple tree, I readjusted the contents of my bag and tightened the strap on one shoe. Christoph saw me and called from the vicinity of the bunkhouse. Unable to hear what he said, I went to straighten and nicked my elbow on a thorn protruding from the bark of the Old One. The momentum, combined with awkward footing and the swinging weight of my overloaded bag, sent me careening around the tree to the northeast quadrant. I grabbed the trunk to right myself. Another thorn punctured my skin, this time at the base of a finger, sinking deep enough to hit bone.

The pain of the wound almost sent me to my knees as Christoph's hammer falls and the birdcalls of a mid-September afternoon deadened to nothing. I tried peeling my hand off the tree in order to tend to the puncture, but the thorn wouldn't release its hold.

This was not the spot Alabastair had instructed—repeatedly— where I should place my hand.

An odd tugging sensation lingered underneath my skin, pulsing within the bloated vein trailing from my inner elbow, down my forearm, to my wrist. The tree was siphoning my blood. I stayed put, head bowed, breathing into the draw until the utter incongruity of the moment gave me the strength to disengage from the thorn's grip. Shiny and black, the slender length was coated in viscous, red liquid.

I licked my wound, remembering Maritza's suggestion that my saliva could both stem the flow of my own blood as well as clean it off fabric. I wobbled on my feet. I was in no condition to deal with the stains on my shirt and I was afraid to grab hold of the tree for stability in case there were more bloodthirsty thorns.

Sunlight turned to a starless night sky without fanfare. The air around me cloaked my immediate environment far more ominously than the darkness of my most recent portal trip.

Yesterday, the foggy depths produced my friend Bas. In France, where the darkness turned clear, sharp, and clean, I was greeted by the Portal Keeper, Gilles.

This murky darkness had an appetite.

I had no idea where I landed. My body stayed frozen in place as my eyes adjusted to the lack of natural sunlight. Shapes became clearer. Trees—tall, straight, with uniformity in the circumference of their trunks. Their branches started some six or seven feet off the ground, reaching out and up at a gentle angle and rising to create a multifingered canopy overhead. Other trees, gnarled and arthritic, had branches devoid of leaves. The tall trees spoke to me of individuals with righteous natures. The others exuded sorrow and defeat.

The portal tree directly in front of me—caught between rising up and curving around—pulsed faintly with indecision.

Coniferous. Deciduous. Non-deciduous. I shook my head, tried to clear my thinking.

The trunks to either side of me were matte black. Where leaves grew, the edges glowed in hazy clouds of white. The backing of a coppery red sky lent the scene an otherworldly cast, and none of the nearby trunks had handy identification plaques. Pressing my back to the tree, I rolled to one side to see what was behind. More forest, ruffled with a skirt of dense underbrush. Beyond—the water, its bloodred surface rippling like liquid mercury.

I had to be seeing things. Water wasn't red. Something was wrong with my eyes.

On the ground around the portal tree, a ragged circle of silver-white bricks peeked out from underneath layers and layers of scattered and decomposing leaves. I compared the leaves on the bushes with those on the ground. They differed, their shapes and color unlike any I had seen before.

There was no sign of a path. Only a modest, half-moon-shaped clearing in front of me. The only way out was to portal home. Or to bushwhack my way through the gloom and see who or what I would meet.

If I could rest assured this was a dream—or if I was twenty years younger and childless—I might have chosen to explore. Instead, I folded to the ground, stuck out my legs, and fumbled with the zipper of my bag. Taking a long draw from my water bottle, I leaned my weight onto the heel of my palm.

Pain washed over me as tiny shards sliced into my skin where I'd made contact with the ground. Jerking my hand away, flecks of blood mottled the pristine surfaces of the white leaves. Whatever cut me was hidden. Having no idea what it was, I stopped myself from licking at the cuts and instead emptied the water bottle over my hand.

The water provided a small amount of relief.

I should have saved some to drink.

I pressed the cut-up area to my pant leg to absorb any fresh blood and used my left hand to access my dagger. Rolling to the side, I guided the weapon's tip under the leaves and flipped the top layer. I did the same with the next layer, and the next, exposing particles of paper-thin glass and a handful of clear marble-sized glass balls.

Charming and delicate, they called to me to peer inside their bubbled surface for clues to other worlds. I almost fell onto my elbow before reason jerked me upright and warned me to be wary of touching anything else in this place.

I stared at the cuts on my palm, each oozing bright red droplets, and pondered the warning.

Ignoring my blood's call and my stinging hand, I used the dagger to nudge a couple of the bubbles and as many shards as I could into the refillable bottle. Someone in my circle of Magicals could figure out what this stuff was. I secured the cap, checked the exterior of the bottle for more glass, then dropped it into my bag.

My dagger called to me. I held the blade close to my face,

admired its honed edge and elegant shape. Pressing the exquisitely sharp tip to my upraised hand I drew a line down my thumb pad and marveled at the beauty seeping out of the cut.

Water tumbling over rocks burbled faintly in my ears. My blood was the same color as the body of water beyond the trees. I licked the red line, ascertained that my blood tasted good and that my saliva did indeed stop the flow and seal the cut.

I was tired.

I wanted more of the soporific effect of my blood on my tongue to take me into sleep. I had days, weeks, months to catch up on. I could curl up right here, my back to the tree, and sleep.

No one knew where I was. No one would disturb me. No one would ever find me—

I almost pressed my hand to the ground again and rethought my strategy as I struggled to stand. No way was I exploring any farther into this place and no way was I going to succumb to the lure of sleep. This was not Paris—at least, not any park in Paris I had ever seen photographed.

I rocked forward, steadied my stance, and gripped my wand in my right hand after sheathing my dagger. Touching the tree and gripping the freely given stick that would see me to the Old One no matter what, I closed my eyes and whispered, "Home."

A dull pulse rippled under the bark.

I repeated my request, "Home." Another pulse, this one a slumbering ka-*thump* that traveled from my palm, up my arm, into my head, pinging against my skull like a metal tongue against the inside of a bell.

I clamped my teeth onto my wand and placed my other hand on the tree. A third pulse, followed by a fourth, followed by protracted silence.

"Home." The letters of the word fanned over the bark. Warm breath assured my fingers this was not a dream. My forehead bumped against the tree, and as I breathed, the bark withdrew itself from my touch.

Darkness filled my gaze when I cracked open one eye.

Crap.

I went to whisper again, inhaled, and caught scents I knew. Ripened crabapples waiting patiently for me to harvest the fruit. Pizza, from the Italian place downtown. Shouting. Car doors slamming. Engines starting. I spat out my wand, peeled my uninjured hand off the bark, and turned to run toward the house. I must have been gone for hours.

As one foot and then the other hit clumps of grass I knew by heart, I winced. There was glass in the soles of my soft leather shoes.

"Help!" I yelled, and then again, louder, unsure if I would be heard over the voices and the cars.

"Calliope!" With a *whoosh* and a *thump-thump*, Christoph landed beside me and hauled me to his chest, squishing my bag between us.

"I'm back. I'm back. I'm okay."

My grandfather held my biceps tight enough to stop circulation and tried to urge me to follow him to the house.

"I can't walk," I said, my knees buckling. He fired a concerned look, scooped me into his arms, and took off.

And up. Into the air.

He landed at the end of the driveway in time to stop the line of vehicles readying to head off of the property. Harper and Thatcher hopped out of their Jeep and ran toward us. I didn't have time to warn them about my feet. I accepted awkward hugs as long as I could then I had to let them know. "Guys, I'm hurt." I rested my head against the front of Christoph's shoulder and asked, "Can you carry me into the house?"

"Need help, Gramps?" Harper, not waiting for an answer, simply slid one arm under my knees and waited.

Christoph nodded. Under his instructions, the three of them got me up the stairs, into the house, and settled on the couch. My mangled yell let them know it was my feet that were hurting every time they bumped the bottoms of my shoes.

Thatcher stuffed a bed pillow under my head and untangled the strap across my chest. He went to drop the bag next to the couch. "Put that on the table, Thatch," I said. "No, not that one. Right here." I waved toward the stack of plates and pizza boxes. "Don't touch anything inside."

"Mom, where were you? Do you have any idea how worried we were? You were gone for *hours*."

This was a new experience, being the one causing others to worry.

I didn't like it.

"I'm sorry. I had this idea that I would go and use the portal by myself and I—" I tensed as Christoph cupped my ankles and lifted my legs "—I took the wrong one."

Harper was about to butt in when Christoph said, "Let's get your mother fixed up first. Harper, get me a plate. Thatcher, find me a pair of tweezers."

"I'll get mine," said Azura. I looked toward the kitchen. The two girls stood with their backs to the island, their eyes round as saucers.

"Sallie, could you make tea for Calliope?"

"I'd rather have a beer," I said, intending to lighten the mood. Christoph was not amused. "Okay, chamomile, please."

"Thatcher, I could use a stronger light than this lamp."

"Gotcha. Be right back."

Christoph's glare grew more pointed. His eyes started to go gyrfalcon; all-black irises surrounded by a band of yellow-gold. "Tell me what you did."

I blew out a breath and repositioned my hips. "I went to introduce myself to Odilon Vigne, scion of Clan Vigne and—"

"I know Odilon. And I know his father. *Why* would you take the portal and go looking for a man like that?"

I shook my head. "No, I met him earlier today. In town."

Christoph tensed. Thatcher showed him a flashlight and Sallie came around the couch, holding a mug. "Can you guys clear the table?" she asked. "Quick. This is hot."

Harper gathered everything into one tall pile and carried it to the counter. Sallie nudged the table closer and set the tea within reach. "Can I get you anything else?"

"No, thank you. This is perfect," I said. I raised my arms, adding, "Hug?"

Sallie dropped to her knees beside the couch and hugged me tight. Her whisper, meant for my ears only, chilled me. "I hate that clan. They've already taken too much from me. They can't have you."

She let me go but stayed curled on the floor. Azura handed the tweezers to Christoph and sat near Sallie.

My grandfather lowered one of my legs to the armrest on his end of the couch and motioned for Thatcher. "Hold the light so I can see the bottom of your mother's foot. Harper, help me get this shoe off."

I gritted my teeth in preparation. They were careful, and it was only when Christoph began to remove the glass that the pain refreshed with every pinch of the tweezers and pull of my grandfather's steady hand. He dropped the pieces on the plate, repeated the procedure on the other foot, and instructed Harper to leave the plate and my shredded shoes on the back deck.

After my feet were cleaned and patted dry, coated with salve and bandaged, I finished my tea. "Do you want to hear about what happened?" I asked, looking over the rim of the mug.

Christoph turned his chair and straddled the seat, facing me. His wings stretched out once, then again, before settling. He rolled his shoulders, propped his elbows on the back of the chair, and cleared his throat. "Granddaughter, what is the first rule of experimenting within the network of magical travel?"

The four teenagers chimed in at once. "Tell a responsible

being where you're going, test your communication device before you depart, and set a return time."

My cheeks turned hot. "I was upset," I said, offering one of the weakest excuses in the book.

"Can you imagine what it was like for me to be standing on the ladder, waving at you, only to watch you blink out of sight?" Christoph flared his nostrils. "I went to contact our druids but, silly me, I don't have a cell phone." He put up his palms. "I know. I will rectify that situation tomorrow. I had to wait for the boys—luckily, they were excited to share their weekend with you and drove home right after school let out."

I again tried to say something. Christoph shut me down. "Granddaughter, let me finish. You scared the crap out of me and in turn, I scared the crap out of these four."

"I'm sorry."

"Apology accepted. Now, tell us where you were."

"First I have to tell you about what I did earlier today. I went into town and had a meeting with someone who upset me very much."

"That was the one with Odilon, right?" asked Christoph. When I nodded, he added, "What did he say to upset you?"

"A lot, most of it having to do with his land acquisition plans." I went to sip my tea and mumbled the rest as I blew at the steam. "And he's forcing me on a date."

Damn Christoph's heightened hearing. "He's *forcing* you? How?"

"He wants to have dinner with me on Thursday night."

"Tell him no."

"I can't." Both our voices were escalating in volume.

"Of course, you can. Just say—"

"He's got pictures of the kids, Christoph," I yelled, sloshing hot tea on my hand. "And you, and Wes. From the mentoring weekend. What the hell else was I supposed to do?"

Christoph exploded out of his chair and stomped toward the

hallway. "Harper, give me your phone. Calliope, I'm calling Malvyn."

"Mom," Thatcher said, sitting in the chair Christoph had vacated. "Tell us about the rest."

"When I got home from my meeting with Odilon, I was frustrated and feeling completely outwitted and disempowered. I decided the best way to combat those feelings was to do something that made me feel brave and strong."

Sallie and Azura exchanged glances between them, and with my sons. I think they were looks of understanding.

"I had a portal adventure last night, after you kids let me know you weren't coming home," I said, "and it was successful. Bas gave me directions for how to get to where I wanted to go and sent me on my way. I figured if it was okay with him, I could travel with very little risk and get myself home safe and sound."

"Wait. Mom. You took a portal last night, too?"

"Yes. I wanted to see if I could do it, and I decided a visit to Tanner would be a good experiment."

"Tanner's in France."

"I know. And I wish my first trip to Paris wasn't so crazy quick, but there you have it. I arrived in Chamonix safely, returned home in one piece, and thought I could duplicate the experience. I packed water and snacks. I even packed my dagger. When I put my hand on the crabapple, in the exact spot Alabastair showed me, I slipped. I ended up making contact with the opposite side of the tree. One of the thorns poked my hand and by the time I noticed, I was in a very strange place." I paused, then added, "The thorn took my blood."

"Creepy." Azura's comment had all four teens nodding in agreement.

"Very creepy," I said. "It didn't take me long to realize I had made a mistake. I cut my hand before I stood up, and then I must have stepped on more of the glass. My wand's a portal key. That's how I got home."

Christoph reentered the living room. "I've spoken with Malvyn and James, and I left a message with Wessel. We need to talk about this dinner date, Calliope, and we need to speak with a Portal Keeper."

"Try Bas. He's on the island."

Christoph nodded. "Let me see to your hands first, then we can reach out to Alabastair."

As my grandfather cleaned the little cuts and applied the same salve, I described where I had been. I recalled more details, including the fiery color of the sky and the bloodred body of water.

"You might have landed in one of the Fae realms," Azura said. "Or maybe one of the Demons'." She stopped short of musing why a portal to another realm was based in my lone crabapple tree.

"What worries me is the blood, Calliope. It's one thing to prick yourself on a thorn and bleed. That's normal." Christoph finished one hand and started on the other. "Pricking yourself on a thorn that draws your blood is not human-normal. There is magic afoot in that quadrant of your tree. Blood magic."

"Du Sang, du Sang." I whispered my family name as he unrolled a length of gauze. "Is there anyone you know who could tell me more about the du Sang side of my family?" Between Odilon Vigne, Maritza's dress of needles, and the Old One's thorns, there was a growing list of beings and objects wanting my blood.

"Your mother and her sister were the last of their generation. Their parents are long buried." He shoved at the chair as he stood. "We need a plan for Thursday, we need to find your mother's grimoire, and we need a witch who knows their way around blood magic."

CHAPTER 13

"L'Runa," I said. "I'll start with her." The witch who had given me hours of her time only days ago answered my call on the first ring.

"Somewhere in your family's records would be a genealogy chart. We need that information." L'Runa went quiet, then added, "And if you know anyone who has access to the Fae network, ask for their help. Just because you're not Fae doesn't mean we should ignore the possibility one of your ancestors was."

I glanced at Sallie and Azura, seated on the floor, heads together over Sallie's cell phone.

Faebook.

"And I should draw a fresh sample of your blood, Calliope. I can bring it to the lab."

"The one at Grand St. Kitt's?" I asked. Hours of ferry rides would mean a minimum of twenty-four hours before any concrete results on my blood would come in.

"No," she answered, "my lab, the one at my house. There are times when I must exercise utmost caution with my clients. This is one of those times."

"It's getting late. Do you want me to come to you?"

"No. You stay home. Those cuts need to heal. If they don't, call Belle." L'Runa paused. "Did you happen to apply a poultice, something that would draw out any residue from where you were punctured or cut?"

"No. But Christoph cleaned everything thoroughly and smeared balm on my hands and feet."

L'Runa sighed. "Please call Belle right now. Explain what happened and let her know I'll be there soon. And in the meantime, wipe off anything you put on your skin, wash again, and leave the area bare."

I hung up, dialed the plant witch, and filled her in. She promised to be on her way within fifteen minutes. Christoph waited for me to hang up, then offered to search through my mother's books once he'd wiped the salve off my hands and feet. Anger made his touch less gentle this time around.

"Sallie? Azura? Do either of you have an account on Faebook?"

They looked at each other, then me. "Of course we do," Azura said. "Show her."

Sallie came to her knees and turned her phone to face me. "We were just messaging a friend of ours."

Like other social media apps, this one allowed its users to choose an avatar as their profile picture. Sallie's black and white image sported kohl-lined eyes, dark-stained lips, and a collar around her neck. "You haven't changed your picture," I noted.

"I'm still kind of in hiding, Aunt Calli."

"So how does someone non-Fae like me access Faebook?"

"Why would you want to do that?"

Good question. I draped my arm over my eyes. I was having a hard time thinking clearly. "I had this idea that if I could see the real faces behind the glamour I would—" I let the thought go, then continued. "I'm trying to learn more about the du Sang lineage. Magicals have directories but my name isn't in any of the ones from across North America. Neither is my mother's name.

So I guess what I'm really asking is how do the Fae keep records of who's who?"

"It's complicated."

"I'm listening." I lifted my arm, opened my eyes, and read-justed the pillow supporting my head. The boys were listening, too.

"Well, for starters," said Azura, "many Fae families are not the heteronormative nucleus of one male, one female. Some family lines are matrilineal, some are patrilineal. As far as I know, I am the result of my father's sperm and my mother's egg, but...?" Azura shrugged. "They sure didn't think twice about leaving me in Victoria to fend for myself when their clan leader asked them to move to some town out in the middle of nowhere."

I let that sink in before asking, "Sallie, you said Meribah and Adelaide were both seeing Odilon?"

Sallie snorted. "Yep. Which I have no problem with, but he's a lot younger than both of them and Meribah's been very vocal at the Flechette Clan gatherings about wanting a daughter."

"She can still get pregnant?" I asked. When both girls nodded their heads, I added, "That's a scary thought."

"Unless Malvyn sealed my parents' house, I can get in, Aunt Calli. And if I can get in, I can bring you the book that has the names of all the Fae clans' family members going way back."

"I'll go with you," said Azura. "Text your work. Tell them you need the day off tomorrow for family business."

"Tomorrow's Tuesday. It's the farmers' market. They'll be pissed."

"We'll fill in for you," said Thatcher, okaying the offer with Harper. "My last class is over at two thirty."

"Can you take a portal?" I asked the girls.

Azura pursed her lips and shook her head. "Definitely not safe for either of us. The only portals we know of are on the Flechette estate outside of Victoria, and the only reason we know that is because when the clans gather, they travel to and from Court from there."

I nodded like this was old news. "Take Tanner's truck. And be careful."

L'RUNA ARRIVED. THE TEENS GREETED HER BEFORE HEADING upstairs and Christoph offered her tea and a snack. She declined food and said yes to tea. "Rooibos, if you have it. With honey."

"I'd love something to eat," I said. "I'm starving." Christoph glared at me.

L'Runa pulled a chair close to the couch, placed her tackle-style box on the low table, and brought my empty mug to the kitchen. When she returned, I pointed to my cross-body bag. "Inside is my water bottle, and inside that are pieces of the glass that sliced up my hand and a few of the unbroken glass balls I found at the base of the tree in the—the weird place."

"Did you call Belle? And did you clean your hands?" When I nodded, and nodded again, L'Runa opened her case, then unzipped my bag and lifted out the reusable bottle. She held it an arm's length away, unscrewed the cap, and waited. Satisfied, she brought the cap to her nose and sniffed. She did the same to the thermos, shaking it gently as she inhaled. The balls hit against the interior metal surface.

"Do you have a sieve?" she asked.

"In one of the lower kitchen drawers."

L'Runa took the bottle to the sink, added water, and poured the contents into the mesh sieve. She repeated the process three times before asking Christoph to hand her a dinner plate. She inverted the strainer over the plate, tapped, then set the strainer on a paper towel. "Leave this," she said, "until we know the composition of the material we're dealing with."

Christoph poured hot water into a teapot and murmured his

agreement. A car's horn sounded. "I'll see who's here," he said, heading out the front door.

L'Runa settled herself on the low table next to the couch and held the plate in her hands. "I imagine you were in pain, Calliope, yet you were able to think quickly and gather these. Good work."

I warmed to her praise. "Have you seen these before?"

She worried at her lower lip and shook her head. "Most witches use natural materials in their spell-making. Sorcerers— as I'm sure you've seen with Malvyn—can add spells to metals. Glass is made from natural materials yet requires intense heat for its creation." She poked at the shards and balls with the end of a pencil. "But I'm not convinced this is glass. Where exactly did you recover these?"

"I portaled from the crabapple tree near my garden to another tree, in a very different place. Leaves were piled all around the base and I could see they covered these things that looked like white bricks, only they were slightly sparkly, like stone that has a lot of mica in it. The leaves on the ground were—" I had to close my eyes in order to picture everything. "The leaves on the shorter, twisted trees were all white. The leaves on the tall trees, which were perfectly straight, were...black, I think, and the leaves on the ground were reddish-black, like the sky, only darker."

"You're saying the color scheme of this place was black, white, and red?" she asked.

"Yes. Including a body of water, which I didn't get anywhere close to."

"Nigredo. Abledo. Rubedo. The stages of alchemical change." L'Runa stared at me, barely breathing.

"What does that mean?"

"It could mean many things, that you entered a place coming to life, or transitioning from life to death, or it could mean nothing. But—" she held up one finger "—given that your family name is du Sang, you are a witch in training, and your land holds a portal tree, I would say we have a situation."

Christoph held the front door for Belle. She hustled to the couch, touching L'Runa lightly on the shoulder before turning her attention to me.

In the background, Christoph placed a teapot on the dining table and made two more trips back and forth, bringing in mugs, a plate of apple slices, and small bowl of peanut butter. "I'm making a grilled cheese for you, Calliope."

"Thanks." I gave thanks Christoph wasn't an imbuer, scooted my butt against the arm of the couch, and sat up. "Hey, Belle."

"Calliope." She came around to the end of the couch, gripped my cheeks in her hands, and planted a kiss on my forehead. "I'll work on your feet. Are you in much pain?"

"A bit," I said. "I think my feet are getting more sensitive the more I use my magic."

"Not an uncommon complaint among earth witches," she assured me. "I'm going to mix up a poultice that will draw out anything that might have gotten in through the cuts. Though I wish we'd done this right away. I'll be right back."

"Do you get nauseous when your blood is drawn?" L'Runa asked.

"No. Go ahead and take what you need now and then I'll eat."

The witch opened a white plastic case filled with phlebotomy supplies and set it on the table next to her thigh. She excused herself to wash her hands as Belle returned with a white enamel bowl. The contents smelled earthy. She pulled a chair to the end of the couch, draped a towel over her generous lap, and slathered a warmed clay mixture over the bottoms of my feet.

"Let me get her blood before you do her hands, Belle." L'Runa went through the motions of donning gloves, finding a vein, and tying a section of rubber tubing around my upper arm. I looked away as the syringe neared my skin. I'd had enough of getting pricked for one day, and I was relieved when she declared four vials was enough.

Christoph handed me a tall glass of water. "Drink this," he said. I followed his order while watching L'Runa label and store the vials. She headed to the kitchen. Belle moved to a different chair and applied the poultice to my hands one at a time.

L'Runa returned with the two plates of shards, waited for Belle to finish, and set the plates on the edge of the table when the plant witch stood.

I eyed the bits of glass while Belle fed me triangles of grilled cheese. The shards on one plate were blood-streaked. On the other, the glass glistened from being rinsed. L'Runa took a seat, unfolded a jeweler's loupe, and held the plate of cleaned pieces close to her face for inspection. "Christoph," she said, "I saw a flashlight on the counter. Could you shine it over here for me, please?"

"What do you see?" I asked.

"They look like hollow marbles." L'Runa thanked my grandfather for holding the flashlight, set the plate down, and turned to face me. "You said you found them at the base of a tree. I think we can assume it was a portal tree. That makes me think these are the equivalent of portal stones." She tapped the loupe against her chin. "You also said you found them underneath layers of leaves. I would deduce it has been some time since this portal destination was last used.

"Do you recall how many layers covered the shards?"

I could picture the answer clearly. "Three. Why do you ask?"

"Knowing how many cycles have passed since there was activity at that portal could provide helpful at some point."

"Do you think Malvyn would know what they are?"

"That is possible," she said. "I'll take one with me, as well as a few of the broken pieces. You should put them in a closed container when we're done here."

L'Runa returned to musing silently. I asked, "What about the colors? The black and white and red."

"Which did you notice first, Calliope?"

"Black," I said, closing my eyes to sharpen my memory. "When I opened my eyes, everything was black. Then I noticed spots glowing white and as my eyesight adjusted, I could pick out individual leaves. Red was last. Red sky, red water, and the leaves around the tree were more red-tinged with black edges.

"Also, the place was absolutely quiet. No birds. I must have been there for hours though it didn't feel that way at all." L'Runa's gaze was unfocused and her body was still as an egret waiting at the shoreline. Wanting to hear any supposition she might be musing on, I had to ask, "What are you thinking?"

"I am thinking you found a long-dormant portal to a forgotten realm, Calliope, and the taste of your blood has caused it to awaken."

L'Runa had no more to add other than she would run my blood through unspecified "tests," possibly consult with other trusted witches about her theory, and that I should prepare a set of samples of the glass shards and marbles for Malvyn. I mentioned to her again that we had Alabastair as a resource and we should share with him, too. Both Christoph and L'Runa agreed, with my grandfather adding he avoided portal travel whenever he could, and this was all strange and unsettling.

"Can you make sure the kids have whatever they need?" I asked, after both Belle and L'Runa had left. I was bone tired and in need of a pit stop at the bathroom and a final stop at my bed.

"I can do that, Calli-lass. Let me help you first."

Christoph circled my waist with his arm as though we were heading off to a square dance. I assured him I could make it to my bed unassisted by walking on the outer edges of my feet.

· · ·

THAT NIGHT, TROUBLED DREAMS KEPT ME FROM A RESTFUL SLEEP. The only thing I remembered of them in the morning was that I was searching for something. Which made sense, given my recent adventures and the current state of my life. Lying in bed, tired and anxious, I couldn't summon any regret about my solo portal trip.

I had found—a place. Or a place had found me, called me to it.

I raised my right arm to the wan northerly light. The gauze bandages Belle had insisted on wrapping halfway to my elbows had survived my restless sleep. Mostly. When I peeked under the loosened section, the cuts were scabbed over. The paler skin of my inner elbow looked normal, if a tad blue. The blood streaming in grayish green rivulets under my skin, did not. A peppery tingle flowed through the soft tissue all the way to my shoulder.

I lifted my other arm, the one not punctured by the thorn. No tingle, only a throbbing palm and thumb pad from where I had sliced my skin with the dagger.

Taking advantage of the quiet house, I put thick wool socks on my feet to cushion the bandages, and slipped my hands into a pair of knit, fingerless gloves. In the kitchen, I prepared a mug of tea then brought it to my room. I had to shuffle to the living room again to retrieve my cross-body bag.

I'd neglected recording my dreams and adventures in my grimoire. The story of the portal tree with its thirsty thorn was too much of an anomaly not to write down. Back in bed, I munched on dried plums and pears, sipped hot tea, and wrote. I even sketched what I could recall of the two kinds of trees, the shapes of the leaves, the placement of the white blocky stones, and the location of the body of water.

I was content to let the morning pass without inserting myself into the kitchen or the teenagers' prepping for school and the girls' trip to Victoria. If they forgot something, so be it. In this moment of recording my magical adventure, I embraced the dual shifts happening within House's walls. Competent adults were a part of my life now and it was okay for me to practice letting go.

I tucked my pen into the grimoire, set the book to the side, and wrapped both hands around my mug. Harper, ever the headstrong older brother, was coming into his gifts, a blend of magics —air magic, shifter magic—I knew almost nothing about.

I was earth-bound. I knew soil and roots. Yet within the circle of my mother's protection, I had also known the sea. And more and more, I was succumbing to the pull of water, moving and still, fresh and salt.

Slipping another pillow behind me, I pressed the back of my head against the headboard and stared up, tracing the straight lines of my room. Unpainted tongue-and-groove boards running vertically along the walls. Walls meeting ceiling. Ceiling needing a fresh coat of paint.

I closed my eyes.

Water.

No straight lines there, unless it was water being forced to follow a man-made path. The night the dolls had whispered me awake they had nudged me into looking for water, and not just any water. A specific open body or moving stream called to them. I had tried to tap into my own memories—one doll represented a much younger me and I had to have that information locked away somewhere. But either I didn't, or I couldn't reach it.

I had tried.

And then I'd gotten worried I wasn't thinking or acting coherently and put an end to my middle-of-the-night search for water on the behalf of inanimate objects.

I snorted softly and sipped the last of my tea.

This thing between Tanner and me was helping me to understand the nature of fire, how to build, light, feed, and temper flames. How to keep banked coals glowing. I could probably do all that, with the right person. Maybe Tanner was my right person. It felt like he could be yesterday and today and probably still would tomorrow, through our individual and collective attempts at normalcy and inevitable calls to adventure.

I smiled at Christoph's response to *my* adventuring, a man of unknown age lecturing his forty-one-year-old granddaughter about portal-travel protocols and realized that caring for and being worried about someone you loved didn't ever really end.

The caffeine in the tea hadn't done its job. I set the mug on my desk, nudged aside my grimoire, and drew the covers over my head.

"CALLIOPE?" THE GENTLE POUNDING AT THE DOOR ECHOED THE throbbing in my head, hands, and feet. I went from blowing bubbles underwater with my mother to answering Christoph's wake-up call with a garbled *mmph*.

"Malvyn's calling," he said. "May I bring you your cell phone?"

"Ask him if I can call him right back." I pushed up to sitting so at least half of me was vertical.

"Okay."

I hauled my heavy limbs out of bed, stumbled to the bathroom, and found resurrection under a steady stream of hot water. My overalls were hanging on the hook on the back of the door. A quick inspection showed dirt and grass stains on the knees. I tossed the garment in the direction of the laundry closet on my way back to my room. Hunting for clean clothes, I vowed to do better at keeping up with essential chores. Once I got my energy and focus back.

"Hi, Mal," I said, holding the phone gingerly in my unbandaged hand. I had to stifle a wide-mouthed yawn before I continued. "Christoph said you called."

"I want to help you prepare for your date with Odilon. We all want to help you."

"Thanks, Mal," I said. "I'm sorry I didn't call you right away."

"Apology accepted. Now, let's schedule a fitting. I have ideas for jewelry, and Maritza is ready to start working on a dress. We would like to come by after lunch today." He stifled a cough. "You do know that when I say date, I don't mean anything other than it is a day and time on the calendar and not a romantic assignation?"

"Of course, Mal. Though I think I prefer *working dinner*, or *stealth investigation*," I teased. Malvyn Brodeur was an elegant, mannered man, and every once in a while, I wanted to crack his cultured exterior just a bit.

He surprised me by chuckling and agreeing. "Calliope du Sang, Stealth Witch. I like it," he said. "Is one o'clock good for you?"

"Perfect."

I tried calling Kerry's personal phone number again. This time she answered on the fourth ring, whispered she would call me right back, and hung up. My phone rang fifteen seconds later.

"Calliope, this man is getting ridiculous," she hissed, foregoing her usual perky greeting. "You *have* to help me stop him and his nonsense. When are you coming back to work?"

"Kerry, I looked over everything you sent me." Guilt got the better of me. "Also, I went into the office on Friday evening and had a look through a ton of old files."

"I *thought* that was you," she said. "You're lucky Mr. Know-It-All hasn't a clue about our paper filing system. All he cares about is what's on that damn laptop he brings to work every day. There's something very fishy about him, Calliope."

"I agree. That's why I took the files and why I'm still looking through them. But listen, there's something I need you to do, and it's going to require your best acting skills." I outlined my idea and although she balked at getting within three feet of my *tempo-rary*—as she continually emphasized—replacement, she agreed to get a selfie with him and send it to me first thing in the morning.

"I know you'll come up with a good excuse," I said.

"You owe me," she countered. "And the one thing I want is to have you back on the job. I'm not the only one who misses you. The old-timers especially, Calli, are freaking out."

CHAPTER 14

By Tuesday afternoon, the first floor of my house looked like a clothing designer's atelier. Maritza, Malvyn, and Alabastair had arrived in Mal's opulent SUV. I once called it a fancy Jeep to his face. He corrected my misnomer. *His* preferred vehicle for carting off murdering Fae and delivering a portable sewing studio was a Mercedes G-Class.

He backed the spotless vehicle up to the house and unlocked the rear door with the push of a button. Alabastair descended from the passenger's side, opened the door behind him, and held his hand out for Maritza to steady herself while disembarking. Bas's attentiveness to Maritza suggested there might be more to their relationship than apprentice and Master Teacher. They were consenting adults and my curiosity was piqued.

I came down the porch stairs, eyes alert for more clues, and let the trio know I would offer to help carry in supplies except that I had cut up hands and feet.

Malvyn handed a dressmaker's dummy on its stand to Bas. Next out were three thick rolls, four to five feet in length and wrapped in brown paper. Mal shouldered those and followed Bas into the house, with Christoph manning the door.

The back seat of the Mercedes was piled with four pieces of vintage luggage of differing sizes, all with stitched edges, rounded corners, and handles on their tops.

"Can you manage two of these, please, Christoph?" Maritza asked, peeking over the rim of her signature black-rimmed over-sized sunglasses.

"Calli, come hold the door," he said.

Today Maritza was wearing a pair of flats that were far more elegant than the ones I'd worn when I went to see Odilon. Without heels, the witch was a few inches shorter than me and still of an indeterminate size. She did not stay a consistent height and silhouette, instead fleshing out or going gaunt depending on the kind of magic she was wielding. Today, her cheeks were rosier and plumper than usual.

She closed the car door with her elbow and led the way up the steps. "I will need a cutting table, Calliope."

"Would the dining table do?" I asked.

She walked all the way through to the combined dining and living room area, set her cases on the floor, and appraised my furniture. "Yes, this should be fine. The surface will have to be cleaned and then covered with an old sheet before we can lay out the fabric for your dress."

"Calliope." Malvyn had propped the rolls against the far wall and seated himself on the couch. The rectangular case he'd sent Bas to retrieve was by his feet. Mal laid out a sketchbook and what looked like a jeweler's tray on the low table. "Could you join me?" He pointed with his fountain pen to the chair catty-cornered to him and nodded his approval as I sat, knees together, ankles crossed.

I had been practicing.

"I thought about creating a few pieces of jewelry for you that would also serve as weapons, both defensive and offensive." He lifted the lid again on his box of sorcerer's supplies and withdrew a few bracelets. The one in the shape of a snake caught my eye.

"Interesting," he said. "Put it on."

I extended my arm, asked for his help winding the flexible metal around my wrist, and held it up for his inspection. "It's beautiful, Malvyn."

"It is. But it is not you, Calliope. I do not associate you with snakes—though they are an ancient symbol of the Goddess and rebirth—but the shape gives me an idea." He flipped the cover of his sketchpad, selected a fresh sheet of paper, and drew, occasionally glancing at my arm. In the background, Maritza spoke with Alabastair, their voices hushed. Christoph had left the luggage by the couch and returned to one of his outdoor projects. I could hear him hammering away.

"This," said Malvyn, "is what I see for you. Mari, what do you think?"

His sister took the offered drawing and stepped closer to the glass doors fronting the back deck. "Vines. Brilliant. You create the piece for her to wear and I shall continue the design on her dress."

"What do you mean?" It sounded like she and Malvyn had already made a decision about what they wanted me to wear.

Mal leaned forward. "Odilon will expect you to come to him prepared to do battle. You're a mother, and he has threatened your children. He made quite a declaration by showing you those images. Make no mistake, Calliope, James and I are as upset about that as you. And Christoph. He and Wes feel guilty, but this is nothing they could have anticipated."

"None of us did," he added. "And now we know there is someone in the mentoring program—adult, child, we don't know —feeding information to the Fae."

"How does this affect what I wear, especially knowing I could be searched?" I shuddered at the thought. I didn't want Odilon's hands on me any more than necessary, given that I was going to be a guest on "his" yacht. A perfunctory hand-shake, perhaps the cheek-to-cheek greeting I had grown used to exchanging whenever I saw Malvyn and James, and that was all.

"The dress Maritza has in mind for you will be simple, elegant, and completely weaponized. Odilon will not expect this. He will, I think, expect you to be accompanied by hidden Magicals and to have armed yourself in a more blatant fashion, with accoutrements typical of witches."

"Like a bracelet?" I asked, curious to know how a spiral-shaped piece of jewelry could hurt someone like Odilon, especially given that he was Fae. Imagining him with an extendable blade at each fingertip, like Meribah and Adelaide, sent a tremor through my body.

"Like a pouch with herbs, vials for locks of hair, the usual clichés." Mal tapped my wrist. "I will take this shape, the curving snake, and create a vine like the ones that do your bidding, Calliope. One for each wrist."

"You mentioned the Vigne crest," I said. "Odilon was wearing gold cuff links. They had strangler figs engraved on them."

He gave a self-satisfied smile. "You will also be adorned with vines and he will see your symbol as a sign of compatibility. We can use that to our advantage."

"This is so not me, Mal." There was a reason I had never taken up a hobby that required me to be on a stage for any reason.

"Everything we create for you is with one goal in mind, to enhance the illusion of the very specific role you will play that night."

"Get the bad guys to leave this island alone?" I joked.

"Ultimately, yes." He returned to his sketches. I returned to vacillating between helplessness and righteous anger. I wasn't helpless, though, and ill-expressed anger had gotten me in trouble. Somewhere in between those two endpoints of my emotional pendulum was the clear head I needed to plot Odilon's exit strategy.

Maritza pulled her own sketchbook from the bag that Bas had

brought in along with Malvyn's case, and said, "Let me show you what I have in mind for your dress."

A few sure strokes, a tilt of her head, and she turned the page to face me.

She'd designed a formfitting knee-length cocktail dress with bell sleeves. The neckline scooped to expose my collar bones and a series of panels shaped my midsection before the skirt flared out. "This is perfect, Maritza. And unlike anything I've ever worn."

The witch who was more than a witch cleared her throat. "At some point, Calliope du Sang, a woman of your potential owes it to herself and those who support her to take a step up and assume her role. The right garment can help us grow more quickly into who we are becoming." She added another flourish to the design. "This garment is being made for you, for this specific event. It may not survive, but it will make certain you do."

"How can one dress do *that*?" If I made it through this dinner, I would ask Maritza to duplicate her design into a dress that lacked the capacity to put my dinner date out of commission.

Tanner would appreciate the forethought.

"With these." Maritza placed her hands on the lid of one of her cases and flicked the latches with her thumbs. This case was filled with rows of wooden spools filled with threads organized by color. There was an entire row of black and most of the threads had the sheen of silk. Packets of needles were tucked into slits on the velvet interior of the case's cover. "These needles were also made by my brother. However, they differ in design and purpose than the ones on your last dress. They also obey my instructions, working in concert with the threads and together stitching spells directly into the cloth."

My laugh was nervous. "This is beginning to sound like a military operation."

"As it should. Think of this dress as sartorial armament."

"Lives are at stake, Calli-lass. We all know this." Christoph entered into our discussion with stealth and promptly veered toward the hall. "I will join you after I shower."

"How do you know how to do all of this?" I asked, sweeping my hand over the open cases spread out around the tables and chairs.

Maritza glanced at Malvyn and cocked an eyebrow. "We were born into a long line of embroiderers. Our parents—who live in Mexico—carry the family name, Bordador, though they both gave up needlework long ago. Malvyn thought *Brodeur* as a last name was better suited to life here in Canada. Brodeur is simply the French variation. My brother may be right, though our father complains about it to this day."

Alabastair placed a tray holding a teapot, cups, spoons, and everything else needed for afternoon tea. "May I serve anyone?" he asked, his gaze on Maritza.

"Please," she said. "You know how I take mine."

My favorite necromancer, whose skin was a pale green when I first met him and was now closer to pale tan, blushed the faintest shade of pink. There was definitely something going on between those two and seeing the infusion of color in his cheeks reminded me I wanted to talk to Bas about the bloodthirsty portal tree.

Maritza picked up where she left off, no difference in the tone of her skin or her delivery. "When one is born into a family with magical elements on both sides, the child stands a better chance of inheriting the prime ability. For Malvyn and I—and our sister, Moira, who passed seven years ago—that prime ability is binding. My niece has an adjacent talent, imbuing.

"Alabastair, for example, was born into a family of necromancers on both sides, bestowing on him an almost guaranteed genetic predisposition. He is one of the most adept naturals I have ever come across." With that, she accepted the cup of tea Bas handed to her and beamed a smile in his direction. He went from pink to deep rose. Maritza patted his cheek. "Now, I must turn my full attention to Calliope's dress. I have decided that my niece, Leilani, will assist with its creation."

Malvyn looked up quickly, exchanged a look with his sister, then nodded. "I agree. After hearing her report about the weekend, we must support the next steps she takes. James and I have already discussed how her ability to imbue food could be transposed to other mediums. Given her heritage, thread and fabric are a probable medium of magical expression, especially under Mari's tutelage."

"We would like to help, too, if we can." Sallie and Azura had snuck in behind Christoph at some point and situated themselves near Malvyn. "May we take a look at your jewelry, Mr. Brodeur?"

"You are welcome to call me Mal, or Malvyn, and yes, see if there is anything in there that speaks to you." He reached out to touch Sallie's chin and give her his full attention. "I haven't forgotten your request."

Sallie paled. "I wish I had a clear idea of what I wanted my collar to look like. That," she said, pointing to the vine he had sketched for my bracelet, "suits Aunt Calli perfectly. I know my collar should be something symbolic, something with meaning, like a pretty butterfly, but butterflies and flowers have never really been my thing." She wasn't able to keep the sarcasm out of her words.

"Lift your chin." Malvyn slid a pair of glasses onto his nose, peered at Sallie, then set the glasses on the table. "Before there is a butterfly, there is a chrysalis. You are in the stage of becoming, Sallie Flechette, and I think—" he uncapped one of his pens, roughed out something on his sketchpad, and showed Sallie and Azura "—this, perhaps rendered in silver or pewter, would be perfect. Once you have clarity about what you are becoming, we can design a new collar to reflect your growth."

He passed the drawing to the girls, who clustered close to me. Using silver ink, Malvyn had drawn three stylized chrysalises in side-view, each with four or five abdominal segments linked by a black cremaster. "*Mechanitis polymnia*," he said. "The clear-winged butterfly that grows within the safety of a chrome-like chrysalis. The covering is an effective defense weapon because its surface reflects its surroundings."

He tapped the page with his pen. "Your parents spent years hiding your magic, Sallie. Perhaps there is some gift to be found in that pain, one that you have not yet uncovered."

Both girls and I were wiping tears from our eyes by the time Malvyn finished. "What did I do?" he asked, looking up. "Did I upset you? I'm so sorry, I didn't mean to and we can design something better—"

"That design is *perfect*, Mal. I love it. And you're right. I *am* becoming and this design will remind me of that. Thank you."

Azura reached for Sallie's hand and squeezed once their fingers were interlaced. "Let's go finish setting up the bunkhouse," she said.

They left through the front door, arms around each other's waists. Maritza unrolled a measuring tape and faced me. "Calli, let's go somewhere more private and get your measurements. I would like to have the dress cut and pieced together by this evening."

We passed Christoph in the hall. I urged him to begin filling Alabastair in on the outline of my portal adventure. "And thank you for wanting to protect me," I added.

"It's one of my jobs, Calli-lass. You know the guilt I carry."

"I do," I said, planting a kiss on his scruffy cheek. "I carry a bit of that myself."

When Maritza and I reentered the living room less than ten minutes later, only Bas's extreme sense of propriety kept him from hauling me outside.

"Calliope," he said, folding his six-foot-plus frame onto a wooden dining chair. "You made an extraordinary discovery.

Now, I have a few questions..." Bas's concept of *a few questions* became a detailed interrogation that he recorded on his cell phone as we spoke. He was able to gather forgotten impressions from me, drawn from each of my senses. I offered to sketch the trees and he readily agreed a visual image would help.

"I take it you're not willing to give a blood donation in order to see the place yourself?" I asked.

"Things that require a blood tax, Calliope, have a tendency to be highly selective about whose blood they desire. Even vampires —though lore and legend would have us believe they are far more indiscriminate."

Bas finished his questioning and excused himself, saying he wanted to spend the rest of the afternoon studying the Old One. He voiced a plan to come and go from the one working portal while testing for ways to access the other three without the use of blood.

MALVYN AND MARITZA LEFT THREE HOURS LATER. A BLACK DRESS of lightweight wool, basted together with long stitches of white thread, hung from the dressmaker's dummy. Maritza insisted the dining table was off-limits to food for the duration of Project Dress Calliope.

Harper and Thatcher were home by five with Leilani in tow, and together with Sallie and Azura had voted to prepare a spaghetti dinner for everyone who wanted to eat. The pervasive warmth generated by all of us being in this together made it hard to be nervous about my imminent dinner with Odilon.

"What can we do to help, Mom?" Harper asked from his corner of the couch, a plate of dessert balanced on his knee. Leilani had left a pan of her swoon-worthy lemon poppyseed cake. I didn't think it would last the night, given the way Christoph was attacking it. Sallie and Azura had each claimed two slices before heading to the bunkhouse.

"I don't know," I said, pressing the last few crumbs onto my plate with the back of my fork before lifting the bite to my tongue and licking the utensil clean. "I do know, however, that I shouldn't even waste my breath saying there's nothing you can do, and you should stay home where it's safe."

"Glad you figured that out," said Thatcher, messing up my hair before he gathered my plate. "Because you haven't heard about our weekend or our superpowers. Right, Harp?"

They bumped fists as Thatcher passed to the kitchen with a stack of dirty dessert plates and forks.

"Superpowers?" I looked to Christoph. "My boys have superpowers? What haven't you told me?"

"Your Thatcher is a natural tracker, Calli-lass."

"And?"

"Harper, do you want to tell her?"

"I'd rather show you, Mom," Harper said. He placed himself in the only clear spot on the floor, right where the living room, dining area, and hallway entrance converged. Turning his back to me and his brother, he peeled off his T-shirt and showed us his back. His wings were in their infancy, a network of milky white ridges and knobs to either side of his spine, all of it covered by translucent skin.

Harper took a deep breath and swept his arms away from his body. Within a minute, a faint glimmer covered his entire back and the armature of his wings disappeared.

"How did you do that?" I asked, on my way off the couch to examine my son's body close-up. "This is incredible."

Christoph cleared his throat. "It would appear that your son has inherited strong genes from both sides of the family, Calliope."

"What are you saying?" Dread dropped a familiar weight into my belly.

"Harper has the Fae ability to create glamour."

CHAPTER 15

I had to duck around Harper, grab a kitchen stool, and sit. There was no way I was going to rain on his parade of talent. We would figure out how to make his wings—and his ability to hide them underneath a coating of magical illusion—positive things.

I took his hands and straightened his fingers. "Can you shoot blades out of your fingernails?" I asked.

"No, not yet," he said, earnest concentration on his face. "Gramps thinks I might be able to manifest falcon claws rather than blades, which I would be totally cool with, Mom."

"Who else knows about this?" I darted a questioning gaze to Christoph, then returned my attention to Harper. His brother joined us, leaning against the kitchen island and crossing his arms.

"Only us, Mom," he said. "Me, Harp, Wes, Leilani, and Gramps."

"What about Sallie and Azura?"

Thatcher shrugged. Christoph joined us. "I thought it best to keep this development to ourselves, which is not to say I view the girls as outside the inner circle. This is simply something I have never seen before and Wes and I—as the adults accompanying a group containing minors—made the executive decision to show you first."

"I trust Sallie and I think she would take badly to being left out." I blew out a fast breath. "Any thoughts on Azura? Did she share her story with any of you? Because I'm assuming she might be with us for a while."

"Her parents see her as a reject, too, Mom," said Harper. "She has all the physical characteristics of the Fae and none of the fighting abilities."

"Not even deadly snowballs?" I joked.

The boys laughed. Harper added, "After this weekend, I'd say she's got potential. She's just frustrated because she can't figure out how to do more."

"Let me think about this. I'm inclined to include the two of them in as much as possible." I looked to all three of my guys. "Sallie considers us her family now. And I think she's been through enough trauma and being separated out."

"I agree, Mom," said Thatcher, "and Gramps, can you explain to Mom about my other superpower? I'm not sure I totally understand it yet."

"It was Thatcher who first noticed Harper's glamouring, Calli-lass. Wes and I ran Thatcher through some fairly standard tests for magical abilities. Not only is he a tracker, he shows signs of being an empath. Which means that, with training, he will be able to discern the true intentions, the true colors as it were, of those he is close to at any given time. Right now, he can sense those in close physical proximity. The parameters of his skill will grow with practice and maturation."

"Can you turn this ability off and on?" I asked, laying my hands on Thatcher's forearms. "Because that sounds like it could get overwhelming, sweetie."

"I can, Mom. Or I will be able to. Wes is looking for help. He thought Rose might have someone in one of the BC covens she uses to train witches who are empathic." He shrugged slightly and smiled. "For now, I put in my earbuds and listen to my playlists. Helps tune out what everyone's feeling."

"Awesome skills, little bro," said Harper, pulling Thatch into a tight hug. "Your magic is all about stealth."

Thatcher patted Harper's back gently. "Yeah, but…"

"No buts. Own your magic. Wings are cool but they are a fucking pain in the ass, and they hurt. All the time."

THE BOYS DECIDED THEY NEEDED AN EVENING OF GAMING WITH their online buddies. I waved them up the stairs. Christoph complained of aching joints and went to his room. I slipped my arms into a cardigan sweater with deep pockets and stepped outside.

The seasonal rains would begin soon, but for this night I could enjoy a cloudless sky filled with starlight. My feet found the circle of stones Tanner and I had uncovered and traced the path, one step at a time. I circled what would become one of the new herb gardens, then reversed my direction and continued back and forth like that until I had worked through the dilemma uppermost in my mind.

I wanted Tanner to be here with us—with me—for the strategizing and for getting me ready for dinner with Odilon. If any territorial male stuff came up, we would deal with it. To my thinking, if he and I were going to explore an intimate partnership, one built on everything my marriage was not, then we had to learn to work together. On pleasurable tasks, like fixing up my house and bringing the property to life again, and on challenging tasks, like digging deeper into the minds of Odilon Vigne and his clan. Because a hostile takeover of this island's riches, magical and otherwise, was not going to happen on my watch.

I found myself leaving the circle of rocks and heading toward the bunkhouse. "Sallie? Azura?"

"Come in, Aunt Calli," said my niece. At the edge of the door-less doorway, a hand grabbed the side of the big piece of fabric that had been hanging in Thatcher's room. "We're awake."

I ducked under and hugged Sallie, then bent to circle my arms around Azura. My cheek came away wet. "Hey, what's going on?"

"We're sad."

"Want to talk?"

They nodded in sync. Sallie unwound a wad of toilet paper, blew her nose, and snuggled next to Azura. "We'd like you to adopt us."

"Sure," I said. "You willing to scrub toilets, rake leaves, and bring me tea?"

They looked at each other, then at me, and burst out in tear-filled giggles. "That's all it takes?" Azura's eyes were red-rimmed and open wide.

"You're both close enough to turning nineteen that legal adoption is moot. But if what you're really asking is for a place to call home for now, then yes, I am willing to provide that for you." I held up one finger. "Pending a family discussion with Christoph, Harper, and Thatcher. I know Thatch especially is concerned about you, Sallie. I also know they'd feel left out if we didn't talk among ourselves first."

"We totally get that, Calliope," said Azura. "You don't know much about me, but Sallie does. Our stories are kind of similar."

"Tell me more," I said, making myself comfortable on the nest they'd concocted out of pillows, blankets, and sleeping bags. The interior of the bunkhouse was redolent with fresh cut lumber and fresh starts.

"Sallie and I met in the homeschooling group. My parents took me out of the Victoria Academy for Magicals two years I think after Sallie left. My parents did the opposite of hers; I mean in terms of them being super controlling of her magic and mine being frustrated at my lack of development."

"You're referring to the collars?" I asked.

Azura nodded. "My parents were convinced I was holding back on them because whatever it was they *thought* I should be able to do did not include making snowballs on demand."

"Where are they now?"

"Somewhere way north of Vancouver? I forget. They go where they're told and when they left Victoria in June, I said I didn't want to go with them. I had already completed all the requirements to graduate high school."

"Are you supporting yourself?"

She nodded. "They deposit money in my account every month, but I supplemented that with catering gigs over the summer. Those're kind of drying up now, but I've got enough to live on if I'm careful."

I shifted position, sitting back on my heels. "Let's keep talking about this. For now, this is your space. Keep it—" I looked around, noted the open suitcases "—neat-ish, okay? The bunkhouse is Christoph's pet project and he wants to have it ready for the rainy season and winter. With your help he might be able to speed up getting the composting toilet and the outdoor shower set up, but that's his domain, not mine."

As I left the bunkhouse, Sallie and Azura were gathering their toiletries for the day's last trip to the house. I veered to the right and unlatched the gate to my garden. Muted voices deep in conversation floated alongside the girls as they passed by, not aware of me at all. I sunk into my old garden chair, which was shedding chipped paint and was on its literal last leg. The commingled giggles of all four teenagers sounded from the window two stories above.

"I was hoping to find you here."

I ran my hands down the tops of my thighs and grinned. "I was hoping you'd come for a visit," I responded. I couldn't see Tanner, or much of anything else on this side of the house, in the dark. He waited until Sallie and Azura passed by on their way to the bunkhouse before peeling away from the crabapple tree and coming to my gate.

"May I join you?" he asked.

"Yes." Tanner shrugged off his backpack and set it the ground. He followed that with his computer bag and a messenger bag I hadn't see him carry before. "You running away from home?"

He crouched in front of my legs and tucked his hands behind my calves. "I'm running toward you, Calliope. If you'll have me."

I leaned forward, taking care not to wiggle the rickety chair, and threaded my fingers through his hair. "Seems everybody wants to rent a bed tonight."

His grin turned sober. "Wes filled me on what's been happening."

"And you've come to take charge and rescue this damsel in distress?"

"I've come to offer you my sword, my lady." We both laughed at that.

"I didn't think a knight could pledge his sword to two ladies at the same time."

"I have been relieved of my duties and obligations to Ni'eve," he said. "As of six hours ago. I would have been here sooner, but it took me a while to pack and once I was on my way, I decided to stop at my old apartment in Montreal to grab the rest of my things."

I glanced at his pile. "This is the sum total of your belongings?"

"Not exactly. The place in Montreal belongs to Wes and it's there for all of us to use. I couldn't carry all this *and* my favorite chair, so—"

"I've never been to Montreal."

"Then I owe you a date." Tanner stood and offered his hands. They were warm when I grabbed hold and straightened my legs. "Is everyone here?"

I crossed the front halves of the sweater across my chest and gave him the roster. "I haven't had *the conversation* with Harper and Thatch yet, y'know, the one about you and me and us sharing a bed."

"I can take the couch or the swing on the back deck."

"How about we set up the tent and I join you out here?" I asked. "You can park your stuff in my bedroom."

"I'd like that, Calli." Tanner handed me his laptop bag, shouldered the rest of his things, and held the gate for me to pass. "And I'd like it if tomorrow you could fill me in on why you're having dinner with Odilon Vigne."

"It's not at all a romantic thing," I said. "It's more of an all hands on deck opportunity to get into his head."

"I know. I understand. And I'm here to help, not get in the way."

WAKING UP TO THE THUNDERING OF TEENAGED FEET WAS NORMAL. Spooning myself into a man's naked backside was not. I snugged my arm around Tanner's waist and pushed into the backs of his knees. The temperature had dropped overnight but the cold did not appear to be affecting the druid's arousal.

I slipped my hand inside his sleeping bag, ran my fingers lightly over the silky skin of his erection, and kissed his spine. "I have to get up," I said. "Four hungry teenagers will destroy my kitchen if left to their own devices."

"Mmph."

"What did you say?" I asked, peeling away from his heat and tucking the big duvet we'd carried from my bed to the tent against his back.

"Coffee?"

I laughed, kicked my legs out of the sleeping bag, and pulled on sweatpants, a stretchy bra, and a lightweight hoodie. "I'll ring the gong when it's ready."

I set to making coffee and opening the refrigerator to see

what we had as far as breakfast supplies. Harper and Thatcher were cranky without full bellies before they left for school. "Can we have a family meeting tonight?" I asked.

Thatcher reached over my back for the gallon jug of milk. "Sure, Mom, but not until seven. I'm taking over for Sallie at the farmers' market."

"Harper?" I said. "Did you hear me?"

"Sure, Mom." He glanced up from his phone. "Can I bring Leili?"

"I'm pretty sure she'll already be here. Her aunt wants her to practice using her imbuing magic on a sewing project." I pointed to the dressmaker's dummy behind him. "Maritza's making me a dress. Mal might be here, too."

"Can you give us a hint about the topic?"

"Sallie and Azura need a place to call home. For now. And they'd like it to be here. With us."

Christoph shuffled through the kitchen, dressed in cropped baggy pants and an oversized long-sleeved shirt, and waved as he exited the house. "I'll be in the yard." A loud *oof* followed him down the front steps.

"Also," I said, "Tanner's back and I want to talk about what that means."

"Sounds good," said Harper. "Thatch, you almost ready?"

"I just got breakfast. Go work on disguising your wings."

I shook my head and smiled to myself. That was easy. "Either of you want coffee or tea?"

"What, and stunt my growth?" Thatcher, easily the tallest one in the house, was standing at the island, noisily scooping cereal out of a mixing bowl with a soup spoon.

"Mint tea, then? Maté?"

"Coffee in a travel mug," he said. "Please."

I didn't bother checking in on Tanner after I reminded all of the teenagers to exercise caution before they left for school and work. If the druid had plans to use his truck today, he was out of luck. The girls were long gone before I remembered he was asleep in the tent, his need for coffee gone.

I made my pot of tea and revisited my garden chair and the slice of sunlight warming its seat. The bottoms of my socks were dew-soaked. I peeled them off, stuck my toes into the grass, and noticed my skin was completely healed.

The yard work Tanner and I had done sent the message to living things underground, and above, that I was committed to this place. And the simplicity of the joining ritual—I swooshed my feet over the grass. Wiggled my fingers into the raised planting bed beside me in search of roots and soil. Raised my face to the sky.

My land was content. I was content.

Christoph's earlier grunting had been replaced with the swoosh of the long stick he used in his movement practice. I sipped my tea and enjoyed the sight of my grandfather's wing feathers fanning around him every time he made a certain move. I was just closing my eyes and hoping for another dose of morning sunbathing when a shout of "Calli-lass!" jerked me upright.

"What?" I yelled.

"Come join me."

"Excuse me?"

"There's an extra stick, the one Wessel uses, propped against the house. I'll teach you the first form. It'll be good for you to get a little exercise."

"Christoph!" I walked to where he motioned the stick would be, left my mug on a step, and strolled over to my grandfather. "You trying to use guilt on me?"

"Not at all, Calli-lass. But regular exercise will help your magic." He stopped midstrike and pointed his stick at me. "Stop rolling your eyes!"

Many moves and gentle whacks across my back and arms later, I had to agree. Feet gliding, then landing, firm and planted, made me feel more in tune with my environment. Even the simplest movements with the stick, repeated over and over again, had my muscles burning and ready for a break. I stuck the end of the pole in the ground and declared myself done. "But you're right. I feel great," I said.

"We do a different sequence that attunes us to the energy available at the end of the day, Calli."

"I might be pinned into a dress tonight," I said.

"All the more reason to practice. I'll bring it up with Maritza. You need more battle prep."

"In heels and a little black dress?" I asked.

"Precisely," he answered. "None of us know exactly what Odilon is capable of. I for one will let you go more easily knowing you have practiced for as much as we can possibly cram into these hours."

I OPENED MY BEDROOM DOOR A CRACK. TANNER HAD SLIPPED INTO the house while Christoph was putting me through my paces. The druid was seated on my floor, meditating. I snuck into the room and around him, picked underwear and a bra that were close enough in color to call them a match, and tiptoed out. Tanner might have purred as I shut the door.

I caught myself smiling again as I collected all the used towels from both bathrooms and started a load of wash. Tanner was finished with Ni'eve and—as he'd explained last night—Jessamyne should no longer be a problem.

When I questioned the *should*, he explained all of the remaining Keepers—no matter their status—were going through a rigorous retraining, and Idunn had threatened to strip the rebellious Apple Witch of her abilities if she did not complete the course to the Goddess's satisfaction. Not having to worry about Jessamyne making further attempts to win Tanner back was a relief. Compared to Odilon though, I almost preferred her over him.

Almost.

A whiff of what I might be able to pull off sent shivers skating over my arms and up the back of my neck. I was used to investigations of the agricultural kind, where dressing for work meant pants and boots that could withstand mucking about in mud. I'd be mucking about in a different kind of mud, looking for other kinds of clues, when I stepped onto the yacht.

Truth be told, I was excited to wear an article of clothing designed to become a weapon, should the need arise, and I was antsy for Maritza and Malvyn to arrive. I kept myself busy with housework.

Rattling water pipes sounded from the downstairs shower. I finished stripping the beds and opened every window to air out the accumulated smells of boys and pizza and stinky feet. The family meeting was going to include sections on personal hygiene and delegating chores.

"Calli?"

Tanner's voice echoed through the downstairs.

"Up here," I said, moving to the landing with the handles of the wicker laundry basket in either hand. Tanner took the stairs two at a time and relieved me of the load.

"Have you seen my truck?" he asked. "And do you want this to go in now or—"

"There's already a load in the washing machine." I went up on tiptoes to plant a kiss on his cheek once we weren't in danger of taking a spill. He turned his head and snaked an arm around my waist as his lips caught mine.

The mint I associated with Tanner from the first time we met was missing. I tasted my toothpaste on his tongue, smelled my soap on his skin as well as the scent of an unfamiliar laundry soap at the neckline of his T-shirt. Underneath all that lay a wilder, wolfier air.

The kiss ended. My curiosity did not. "The girls took your truck. And why do you smell like a wolf and—" I took another deep inhale through my nose, letting his scent skim my tongue, as well "—spruce trees?"

"I might have crossed above the tree line outside of Chamonix and chased a few marmots for sport." He grinned and shifted. "Point me to the laundry room?"

"It's more of a laundry closet and why were you chasing those adorable little guys?"

Tanner dropped the basket and opened the louvered door to the narrow room. "Wolf wanted one last run before we left."

I slid my arms around his waist from behind. The washing machine was in its final cycle. "How is Wolf?"

"Wolf is healed," he said, spinning to face me and drawing me tight against his front. "Completely, one hundred percent healed." He cupped my shoulders and pressed me away. "Fill me in on the kids and cars and schedules."

I was about to when a vehicle horn sounded from the driveway. "I think that's Maritza," I said. "Time to make *another* dress."

Tanner's offer to take over laundry duty was muffled by the back and forth chatter between Maritza and Bas. The witch had left most of her supplies at my house but had taken her needle and thread case home. Her sunglasses dangled from one hand, her case grasped in the other, and Bas had his knuckles raised to the door frame.

"You're here," I said, trying not to wiggle and bounce. I was not a puppy, and these were not my new owners. I was a witch getting ready to have dinner with a man of unknown magical might, and there was serious work to be done.

CHAPTER 16

T anner took over the corner of the living room, with its semi-falling-apart armchair and floor lamp. He found a side table big enough for his laptop and set up a temporary work space. This way he and I could continue researching the land ownership questions while Maritza pieced together the dress.

"Do you need me to bring in anything else from the car?" Bas asked. "Or assist you in any way?"

"I think not for now, Alabastair."

"Then I shall excuse myself. Calliope, may I have your permission to continue my investigation of your crabapple tree and the four portals?"

"Bas, yes, of course." The look on Tanner's face reminded me there was more I hadn't told him. "Tanner, I had another portal adventure after I saw you."

"Did something happen on your way home from Paris?" he asked. "Or Chamonix? Were the dryads fresh with you, because—"

"Excuse me, Calliope? Before you and Tanner talk further, would you mind changing? I brought an appropriate undergarment for you," Maritza said, settling into her couturier's voice. "Do you have an underwire bra?"

"No." After my Blood Ceremony, when my body had changed, I tossed all my old bras. My breasts were miraculously firmer and a full cup smaller. I splurged on new underwear, though the silk panties Tanner gave me were in a whole other league than organic cotton hipsters.

Maritza assessed my chest area and said, "We'll work with what you have. Please put this on." She handed over a bag. Inside was a slinky black slip. I held the featherlight whisper of silk against my body and couldn't help searching Tanner's face for a reaction.

He liked the slip. It would go well with his gift of Parisian lingerie.

"Calliope. Tanner. No flirting. The pieces of this dress must be assembled by the time Leilani gets here after school. She and I will finish the embroidery tonight."

Properly admonished, I went to my room to change. I wore my bathrobe over the slip and returned to the queen bee in charge of the day's main event.

"Stand here," Maritza said, indicating a spot in front of the sliding glass door. I draped the bathrobe over the chair at the head of the dining-table-turned-cutting-table and faced the witch. She lifted the basted garment off the dummy and held it in front of me. There were no closures on it yet, just a number of pieces, six or seven, of black fabric basted together. I extended my arms forward and accepted the dress.

Maritza slid a pincushion cuff onto her wrist and stepped behind me. Her touch was gentle. Her everyday manner could be abrupt, straight to the point, but when it came to working with cloth and her magical needles and threads, another aspect of her persona rose to the surface. I found the touch soothing.

Tanner coughed discreetly. "Calliope? You used the portal

again and something happened. Could you tell me about it, please?"

"I went out to the tree. I think it was late morning. I put my hand on the section Bas showed me the night I visited you, but then I slipped. My hand landed on a thorn, and it hurt, and it wouldn't let me go." I explained what followed and finished with my confusion about how long I thought I was gone versus the seven or eight hours that had passed with Christoph frantic and everyone ready to mount an all-out search for me.

"I have never been to a realm such as the one you described, Calli, but I've read much of the available lore."

"And?" I asked, thinking Tanner had an inkling he was hesitant to share.

"And I'm surprised you got out of there alive."

"Why do you say that?" I'd gotten cut on shards of glass, not shards of bones, and hadn't sensed any living beings, other than the trees.

"I don't think you were there long enough for whatever inhabits the realm to have noticed you." Tanner rustled one of the stacks of papers then patted it with his palm. "But you left traces of your blood around the portal tree. Which means anything that lives there could potentially follow you here."

Maritza murmured her agreement. I let that sink in before I spoke. "Let's look at this objectively. Wes and Kaz could tell right away that the crabapple tree was a portal and that it led to four different destinations. We now know two of those destinations. With Bas's help, we might know where the other two connect to soon. And he might also figure out a way for me—or us—to get to the bloody place again."

I took a deep breath and tried to stay still when Maritza asked me to stop fidgeting. "That place is connected to this tree, on this property, and I don't think it's in any way random. We just have to figure out why it's here. And," I added, "why it was abandoned."

"You're right, Calli."

"And if Christoph is right about me being the last of the du Sangs, then I think it's incumbent upon me to go there again and explore." There, I said it. Voiced the vague notion that had been needling me since my return. The Old One wanted me to see the place where my blood was as good as currency.

"Then I will volunteer to go with you."

"Good." I turned when Maritza asked, my back now to Tanner. "Now that we agree on that, what're your thoughts on the surrounding properties?"

"We still don't know who owns the property to the northeast of yours. Records have it in blind trust," said Tanner. "As with the property across the street. We can't even tell if they're the same blind trusts, though given the same law firm is named, I'd guess yes."

Tanner focused on the screen in front of him, pen in his mouth when he wasn't jotting notes onto a pad of paper.

"Calli," he said, glancing at me. His smile smoothed the lines of concentration jamming his forehead. "Earlier, Kerry determined that Doug—or the Flechette company—owns two of the properties that abut yours, to the north and south. I want to show this to Bas." Tanner stood, holding his laptop, and stepped around the low table and boxes of sewing supplies and went out the front door.

Maritza came around in front of me and assessed her work. "The bodice of the dress must fit you like a lambskin glove, Calliope. Snug, yet pliable. The rest of the dress will hang from that foundation."

"What about the sleeves?" I asked. I felt overexposed, even knowing the dress had a long way to go.

"I will fit them to the dress once we have the bodice right. But here," she said, reaching for two pieces of black fabric on the closer end of the table. "Let's slip these on so you can get a sense of how they will hang." Maritza guided one sleeve onto my arm, pinned the top to the shoulder seam, and repeated with the other sleeve on the other side.

Tanner and Bas reentered the house, bringing with them a rising breeze that teased at the possibility of rain. Tanner's gaze swept me head to toe as he passed and returned to his corner armchair. Alabastair took a seat at the table.

"Tanner, Alabastair, what do you think?" Maritza stepped away. Slightly afraid of the pins, I shifted side to side, enough to give my admirers a two-hundred-seventy-degree view of the me in the dress.

"Stunning," Tanner said, eyes on me and not whatever was on his screen. "Both the garment and the wearer. I have a feeling the dress is going to be a work of art, Maritza." He winked at me and added, "Calliope's already perfect."

My body heated from the top of my head to the bottoms of my feet, and suddenly I was worried about sweating so much during the dinner with Odilon that he'd be able to read me right away.

"Exquisite." Bas kissed his fingertips.

After unpinning the sleeves, Maritza's fingers flew over the front panels, tugging here, pinning there.

"Did you two find anything interesting?" I asked Tanner.

"We compared the assessment maps to get a feel for property lines. The parcels to the north and to the south are the two owned by the Flechettes. As far as records show, there have been no homes built on those properties in decades. I haven't drilled down far enough to see if the names of past owners of the parcel to the east, which abuts the area near the bunkhouse, and the one across the road are in the records.

"I think it would be worth a few of us reconnoitering all four parcels," he added. "Soon. As in, today. See if we find any property markers."

I liked his idea. "Christoph's here. He'd go with you."

"I'd like to see who else is available. The more the merrier."

"Call River," I suggested. "He had a date with Airlie on Friday night, and I think he should fill us in on how it went."

Tanner chortled and took out his phone. The call rang through as he stood and went to the back deck. I could hear him through the glass, and it sounded as though River was ready for more exploring. "He'll be here after lunch, and he's calling Wes to see if he's up for an adventure, too."

As far as I was concerned, the bigger the group the better. They were also more likely to know if anything they came across had its origins in magic. "Before you guys head off," I said, "would you mind testing the wards around the house? If we're going to be nosing around on the Flechettes' land, I want to know they can't retaliate if you get caught. And if you do," I added, "we can use my connection at the police station."

Tanner gave a soft growl as he resettled and drew his computer onto his lap. He and Jack Kaukonen, my friend from high school, had been in their wolf forms during the showdown in August. Meribah's, Adelaide's, and Doug's fates were decided in the field, per an agreement between Jack and Malvyn acting in their official capacities as an officer of the RCMP and an enforcer, respectively.

It was six weeks later and still no one knew of Doug's twin brother Roger's whereabouts. My gut said he was in hiding. Roger especially did not seem to function well without his mother's guidance, twisted as that maternal influence was.

"This fitting is complete." Maritza circled behind me once again. The dress loosened as the pins in the back panels were removed. I shrugged out, careful not to disturb where Mari had added more pins in front.

"Should I stay in the slip or—"

"You may get dressed, Calliope. And if you would be so kind, I could use a bite to eat. Black tea if you have it, lemon, no cream, and a selection of tea sandwiches? I couldn't help but notice the fresh dill on your counter. Perhaps cucumber for starters?"

Maritza dismissed me with a turn to the table and bent to her work.

"Tanner, Bas?" I asked. "Are you two ready for lunch?"

"I would love to stay, Calliope, but I think my time would best be spent consulting with a peer who may be able to assist us with the mystery of this new portal. He is of impeccable character and I will swear him to secrecy." Bas hugged me, then turned his full attention to Maritza.

Tanner stretched, popped a few vertebra, and yawned. "Yes. I want to chat up Christoph, see what he thinks about the idea of slapping on an inspector's badge and tromping through the woods."

THE QUESTION OF WHO THE BLIND TRUST OWNER BEHIND THE LAND across the street and the smaller parcel at the far end of my property was gnawed at me while I moved through my kitchen. I shooed Tanner and Christoph out. I didn't need their help. I needed space to think.

Christoph reminded me he wanted to have a look through my mother's books. Given the looming deadline, I washed and dried my hands and went to my bedroom before assembling the sandwiches. I removed the *Good Housesweeping* volumes from the shelf underneath my desk and placed them on Christoph's bed in my old office.

Slicing the cucumbers paper thin and cutting the crust off the bread allowed me space to empty my head. I had no memories of neighbors who might have lived across the street, no sudden recall of past events. I finished making lunch, called everyone in, and set the first tray on the table on the back deck. While I finished making pots of tea, River turned into the driveway. Peeking through the kitchen window, I could see he had a passenger.

I yelled for him to come in as soon as he gave a quick rap

against the door frame. He was preceded by the water witch. Both had bright pink cheeks and a sparkle in their eyes. River, who usually gave off a sense of calm that could affect everyone in his proximity, was fidgeting with his keys.

"You're Airlie," I said, acknowledging the obvious. "It's so nice to finally see you again."

Airlie held out her arms and we exchanged a quick hug. Where the druids all carried an underlying musky, earthy scent, she radiated a fluid sensuality. I was inclined to like her on the spot. "You two are just in time for cucumber sandwiches and tea."

"That sounds lovely." Airlie stepped sideways into the house, giving River room to enter. I got another hug and directed them to the back porch.

"The bathroom is down the hall if you need it." Which reminded me I had wet towels waiting to be put in the dryer. "River, can you carry the tea tray to the back deck?"

I had the closet's louvered door open when Airlie stepped out of the bathroom. She tapped my elbow and leaned against the door frame. "River told me why Tanner called him here today. May I tell you something?" she asked.

"Of course," I said. My radar leaped at the excitement rolling off her body in tentative waves.

"I sensed a body of water right before we turned into the driveway. I didn't want to say anything to River just yet, but if you would like to go exploring, I am feeling such a call from across the road that it hurts to ignore."

I emptied the lint filter, replaced it, and shut the dryer door. "Would River feel the call, too, seeing as otter is one of his forms?"

"Perhaps?" she said, turning to follow me. "But perhaps not."

Intrigued with her answer, I found a smaller tray and loaded it with sandwiches and a bowl of washed grapes and added plates for her and River.

. . .

TANNER SKETCHED A ROUGH MAP OF THE AREA FOR US TO ORIENT ourselves. After lunch, he organized the two other men and they debated possible approaches. River suggested they begin with the parcel to the north, which happened to be where Doug and Roger had first tried to enter my property. I waved the trio off and brought a lightweight quilt to Maritza. She mentioned she wanted to rest for twenty minutes, adding the swing on the back porch would be a fine spot for a nap and that she would not need me once she was refreshed.

Airlie nudged my side and pointed to the front door. *You ready?* she mouthed.

I gave her a thumbs-up and whispered, "Let me switch out the stuff in the clothes dryer then we can go." She insisted on helping by folding the still-warm towels as I stacked the dishes from lunch and put away the perishables. Once I used the bathroom and brushed my teeth, I declared myself ready.

Airlie crossed the road after me and waited on the verge as I slipped off my flip-flops and stepped onto land that was not mine.

"You're an earth witch, right?" Airlie asked. She stepped next to me. I looked down to see she was also barefooted.

"Yes, and I work best when I can make a direct connection to the ground."

"I work best skyclad, but this will do." She adjusted her flowy dress and followed me into the underbrush, where curling fronds of ferns waited, then tugged on my arm and made me stop. "Calli, wait a moment, please. I need to find something to use as a dowsing branch."

I surveyed the nearby trees. "We might find suckers around that old apple tree," I said, pointing. Blemished, misshapen fruit decorated the branches of a tree that had never been pruned. I led the way, and Airlie used her knife to cut a supple branch for herself and one for me.

"These should do the job. Do you know how to hold them?"

When I shook my head, she took the roughly Y-shaped branchlet and curled her fingers around the slimmer ends, her palms up and elbows relaxed at her sides. "Close your eyes to connect with dowser and get an initial read on the land."

The long end of the branch bounced a bit. I loosened my grip and let the moisture inside the green wood guide me. "I felt something!" I said, and Airlie grinned.

"Me, too." She lifted her chin toward a rise in the land. Neither of us could see past it for the trees. "I'll go first. If you feel anything nudging or pulling you in a different direction, let me know."

We placed our feet with care. I rarely walked the woods with someone who appeared to share my sense of reverence. I might have developed a girl crush on Airlie as I followed the lift of her knees and the soft landing of each of her steps.

"This is fun," she said, a giggle in her voice.

I agreed, adding, "I find I have to keep stopping to close my eyes and reconnect with the stick. Does that happen for you?"

"No, but this is second nature to me. I don't usually carry a dowsing stick, but you and this land are new to me." She paused and raised one hand for me to stop. "Now you have a new tool for your toolbox, and I think we're getting closer to a small body of water."

Waving me closer, she lowered her voice. "You ever come across water sprites?" she asked.

"No. I've met a couple of hidden folk who tend to orchards. Are the sprites like that?"

"Mmm, not exactly. The sprites are protectors of the waterways, and if they don't like me—or you—we'll know pretty quickly. That is, if there are any here." Airlie set down her stick and took hold of my wrist. "Let me stay connected to you. Water sprites are mostly found in fresh water areas. They're related to selkies, which you'll find along the coast. Selkies require salt water."

"Have you ever met a selkie here on Salt Spring Island?" I asked.

"No, but River or Wes or Kaz might have." She looked back at me. "If you're really curious I would ask them."

We continued to the rise we had seen from the road. The trees here grew close together and the underbrush gave a sense of being crowded, but I'd seen a couple of narrow deer trails along the way. I stood next to Airlie and followed her gaze.

A dilapidated building occupied the center of what might have been a purposefully cleared section of the property. An ancient bigleaf maple, its massive trunk gray with age and split in half, graced one side of the Craftsman-style house.

At least, I thought it was a Craftsman. Two dormers rose from the roof like eyebrows, shaggy with an overgrowth of moss and lichen and other small plants. The building looked as though it had shrugged one day, too weighted by the world, and was slowly sinking back to the ground.

"Wow," Airlie said. "This is eerie and gorgeous. I don't see a pond, but I know there's one here."

"Should we keep going?" I asked.

"I'm up for it if you are."

Within a few steps we left the woods behind and entered a field of dried grasses, pockmarked with shallow dips and hiding frost-heaved rocks. Lilac bushes graced the sides of what was left of the front porch and as we rounded the side of the house, the source of Airlie's sureness appeared.

The area behind the house was a marsh. Edged with cattails, sweet gale, and clusters of invasive purple-flowered hardback, the wetland extended to another ridge of forest and the rise of the hill I could see from my house. The iconic trill of a marsh wren called us to explore further.

"This is lovely," I said, basking in the warmth of the sun on bare skin. Though islanders welcomed the start of the impending rainy season, within another month or two we'd be commiserating the loss of days like these.

"I think we should go back to your house. I sense River is uncomfortable that I'm too far away for him to easily reach me."

"You two can do that already?" I asked.

"When you're bound by water, it doesn't take much to feel the other in ways that are unlike the other elements."

We took another long look at the marsh and turned toward the ruin of a house. Only, the back side was not like the front. I continued through the grass, lining myself up with the center of the porch. My foot hit a man-made trail. I stepped onto packed pebbles and dirt, glanced to the marsh and to the house, and deduced someone—or something—had created a deliberate path from the watery area to whatever was behind the sheets of plywood hammered over where a set of steps would be.

"Calliope, I don't like the feel of this," said Airlie. She hovered her foot over the path and pulled away as if shocked. "Something is not right. I want to leave. Maybe come back with the druids. And tools. Or weapons."

"Weapons?"

She nodded and began walking away.

"Wait, I'll go with you," I said. "Let me get a reading first, okay?"

"Okay. But do it fast. This place is creepy."

I dropped the dowsing stick and stepped both feet onto the path. Loosening my joints, I closed my eyes and rooted downward, sending out tendrils of inquiry to the plants on the land, letting them know I was here and asking if they knew anything about this place.

A trickle of movement. Pipes maybe, or an underground stream. One person—no, more—and they hadn't been here recently enough for me to sense the echo of their steps. What caught and held my attention was how similar this was to what I felt the day I walked onto the Pearmains' property and found them bound by the Catatonia spell.

I tugged my cell phone from the pocket of my fashion-backward-yet-handy cargo pants and took pictures, including a panoramic view of the back of the house to the marsh.

"I got what I need. Let's go."

Airlie and I were wordless as we walked to the rise and through the underbrush. It was cooler here under the protection of the fir trees, and I was relieved to put my feet on familiar land and feel its welcome once we crossed the road.

"I need to hydrate," said Airlie, "and lie down with plants. Do you have a garden, or—?"

"I have the perfect spot." I led Airlie around the side of my house, opened my garden's gate, and showed her the chair. "Its joints are loose but if you sit carefully, you should be fine. I'll get you the water."

"A pitcherful, please."

I waved and headed for the front steps. The inside of the house was the perfect temperature, and Maritza was seated at the dining table, the pieces of the dress spread before her.

She raised her head, turned her torso, and stared at me.

"You smell of death."

CHAPTER 17

"I have to bring this to Airlie," I said, pointing at the handblown glass pitcher filling in the sink. "I'll be right back." Troubled by Maritza's declaration, I added turbinado sugar crystals and sea salt and stirred, then cut up the rest of the lemon left over from tea and added the slices to the water. I hustled the pitcher out to the water witch, an empty canning jar and a cloth napkin in my other hand, and plucked a couple of mint leaves on the way. Airlie downed the first glass I gave her and cradled the refill in both hands.

"Thank you," she said, leaning into the chair. "That was close."

"Maritza said she smelled death on me."

Airlie pressed her lips together and nodded. "I smelled death coming from that house and the marsh and it wasn't the natural, seasonal decay we expect to scent at this turn of the wheel."

"I can't wait to hear what the men have found." I patted her knee. "Are you okay out here by yourself?"

"Your garden is lovely, Calliope, and perfect." As if to underline her pleasure, several tall stems of rosemary and lemon balm bent in Airlie's direction and caressed her cheeks. Her features softened as she closed her eyes. I went to leave her to her rest, then turned on my heel.

"Airlie?"

"Yes?"

"Can a witch have strong affinities to two elements?"

She tilted her head and shielded her eyes. "The answer is yes, but it's a very complicated yes. For instance, your base element can be earth—like both you and Belle. If that leads to an affinity with plants, you might develop an interest in plants, and plant medicine, like both Belle and Rose. And then develop further skills as a healer. Why do you ask?"

"Do you have a secondary affinity?"

"I do." Airlie closed her eyes, lifted her face to the sun and took a long drink of the warmth. "Being a water witch has led me to many a fork in the stream."

"A fork in the stream?"

"Yes, a place where I would have to divide myself, and potentially divide again and again in pursuit of the answer to a question, or simply because I was intrigued by an idea. It's all rather complicated because I have no anchor." She inhaled and exhaled noisily for three or four breaths, then added, "Without an anchor, I might not find my way back to my body."

"Which would mean you'd die?"

She nodded. "It would be a death of sorts, yes. My body would likely remain. My mind? Not so much. So let me ask again, Calli, then I really do need to rest. Why do you ask?"

"Because even though I am an earth witch, I keep having all these nighttime dreams and daytime visions and visitations where I am underwater, often with my mother."

"Your mother is dead. Are these perhaps memories from when she was alive?"

I swallowed back tears and whispered, "Yes."

"But not all are memories?"

"That's correct."

Airlie lifted her hand to me. I took it, letting her cool touch soothe my agitation. "It is very, very rare, but not impossible, to be a doubly-blessed witch. If you have been so gifted, your training will need to shift." She squeezed my fingers. "I shall help you."

I left her being ministered to by assorted flowers and herbs and walked the inner ambit of my property. Maritza's comment about smelling death continued to unnerve me, and Airlie's answers to my questions only added more uncertainty. I passed the bunkhouse, with its newly shingled roof. Christoph was in the process of adding a deck all the way around, nothing fancy but wide enough to accommodate an outdoor shower at one side and a couple of chairs in the front. The woods behind the outbuilding were alive with bird activity, perhaps set off by Tanner and the others. I kept walking, at one point lifting my arm and letting my fingers trail along the invisible wards.

Emerald-green light shimmered, a sheer curtain running the full height of the tallest trees all the way to the ground. The wards were solid, healthy. I was intrigued to see what they looked and felt like from the other side. I almost barged into the under-growth—the salal bushes were predisposed to liking me—but after the earlier adventure with Airlie, going alone didn't seem the wisest choice.

I continued, keeping the woods to my left and following the edge of the grass to the driveway. Staring across the street at the rise in the land and the trees along the low ridge, I felt a faint call tug at my feet. I closed my eyes and rooted down, scuffing away the little rocks digging into my toes, and waited.

Water.

Was this what the dolls had felt, that night they made me take them for a walk? Water, clouded with rotted plant matter and tasting of...salt? The water found its way from below the ridge to the drainage ditch running parallel to the road.

Pushing my search farther, I hit more water. Fresher.

Untainted. Bubbling up from the artesian well feeding the marsh before making a slow flow toward the house.

My land was downhill from the larger of the two mystery properties. The marshy area Airlie and I had seen appeared to be healthy. There was lively bird activity. But something there had bothered Airlie. Though we hadn't gotten close enough to see the plants and test the quality of the water, we could do that later today with reinforcements. I imagined if we told River and Tanner about our adventure, they would insist on going with us. I could bring the sample kit on permanent loan from work.

Vehicles sent vibrations through the surface of the road, sounding their approach. I opened my eyes to see the Jeep, followed by Tanner's truck. The arrival of the teenagers meant it was getting close to five. I'd been meandering longer than I realized.

"Is Leilani here?" Harper cut the Jeep's engine, grabbed the roll bar, and stood.

"I'm not sure," I said. "Cover your car. We might get rain tonight." I waved to Sallie and Azura and reminded them to roll up the truck's windows.

"We'll make dinner." Sallie brushed a kiss across my cheek as she passed. Azura followed, weighted down with cloth shopping bags filled with the day's excess produce harvest.

Maritza was standing in front of the dressmaker's dummy, working on the bodice portion of the dress. The center panel, which would hug my ribs along with four other panels and drape from there, hung below. I stood at her side and marveled.

"The black-on-black stitching will hide the magical objects they depict," she said.

"How can you see to do that?"

"Watch." Maritza pursed her lips and blew across the fine wool cloth. The designs she'd embroidered glowed the pale green of the innermost celery stalks. Vines, complete with leaves and thorns, rose in vertical, sinuous paths up the front of the dress.

Along the scooped neck of the bodice's top, the outline of a linked chain created a collar motif. "This chain here," she said, tracing the scoop with a finger, threads glowing a pale gold in its wake, "links you to the Brodeurs. It is our contribution to your protection. My brother spelled the thread to prevent you from sharing information that is not yours to give."

I brought my hand to the base of my throat, touching the vulnerable softness in the hollow. "What will I say if Odilon asks me a question and I cannot answer?"

Maritza tapped her chin with a thimble-covered fingertip. "Drop your napkin? Spill your wine?" She waved away my question. "You'll come up with something."

I didn't think verbal adroitness was one of my strengths, but I had proved myself capable of coming up with solutions under duress. Forewarned, I could do this.

"These vines are yours. I basted this panel to the bodice to see how the vines and the chains look together. Once I have finished, we will brew a tea of plant matter and blood and imbue the cloth."

"I assume you mean my blood?" I asked.

"Yours, Harper's, Thatcher's, and Christoph's."

In other words, my closest living blood relatives. "Why include them?"

"You four are connected via the blood of family. You are connected to this land via your Blood Ceremony, and the vines that grow here have bound themselves to you. It is to your advantage they have tasted the blood of those who would do you harm, and it is to their advantage to know the blood of those they should not attack." She swept her hand over the stitches and the color vanished. I had to look very closely to see her needlework, and once I put a bit more distance between me and the fabric—say, the width of a dining table set for two lit by candles—I could not detect either the vines or the chain.

Leilani's voice joined the ones already chattering away in the kitchen. Maritza leaned closer to me and whispered, "This will be my niece's first time working with magic-imbued thread."

"Will she embroider more vines?" I asked.

"No. The front section is complete. Three more allies are needed to grace the sides and back of the dress, one from each of the four base elements. The vines represent your connection to the earth and living things. I was thinking a pair of wings on your back would connect you to air and further strengthen the bond with your grandfather."

I nodded. Those two design motifs were simple enough understand and, potentially, activate. I also had Benôit's rings. "Feathers would be useful, perhaps in the sleeves," I said. "I use those to communicate specific messages with Christoph."

Maritza agreed. "How many feathers?"

"Three. Also, I feel connected to both my mother and my father through the element of water, especially salt water. My mother and I swam together often, and my father—" I choked up. In that moment I realized I didn't feel any kind of a real bond to Benôit. "Christoph told me my father had a selkie's skin and that he chose to live an aquatic life. No one seems to know what happened to him."

Maritza touched me lightly between the shoulder blades. "Seeing as you will be dining on a yacht, which requires being on water, I think it would be wise to call upon your memories. If you end up in the water, your mother's presence should have a calming influence."

"You can add a seal," I said, decision made. Ending up in Ganges Harbor was not on my after-dinner to-do list, but if the magical shit hit the magical fan, I'd jump. "I don't mind. And for Genevieve, kelp." Every underwater memory was accompanied by the sensation of seaweed flowing across my skin.

"And fire? Any associations there?"

"Tanner," I said without hesitation.

"The druid?" Maritza raised both eyebrows.

"Mm-hmm, the druid. Let's just say there is a slow fire building and I am enjoying basking in its glow."

"I understand." She patted me again, adding a little circular rub this time, and asked, "What image would help you connect with what you feel for him?"

I lowered my voice. "I sometimes see golden sparkles around his head and in his eyes."

Maritza moved away from where we were speaking, kids still loud in the kitchen, and bent to open one of her cases of supplies. She placed a stack of round tins on the table and twisted the lids off one by one.

Filling the containers were metallic sequins in shades of gold, silver, and copper. I pointed to the brightest of the golds. "That one," I said.

"Perfect. Once the embroidery is finished, we can embellish the dress with these." Maritza tilted her head and squinted at the dress. "The question is, where? Scattered all over. Or concentrated or—" Her voice drifted off.

"I would vote for scattered all over. Front, back, and sides."

"I can see your point. We must also consider how the fire used in the creation of the metal will interact with what is around it. Water could douse fire's power, whereas air could feed it. Earth can contain fire and assist with increasing its intensity. There are alchemical interactions to consider here. This is no simple frock." She waved her arm to encompass the table and the dressmaker's dummy. "This is a sentient dress, Calliope, and you will be its master."

With that, she dismissed me, secured the lids on the tins, and set aside the one containing the gold sequins. Unnerved as I was by Maritza's proclamation, I let her know to call me if she needed help. I repeated the same to the teenagers piling their plates high with rice and stir-fried vegetables and pocketed my cell phone before stepping outside.

The sun had set behind the hill that shaded my property and

the sky was filling with gray clouds. The rain I had been sensing all day inched closer. Walking to the northerly side of the house, where I had once hidden Tanner's pouch in a hollow in the foundation, I listened for men tromping about in the darkening woods.

I heard nothing and decided it was time to look for the men. I started with phoning Tanner. When my call went to voicemail, I tried River. Same thing. I trudged back inside and shrugged into a rain slicker.

Walking clockwise around the house again, still hearing nothing coming from the section of the woods abutting Flechette-owned land, I discovered Airlie had fallen asleep in the garden chair. "Hey," I said, knocking at the gate, "do you want to go inside? You're welcome to finish your nap on the couch or on my bed."

Airlie popped up to sitting and palmed her forehead. "I—I was resting and sensing into the waterways in the area and the coming rains, and I guess I fell asleep. What time is it?"

"Five thirty," I said. "River and the others aren't back and they're not answering their cells. I'm a little concerned."

She stood, stretched, and took the few steps to the gate. "I'll go with you. Give me a couple minutes to use your bathroom?"

"There are jackets and sweatshirts in the closet by the front door if you want another layer."

While I waited for Airlie, I walked away from the garden, closer to the heart of the open space. I found it curious that the Flechettes owned the properties to the north and south of mine, and the ones to the east and west were in mystery hands. The water I tracked earlier ran in a lazy flow from the northwest to the southeast.

The map I copied from my mother's book was stashed with the gardening tools. I found and unfolded it. Airlie arrived as I was deliberating where to start.

"I brought my phone, too," she said. "We might need the light.

There's no message from River." She zipped up the sweater and leaned over my shoulder. "I wonder if we should begin with the section to the east. I feel a pull in that direction."

Airlie's admission reminded me I could reach Tanner using the wolf pin. "I'll be right back."

I ran to my bedroom and opened the little square box. The white wolf blinked its eyes as I slid my nail between the top and bottom halves of the pin. Milky quartz, striated with black lines, waited for my cue.

What was my cue? Crap. Tanner had said I should sing a lullaby to the pin to deactivate it, but I wasn't sure how to fire it up. "Dammit, Tanner, where are you?" I rubbed my thumb over the quartz and was rewarded with an answering tingle. I hustled down the hall, noting Lei-li and Maritza working side by side at the dining room table.

"I think we can use this to locate Tanner," I said to Airlie as I uncurled my fingers and showed her the pin. The quartz's faint glow held steady. "But I have no idea how. We got distracted before he could finish explaining to me how object-based magical communications work."

"Druids can be very distracting," Airlie agreed. "I'm not keen to rush things with River. The saying 'Still rivers run deep' is triply true with that man." She took hold of my wrist. "Let's find them before we start comparing notes on what it's like to date a druid. I'd suggest placing the pin, opened up just like you have it, in your palm and then straighten your arm in front of you."

I did as she suggested. Airlie put one hand on my hip and pushed me toward a more central spot in the open yard. "Now, start to turn in a circle—slowly, Calli, slowly—and watch for any changes in the color of the stone or the intensity of its glow."

The quartz cooled to the south and west and brightened as I passed through the north into the east. Airlie urged me to repeat the circle once more. The stone gave us the same results.

"Okay, looks like we're walking thataway," she said.

We passed to the left of the bunkhouse and entered the woods. As gray seeped over the washed-out blue sky, I had to rely more and more on feedback from my feet and ears. "I'm turning on my flashlight app, Airlie."

"Me, too."

We kept the phones pointed down and our gazes ahead. When I looked over my shoulder I could see the lights inside the house. I didn't want to go so far that we'd get lost. "Let's try calling them again," I suggested.

Airlie nodded and dialed River. He answered right away. "Hey, where are you guys?" she asked. "Hold—hold on a sec, River. Calliope's with me and I'm putting you on speakerphone."

The connection was crystal clear and there was no mistaking the excitement in the druid's voice when he said, "We found another underland."

Heavy wings swished overhead and brushed the bent tops of the fir trees. I looked up, spotted the two bats who were hanging around the house regularly now and another larger flying form with a wider wingspan. "Christoph," I whispered. This was only the third time I had seen him in flight, and both other times he had been coming in for a landing or taking off. He dipped to one side, circled, and headed toward home.

"Wait there," was the last thing I heard River say before he hung up.

"They're going to find us in the dark?" I asked.

"I bet they're going furry." Airlie giggled. "I love seeing River when he's being all ottery. What about you and Tanner?"

"So far, I've seen him in his wolf form twice and both times were under extremely stressful conditions." I shut off the light. As my eyes adjusted and my ears tuned in to the rise of night sounds, shuffling bushes and snapping sticks announced the approach of the four-legged druids. Tanner loped into view first. River, with the otter's rolling gait, was second. He went right to Airlie, rubbing a circle around her ankles and calves. His otter was much larger than the river otters I'd seen since first moving to the island, which made sense. There was a lot of mass to displace.

Tanner's wolf was bigger, and its fur coat had more dark silver patches than six weeks ago. He rubbed alongside my leg, his back almost the height of my hip. "You're gorgeous," I said, grabbing his scruff. He lifted his face and nuzzled the offered cheek.

Airlie and I followed the otter and the wolf, one chattering, one chuffing, through the woods and into the clearing. Both animals looked at each other, then us, and raced for the secluded side of the house.

"Has River let you watch him shift?" I asked. I vaguely remembered Tanner shifting from wolf to naked human on my lawn the night of my post–Blood Ceremony party. And my friend Officer Jack had insisted I thaw an armload of red meat for his post-shift appetite.

"No. I've gotten the impression he and Wes and Kaz make the change among themselves with ease. I imagine doing it in front of humans is a rather intimate experience."

We entered the house. The sewing project had been neatened, the dressmaker's form set near a corner, and Maritza and Leilani were gone. Cleaned plates were stacked in the dish rack and an explanatory note was pinned to the sheet covering the dress. The witch would return in the morning to work on the other panels.

Christoph appeared agitated. I gave him a hug and asked what they had seen.

"Odd spell-crafting, Calliope," he said. He carried the scent of decay. I leaned close to his shirt and sniffed, wanting to confirm the smell was clinging to his clothes and wings and not coming from inside of him.

"I'm not sure if that's what I'm smelling, but I agree it's odd." I let him go and surveyed the kitchen counters and the stovetop. The teens had left a note for us to help ourselves, and Harper had added a postscript on the back that made me smile. "Thatch and I talked and we're good with you and Tanner. Love you."

I folded the note and tucked it into my pocket.

The covered pot and wok were warm to the touch. I lifted each lid. "Are you ready for dinner?" I asked. "There're leftovers here, but not enough for the five of us."

"Ravenous. Let me help."

Tanner and River entered, clad in sweatpants and T-shirts. I asked them to move the dining table closer to the wall and reconfigure the chairs and odd tables so we could sit together while we ate.

Christoph had taken up his favorite spot in front of the refrigerator, door open and confusion on his face. "Calliope, shall we continue with the stir fry idea? I see a lot of vegetables in here in need of cooking."

"Toss them in the sink. I'll rinse and chop if you cook," I said, pulling out a larger pot.

Half an hour later, we had big bowls of rice, rice noodles, and vegetables. River volunteered to make a batch of his secret peanut sauce, adding a fragrant sweet and sour spiciness to the air.

The five of us seated ourselves across the array of chairs, cushions, and the couch. Christoph shook out his napkin, placed it across his lap, and raised his fork. "Magicals, report."

CHAPTER 18

I darted a glance at Airlie and tilted my head toward the front
of the house. She nodded and pointed to her chest. I gave her
a thumbs-up. "Calliope and I had a bit of an adventure," she
began. "After the three of you left, she and I exchanged…impres-
sions, and decided to explore the property across the street."

"We took our phones," I added, leaving out that I'd forgotten
to stick my wand in my pocket or strap my dagger to my thigh.

Airlie continued, "We both felt called, me through the waters
and Calliope because—"

"Because I want to know who's behind the blind trusts," I said.
"I really dislike not knowing who owns those two plots, especially given we have proof the Flechettes surround me on the two
other sides."

"I showed Calli how to use a dowsing stick and once we were
over the rise, the one you can see from the road, the property
flattened out." Airlie used her hands to illustrate the progression
of our adventure. "We saw a house. Old, built in the early 1900s.
Dilapidated. But…soulful somehow. There's a story in that place,
but we didn't get close enough to figure it out. Instead, we
continued around the house. We both sensed water flowing

underground, and I could feel the presence of a larger body of water. Sure enough, there's a lovely marsh in the back."

I took over. "We didn't get too close to the marsh. There's a straight path that leads from the marsh to the back of the house, and there's something there we think needs investigating." I opened my phone and brought up the panoramic image. "Take a look."

Tanner and River watched the screen, then handed the phone to Christoph and showed him how to run it again. "When I read the ground, I got sensations similar to what I'd felt the day I walked onto the Pearmain property, discovered the severed heads, and met Tanner."

"Can you describe it to those of us who weren't there, Calli-lass?"

"It's like there's a deadness to the ground—an emptiness, loss of life, loss of awareness. What I find particularly...interesting... is the contrast. On the one hand, you have this house that is rotting away, there's no sign of a driveway or of vehicles passing over the fields, yet there's a big piece of plywood at the back where a porch door would be, or the outside entrance to a cellar."

Saying that sent shivers up and down my spine. "Oh, and the other thing. Airlie, you were in the garden when this happened. I did some sensing at the driveway, right where it meets the road. The water flow from the marsh toward the old house is a trickle, but it's clear—fresh. The water flow from the house to the drainage ditch smells a bit rank. And I know this sounds extra strange, but I think it's salt water."

"Any chance that house is situated on one of the rumored salt springs this island is named for?" Tanner asked.

I shrugged, turned my hands palms up. "Maybe?"

"I think it's odd that you didn't sense a flow from the marsh all the way to the road." Christoph's face was a map of questions. "Let's table further discussion of that property. I'd like to tell you two what we found, and then maybe tomorrow morning we can all go across the road and see if our findings are somehow tied together. River? Tanner?" Both men nodded. Christoph cleared his throat. "We think we found another underland. Tanner, you said you had pieced a map together?"

Tanner seated himself in the overstuffed chair in the corner. His laptop was on the little table beside, and the papers we'd snuck out of my old office were stacked on the floor. He rifled through the topmost ones, opened his laptop, and said, "I want you all to see these."

We set aside our plates and cleared more space on the rug. I hadn't been on my hands and knees in this part of the house in a long time and the dust and dirt was seriously embarrassing. "Please ignore the lack of vacuuming," I said, making a note to add that, along with sweeping, to the teens' chore list. "My minions have had a lot on their minds."

"You know there's a spell for most any household task, Calli?" Airlie's smile was sweet, and her wink suggested she might be teasing me. "Including timely reminders for the minions."

"I'll look forward to the practical magic section of the Basics of Witchcraft course." I returned my attention to the papers Tanner was taping together. My eyes caught what he was doing before my brain registered. "I'll be right back," I said.

When I returned, Christoph was standing, arms crossed. Everyone else was seated on the floor or sitting back on their heels. I handed a yardstick to Tanner and set a jar of pens and pencils on the floor. "This should help."

He thanked me, chose an orange colored pencil, and began to trace the property lines. "I want to draw everyone's attention to the shape that is made when these properties are viewed together." Tanner made three long strokes and lifted the ruler, leaving an inverted triangle bisected by Fortune's Folly Road. He tapped the uppermost section. "This is where Airlie and Calli were today. Calli, this center section is your property, and the lowest part of the triangle is where we found the underland. It's positioned roughly like—" he sketched in a small rectangle inside the bottom tip of the triangle "—this."

River plucked a red pencil from the jar. He darkened the property lines. The inverted triangle now had two squarish side pieces. The top of each paralleled Fortune's Folly Road. Viewed as parts of a whole, the borders of the five properties formed a point-down wedge driven into the center of a horizontal rectangle. The druid added, "I suspect the properties comprising the triangle were once a single plot."

"Keystone," said Christoph, pointing to the overall shape of the three plots of land. "Calliope's property is situated at the center of a keystone."

"In masonry, the placing of the keystone locks everything else into position," River offered, tapping at the hand-drawn map. He swept his finger from my land, down to the Pearmains', then again down the other side, to an unmarked property.

A couple of low whistles circled the group. My chest sank at an implication I didn't fully understand. "Are the property lines too exact for it to be a coincidence?" I asked.

"I would say yes, Calli-lass. This looks very deliberate."

Airlie picked up a pencil and asked, "May I?" She leaned forward, rested on one hand, and sketched in the house across the street, complete with the marsh and the path.

She handed the pencil to me. "Add what's important about your land," she said.

I drew the outlines of my house and garden, drew a circle where the Old One grew, and added a compass rose, noting the designations of the cardinal directions. I was beginning to see what Tanner, River, and Christoph had noticed. "Everything lines up perfectly," I said. "The lowest point of the triangle connects to the midline of the top property, exactly east to west. The stone circles Tanner and I started to uncover sit on the midline."

"Not only that," said Tanner, bringing up a satellite-style image on his laptop. "Here's the Pearmain property, here's where their underland is situated, roughly. And here's the one we found."

Using the eraser end of the pencil, I traced a straight line from one to the other and asked the obvious. "Do you think they're connected physically or by whatever type of magic is involved in the creation of an underland?"

River nodded. "Yes. I do think they're connected."

"How do we figure out if that really is an underland?" I asked, tapping the tiny rectangle with my finger. "And how do we get the Flechettes to sell these two pieces? The way things are going around here, I'm going to need more land and another house."

"I'm sorry my room's not bigger," I said to Tanner after we'd said good-night to everyone and brushed our teeth. He was trying to keep the contents of his backpack contained to the one clear corner of my bedroom. I had no space to offer in my bureau and my closet was in dire need of reorganization. I found a couple of empty hangers and made a peace offering of them.

"I know now isn't the time to talk about living situations, Calli, but River and Wes and Kaz and I have been low-key looking for a place to rent here on the island." He folded two pairs of jeans over one hanger and put it on the space I'd cleared on the closet rod. "Not only is it expensive, there's not much housing stock to pick from."

I undressed, then tugged an old T-shirt over my head. "Now that the four of you have sampled the local witchy offerings, you're thinking about putting down roots, making a claim?" I tickled Tanner's side and he swatted my hands away.

"Kaz and Belle dove in the deep end from the beginning," he said, dancing away from my wiggling fingers. "There's definitely something going on between Wes and Ro, but he's not talking, and River—" he shook his head and pinned my arms to my sides while trying to get his jacket onto the last hanger "—River hasn't been with anyone in a long time."

"Is there a story there?"

"There's a story there and it's not mine to tell."

LIGHT RAIN PATTERED AGAINST THE WINDOW AT THE HEAD OF THE bed, lulling me back into sleep. Every joint in my body had softened. Tanner was sleeping on his side, with one arm lying across my waist. I rolled so my back was to his chest and succumbed to the watery lullaby.

When the underland called, I was ready. The pull of the tide rolled me under, as so many of my dreams did, and took me to the cold waters of the Atlantic where I swam with my mother—and maybe my father.

This time, I followed the fronds of her long dark-brown hair to a secret place, an underwater cave protected by a breakwater. Mama ran her hand over a string of translucent egg-sized pearls protected by a clear, gelatinous sleeve and clumps of rockweed. Trailing after her, I draped the pearls around my neck, giggling, bubbles streaming from my mouth, almost out of air. My mother's gentle scolding, her reverence when she took the slippery pearls from around my neck and replaced them in the common seaweed.

I awoke to the scent of the beach in the morning. The air was still, and the tide was on its way out. Tanner wrapped his arms around me and pulled me to his chest. From one breath to the next, I went from sea to sun-baked grass and the wildness of a wolf on the run. I felt for my druid. He reached past me, placed a condom in my hand, and whispered his desire to join me in my dreaming.

With him inside of me I returned to the waters where this time my body responded to the push and pull of shallow waves smoothing the shoreline, ebbing and flowing, ebbing and flowing until one strong wave pulled me out, and the next one drove me to dry land.

"I could get used to having you in my bed," I murmured.

WE OVERSLEPT AND BREAKFASTED WITHOUT COMPANY. CHRISTOPH hauled Tanner outdoors for more hammering. Maritza arrived promptly at ten, requested herbal tea, and after I brewed a pot using fresh-picked peppermint leaves, I went to my desk.

L'Runa's email popped out at me with the subject line, "YOUR BLOOD IS UNUSUAL."

My right hand and arm buzzed faintly. I shook out both arms, looking to slough off the sensations that had been present ever since the thorn on the Old One had taken my blood and the shards of glass had cut my palms and the bottoms of both feet.

I read further, to L'Runa's offer to bring me the results and her interpretation. I let her know I expected to be home all day. I didn't mention I had a date, only that I would not be available after four.

Still feeling the pull of my dreams, I slid my weighty grimoire off my bureau and carried it to my bed. The strongest image from last night, of pearl after giant pearl connected within the clear, slippery sac, warranted recording.

Situating myself atop my duvet, I stroked the ruby-colored leather cover. Maritza had said she would bind the mostly blank book to me. Could she do that today? Now? I traced the slender river of silver gilt as it swirled around the top, bottom, and sides of the cover. Extra flourishes decorated each of the four corners.

I peered closer, looking for faces, or anything that might turn out to be a hidden clue. When a repeating motif triggered a faint memory, I scooted off the bed and went out to my car. I had two magnifying glasses in my sample-collecting kit and brought them both into the house.

"Is that you, Calliope?" Maritza asked, her head bent over her work.

"Yes," I answered. "Did you need something?"

"No. Do you?"

I turned the larger magnifier over in my hands. "Would you have time to bind my grimoire to me today?"

"It will want your blood."

"Doesn't everything want my blood these days?"

"You are a du Sang, my dear. Now that you—and everyone else it seems—know that, you're going to have to get used to the fact that in the magical world, blood is currency, and yours is worth more than most." Maritza lifted her head. I wasn't sure if something outside the sliding glass door had drawn her attention or if she was simply getting a kink out of her neck.

"This is news to me," I said.

"You have more power now than ever, Calliope. May you use it well." She turned in the chair. "I have another panel to embroider then I shall take a break before Leilani arrives. Bring the grimoire here when I call, and we shall do the abbreviated version of a binding. It takes far less time."

"And far less blood?"

"That, too."

Maritza's concept of abbreviated took half the time I expected. My contribution was a bit of saliva and a scant three drops of blood.

She began by unfurling a long piece of white silk thread from one of the spools in her sewing box, ordering me to moisten the inside of my mouth, and asking me to run the thread over my tongue. "Make sure the entire length has absorbed your saliva," she said.

At the burial mounds, I'd seen her empty a vial of soil mixed with dried blood onto her tongue, then spit it out. This seemed much less unusual, until she took the wet thread and tied it around my grimoire widthwise. She then placed the book in my left hand, pricked my ring finger with one of her ubiquitous needles, and squeezed out three drops right onto the knot.

Placing my right hand on the cover and over the knot, she chanted in French. In my head I was signing up for one of those online language learning courses because all signs were indicating that French should be my second language. When she finished, she glanced at her watch, counted silently, and after however many seconds she deemed were needed, declared the binding done.

"Do I need to leave this on my altar overnight?" I asked, drawing the book to my chest and shaking out my right hand.

"You may leave it wherever you want. Eventually, it will choose its favored location on its own." At the sound of Leilani's arrival, she added, "And if you're lucky, that location will be in the house. Goddess help you if your grimoire prefers to exercise its right to travel."

I swallowed, waved to Lei-li, and began my preparations for the evening's main event.

CHAPTER 19

Hooks and eyes down the back of my dress secured and front seams aligned, I locked my dependable electric car and walked across the parking area, pebbles and gravel crunching under the thin soles of my pumps. To call the rut-filled expanse of dirt a parking lot would give it more credit than it deserved. Dropping my key fob on purpose, I crouched. My fingers wanted to get a baseline read on the soil and I wanted to communicate with the tangled mess of weeds and vines decorating a stand of trees shortened by high winds.

The vines acknowledged my presence with a surprised tug. After the equinox ritual I suspected every vine on the island was now part of my network of allies.

Fingers on the ground calmed my trepidation and confirmed what I suspected. The Flechettes' magical signature, slick like oil on water, was here in abundance. Odilon's addition was the rainbow of hues shimmering over the Flechettes' greenish-black surface.

I stood, flicked my fingertips across my thumbs to remove the specks of dirt, and resumed my mission. Once the first high-heel-encased foot stepped onto the ramp leading to the dock at which the *Merry Widow* was moored, there would be no turning back. The wool dress swished around my thighs. Unlined bell sleeves soothed the goosebumps threatening to erupt across my skin. I appreciated that the dress hugged me tight through the chest while leaving me room to breathe.

This was going to be a disaster.

No, it was not.

I had wanted to look as though I had taken some care with my appearance without going overboard. Anyone who knew me from my days mucking about in their fields and orchards would never believe this version of Calliope Jones, inspector for the province's Agricultural Commission.

This version was Calliope du Sang, witch and badass. The cuts on my palms and across the tops of my feet were protected by minuscule pieces of bandages, spelled to look like skin. I lifted my clutch to hide my grin. If Odilon was watching and caught me smiling at my bravado and giggling from an overload of nerves he might think my purse was wired. I didn't want to suffer a frisking of the human or magical kind.

Nor did I want to relinquish my custom-made bag or the luxurious shawl.

I made it down the ramp without catching a heel on the slats. "Put your weight on the ball of your foot," Maritza had said. That instruction—and the sticky-backed cushions she'd affixed to the inside of each shoe—worked to keep me upright. When I made it to the landing and looked around, the marina seemed deserted. Odd for this time of year, especially on a Thursday night, though weather predictions for the Salish Sea Islands gave us a mix of clouds and sun all weekend.

To my right, the restaurants alongside the harbor were lively with patrons with more outdoor tables occupied than not. I kept my head high, gazed straight ahead, and relaxed my shoulders. I even managed a friendly wave when someone called my name and offered a compliment. Turning away from the bustle, I stepped over a break between one dock and the next and reached the point of no return.

The only boat moored in this area of the marina was the Flechette yacht. A broad-chested man dressed in all black—from his baseball cap to his slacks and the polo shirt with a logo on the left side of his chest—waited midway down the dock. On his feet were high-tech sneakers, his stance was wide, and his elbows were bent. As I drew closer and he removed his cap and sunglasses, I almost hightailed it back to my car.

Roger Flechette.

That *fucker*.

I stopped before I was within his arms' reach to gauge which of my dress's hidden talents I had time to awaken first.

Odilon's voice interrupted my calculations.

"Calliope, how good of you to join me." He stood on the foredeck, hands resting on the polished metal rail. The evening breeze molded the fabric of his sharkskin gray pants to the sides of his legs. I had no intention of staring. The impeccably dressed man watching my every movement was a predator, his body formed to an unnatural perfection by his glamour.

I kept my distance from Roger. He flared his nostrils slightly, enough that the movement drew his upper lip into the ghost of a sneer and lifted the curtain of his glamour for a second. I pretended to not see the blade-like nails teasing from each of his fingertips and turned to face my host. "I forgot to wear boat shoes, Odilon. Do you think you could escort me, rather than Roger? I'm afraid he and I don't play well together."

"Roger is my new head of security. He takes his job very seriously." Though Odilon laughed, his features barely softened. He moved to the retractable stairs, descended, and positioned himself between me and my ex-brother-in-law. Roger made a token show of stepping back as Odilon walked toward me. "If you would please give me your purse. Roger assumes everyone who is not one of us is out to kill me."

Roger grunted. Odilon added, "Even those who profess allegiance to Clan Vigne have designs on the length of my life." He unclasped my bag and showed it to Roger, who sheathed his claws and poked through the meager contents until he was satisfied a tube of lip gloss, a set of tarnished keys, and a packet of tissues weren't lethal weapons.

I kept my gaze to the side of the boat, tucked my dress against the backs of my thighs with my clutch, and took the steps ahead of Odilon with as much calm as I could muster.

I did it. I was on the yacht for the first time since Harper and Thatcher were eleven and almost thirteen and had done something that earned Meribah's displeasure and our banishment. Once again I tamped down the nervous giggle rising in my throat. I was about as adept at maneuvering on this social gameboard as I was walking with confidence in these heels.

"Would you like the grand tour?" Odilon asked. He was standing behind me with a statue's stillness, and I could sense him working to control his heart rate. While I knew he, like most Fae, kept his real features under a constant glamour, I was on high alert for which face he would wear tonight.

I shifted, keeping my grip on the railing until I had my sea legs. Odilon moved in front of me before I answered, "If you would like." Better to map out escape routes, see who else was on board, and burn up the time allotted for this outing.

He led us clockwise around the yacht. The exterior walkway included three levels of decks and short sets of steps in between. I appreciated the long ovals of anti-slip material, set at a patterned angle all along the walkway.

Everywhere I looked metal gleamed and wood and glass shone. I really didn't want to gawk at the redesigned furnishings. My intention was to notice the details as an investigator, not an unwilling dinner date. That became easier when I reminded myself Odilon Vigne had invited me here under threat of doing harm to my sons.

I straightened my spine and followed him down the stairs.

The smell of food as we entered the yacht's interior had me salivating. A white-hatted chef and his assistant paused in their preparations, nodded, and waited until we had passed before picking up their knives.

Odilon closed the door to what I recalled were the sleeping quarters and led the way out through a short corridor to the bow. "We replaced the decking with teak," he said and again offered me his hand.

I stepped up, paused, and stepped up again. In the background, the hum of the engine revved and the yacht motored forward. "I wasn't aware we were leaving the harbor," I said, swallowing.

"Just a little ways. The bioluminescence is out tonight. I hear it is a special phenomenon to witness. We'll moor near Chocolate Beach." Odilon had moved to the forwardmost section of the bow and seated himself on one side of a V of padded seats. I joined him, tucking my dress under me as I sat.

"Did you want to begin questioning me now?" I asked.

"Not really." He gazed out over the harbor and rested his elbow on the railing. Sailboats and houseboats and kayakers on sunset paddle tours meant the yacht had to negotiate its way through the harbor with care. A waitperson brought a tray of canapés and asked for our drink orders. Odilon slid a device from a front pocket of his slacks and pressed. Two tables on tubular bases rose from the decking. The server placed the tray on the surface nearest me and waited for my answer.

"An aperitif," I said, "whatever you have."

The waiter looked to Odilon. "My guest will have a Lillet, white, with a twist. I will have the Glengoyne."

A burbling came from inside the base of the table nearer to Odilon. He rested one hand, fingers splayed and softly patting, on its empty top. His gaze roamed the open water ahead of us.

His demeanor seemed off. I was expecting a cold, controlled, manipulative man, here to make my knees quake and my feet sweat. Instead, Odilon appeared distracted. I looked to the water, saw nothing out of the ordinary, and considered shaking open the shawl and cocooning myself in its finely woven protection.

I decided the cool air would keep me alert.

The waiter returned with a small tray, two highball glasses, and a candle in a glass. Setting down cork circles first, he centered my drink, then Odilon's, and turned to go. "Armand. Wait." My host turned his entire body to face me, and for the first time I felt him become present, as though a silent partner had hung up on his call and he could give me his full attention. "Is there anything else you would care for?"

"Please let the chef know I don't eat meat, fish, or shellfish," I said.

Armand nodded. Odilon dismissed him and reached for his glass. "To you, Calliope Viridis du Sang," he said, staring at me as the glass met his lips. I sipped, the Lillet dry and sweet, and set my glass back on the coaster.

"Why did you insist I have dinner with you?"

"I have become aware of the existence of a race of beings that once inhabited both this world," he said, indicating the water and islands surrounding us, "and the realm of the Fae. They are thought to be approaching extinction. I wish to help them… increase their numbers."

"And how would you do that?"

"By providing them the environment they need to reproduce safely, without fear of predators or those who would steal their young."

"Is this personal?"

Odilon answered by shrugging one shoulder and popping an olive into his mouth. "It would demonstrate my ability to see a difficult task to an extraordinary conclusion."

"What is this race?" I asked. "And what happened to cause them to disappear?"

He wiped his fingers on a square of pressed linen and fit his hands to the curved top of the empty table. With a concerted push, the wood swung to the side on a dowel hinge, revealing an aquarium lit from within.

"Come," he said. "Look inside."

I scooted forward, positioning my knees away from Odilon. I searched for fish or some other underwater creature's form, expecting something otherworldly and exotic. All I could see were bubbles aerating the water. As my gaze adjusted, a cluster of tangerine-sized glass balls floated, unmoored, in clear, gelatinous casings. I leaned forward, tempted to scoop one of the casings into my hand.

Calliope, be careful with those.

But, Mama, they are so pretty.

We have to give them time to grow.

What will they become?

Mama's smile was sad. *Your sisters,* she said.

I clenched my jaw and willed my actions to appear…normal. I leaned away from the aquarium, sipped at my aperitif, and asked, "Balls?"

"Ova, Calliope. Fertilized eggs. The host mother died, and these may be all that is left of the Melusine. They have been kept in stasis, awaiting the feeding that will trigger their awareness and cause them to resume their development."

Crossing my legs and cupping my glass, I stared at Odilon's face. "What are the Melusine?" I asked. The artfully prepared canapés were going to waste. I speared a grape and a cube of cheese, placed them in my mouth, and chewed. Odilon was not going to find out from me that I had empty Melusine eggshells at my house, or that my hands and feet had been cut on their broken pieces.

Or that, in a dream, my mother had called them my sisters.

One could conjure anything in a dream state. And that's all it was—a dream, a vision, something I was having plenty of lately.

"The Melusine appear human. They walk as humans, on two legs, yet they require regular, uninterrupted immersion into water so they may release the fishtail that makes them unique."

"So they're mermaids?"

"As the name would suggest, a maiden of la Mer needs access to the sea and salt water. The Melusine were thought to be solely a freshwater creature, though these ova were discovered in an area where the salt and fresh waters commingle..." Odilon's voice drifted off. He returned his gaze to the tank.

"How were they discovered?"

The waiter—Armand—appeared and announced dinner was ready. Odilon maneuvered the top of the tube back into position, covering the aquarium completely, and pressed the button on the device he'd kept nearby. The tube slid down, its teak wood top coming to rest flush with the deck.

He stood and offered me his elbow. "That is a story I know you will wish to hear."

Lights inside the boat were low, allowing me to marvel at the star-filled sky. At some point during our conversation, the yacht had come to a stop and was now at anchor. As Odilon led me to dinner, I caught a glimpse of the midden beach on the island off to my right. The expanse would glow pale gray-white all night long, as though the bits of crushed shell had captured both sunlight and moonlight for all the decades and centuries of their layered existence.

The dining area the staff prepared for us was on the stern deck. Two propane heating towers were lit, warming the outdoor space. Armand held an upholstered chair for me. Odilon sat to my left, giving us both a view to Chocolate Beach and the silhouette of the island beyond.

"Tomato bisque with mint sauce." Armand slid low, wide soup bowls onto our plates. "Wine?"

Odilon approved the sample the waiter poured. I nodded when Armand indicated my glass, thinking I would only sip. He bowed slightly and left, leaving Odilon to cup the bowl of his wineglass and lift it to eye level. "To the Melusine," he said, holding my gaze.

"To the Melusine," I answered, following his gesture before bringing the rim of my glass to my lips. The wine, a young red if my tongue was still any good at deciphering vintages, was exquisite. I set down the stemware, draped the heavy linen napkin across my lap, and tasted the first spoonful of soup. "Armand chose well."

"The wine is from the Vigne vineyards, and yes, I chose Armand for more than his skill at serving hors d'oeuvres."

Small talk. What an apt designation for words that had no meaning. I wanted to clear the table with a swipe of my arm and demand Odilon share everything he knew.

"You were telling me how you came into possession of the ova," I said, fidgeting with my matching rings. The metal bands were growing looser.

"I did not find them. Someone in my..." He hesitated before finishing his sentence. Sipped at another spoonful of soup. "Someone I acquired for their knowledge of intercoastal water-ways along the Atlantic seaboard found them. A male was guarding the eggs."

"A male what?" I asked.

Odilon leaned away from the table, allowing Armand to remove his bowl. The waiter took my plate as well when I indicated I was finished. He returned with two plates. "Ravioli stuffed with local wild mushrooms, in a sage and butter sauce."

My host refilled his glass. "Bon appétit."

"Bon appétit," I answered, cutting into the oversized ravioli. If there was to be a battle ahead, my body could use the calories. The pasta melted on my tongue. As I chewed, I belatedly searched my dress for reactions to any of the food or drink I'd had thus far. All was quiet on the possible poison front. I was relieved.

"The one who found the eggs was wearing a selkie's skin." Odilon picked up his story. "The male guarding them was a simple rockfish. Not a Magical. Rockfish are extremely vigilant when it comes to protecting the unborn."

"Did your employee kill the fish to get the eggs?"

"Mais non." Odilon's face registered disgust. "That would have been a cruel and tragic end for a creature simply doing the job it was born to do."

"How long have the eggs been in your possession?"

"They have been under my *protection*," he said, emphasizing his rewording of my question, "for decades."

My fork stopped on its way to my mouth.

"Thirty-six years, to be exact."

I returned the uneaten bite to my plate and daubed at the corner of my mouth. I managed to take a sip of the wine and return the delicate glass to the table without spilling a drop. "Who found the eggs for you?" I asked, trying to steady my trembling vocal cords.

"His family was Clan Courant." Odilon cut his second ravioli into thirds, chewed his bite slowly, swallowed, and added, "His first name was Benôit."

"Does he continue to work for you?"

"He is here, on this boat, resting as we eat."

The vines sewn into the dress squirmed. Embroidered wings, anxious to unfurl and beat at the air, tugged at the skin between my shoulder blades. The two rings Christoph gifted me grew heated, expanded, and threatened to slide off my thumbs.

"My father's name was Benôit," I said. I tried to make it look as though I was debating which piece of ravioli to spear first, not throw my wineglass to the deck and scream at him to show me *his* Benôit.

"What a small world."

As if on cue, Armand appeared and said, "Dessert has been

plated and is under the cloche. If there is nothing else you need, I shall depart. The rest of the crew has boarded the tender."

"*Au revoir, mon ami.*"

"*Au revoir et bonne nuit, mon prince.*"

Armand donned a navy pea coat and disappeared. I set my utensils on the tablecloth and slid the rings off before they fell onto the deck. I tucked one into each of the dress's side pockets.

"Does this mean we're alone?" I asked.

"*Seulement nous trois,*" Odilon answered.

An engine starting up from the other side of the boat underlined his answer. As I stood, swearing silently at my lack of French, my napkin slid down the front of one leg and landed on my shoe. I stepped on the linen and walked to the railing. A single-engine craft, with four men on board, moved through the inky sea, away from the yacht.

"You were right about the bioluminescence," I said. I watched the boat's wake glitter in an ever-widening inverted V against the dark backdrop of the water before the flickers of light faded along with the sound of the motor. "It's beautiful."

"I would trade you something for this Benôit."

"What do I have that you could possibly want?"

"Your blood." Odilon was next to me, the fabric of his shirt and pants brushing against my dress and sleeves. "Calliope. Viridis. Du Sang. Have you never wondered at the meaning of your name, why clan names carry weight from one generation to the next?"

"I never knew my true name until a few days ago," I said, turning to face him. I could barely contain my fury.

"Then you know nothing of Clan du Sang, of the legacy left by your ancestors, especially the females?"

"Not. One. Thing." As soon as my confession left my lips I knew I should never have highlighted my ignorance, especially not to this man.

"Oh, Calliope." He tsk'd three times, shaking his head. "Had I known this I might have chosen a different route."

"A different route to what?"

"To getting what I want."

He pointed to the delicate bracelets encircling both of my wrists, slipping his index finger between the warmed metal of one and my cooling skin. "My clan's symbol is similar to these vines you wear, Calliope, but ours is no decorative frippery. When we find a host—willing or not—we act the patient admirer. With time we surround the host, be it a being or a business, until all that is visible is our new creation.

"Clan Vigne acquires and consumes. We do not work side by side; we do not create balanced alliances—we devour and remake anew. I have grown impatient with my inability to fix this situation with the Melusine, to unravel their mystery."

"Would it kill you to change your methods this once?"

"No. But it would kill the Melusine." He held my elbows. "Will you give them life, Calliope Viridis, verdant one? Will you share your blood, as the du Sangs have done for generations?"

Every thread Maritza and Leilani had stitched onto my dress tugged to be released. I had to keep my physiological responses within my normal range, or the symbols would begin to act. "What do you mean, share my blood?"

He squeezed my wrists. The metal Malvyn had shaped bit into my bones. I kept my features impassive as he leaned back and turned his head slightly to one side. "A simple donation, much as you would make at a blood bank. One pint should be enough, though I would require you to remain nearby in case my research is incorrect, and more blood is needed to sustain the Melusine's growth."

In that moment, I understood why Odilon dangled the possibility of a threat to my sons in order to secure what he wanted. Harper and Thatcher carried the du Sang blood. And as far as I knew, I was still fertile.

Fuck. "Will you give me time to think?"

"You have until the banker's notes on the three properties I plan to claim come due."

"And when is that?" I asked.

"Tomorrow at the close of the business day."

Odilon released his hold and left my side, walking to the very back of the boat to where a miniature dock was attached. Beside it was another tender. "Come," he called, gesturing to the boat, "I'm taking you to Chocolate Beach."

Stunned, I picked up my clutch and shawl and followed him. I held the hand he offered, not bothering to hide how badly I was shaking, and sat where directed. Odilon wrapped my shawl around my shoulders when his observation that the temperature was dropping elicited no response.

We neared the midden beach. Odilon cut the engine. As we drifted closer, he handed me a plastic bag. "Put your shoes and your other things in here."

I clutched the metal gunwales and looked over my shoulder at the carved marble planes of his face. "Why?"

"Because this, Ms. du Sang, is where you get off."

CHAPTER 20

Had I brought my wand and cell phone, I doubted Odilon would have returned them to me even after helping me alight in the shallow water. I kept the plastic bag above my head and placed each foot with care, weighing the barnacled surface of every rock against the slipperiness of the seaweed until I made it out of the water.

Odilon wasted no time returning to the yacht, pulling anchor, and motoring toward the marina. I was left with a darkening sky and a rising wind that presaged a change in the weather. The wine from dinner soured in my belly and the tomato and mint that had seemed so well suited in a soup tasted vile on my tongue.

Calliope, be careful with those.

But, Mama, they're so pretty.

We have to give them time to grow.

What will they become?

Mama's smile was sad. *Your sisters,* she said.

I had sisters. I dropped the plastic bag and glanced at my empty palms. No, I had a dream and in that dream my mother said things.

Yes, but Odilon said things, too. And Benôit was on the boat. And I had a decision to make, though there was only one acceptable answer to the question.

My feet stung. I had to find a place to sit and think.

The pearly vertebra of my spine snapped into formation. I stayed vigilant as I crossed the beach, with its deep bed of crushed shells, to a pile of driftwood and sat on the damp hunk of wood. The bottom eight inches or so of my woolen dress was soaked and dripping, adding weight to the already heavy garment. The elements Maritza and Lei-li had stitched into the dress resumed bidding for my attention.

Yes. Yes, I would give my blood to the Melusine.

On my terms.

I brushed chips of broken shells off my hands, set the plastic bag next to me on the wave-smoothed log, and dug into the dress's side pockets for my father's rings. They were cold to my touch and had shrunk so much in circumference that I couldn't get them on over either thumb's top knuckle. I tried every other finger on each shaking hand until I was able to wedge the metal rings down my pinkies.

Closing my eyes, I worked to soothe the wings struggling to free themselves from the backside of the dress. I recalled Christoph's feathers and how it calmed me to run my fingers over them until all of the barbs lined up and lay flat.

Vines growing on the narrow island where I was currently marooned responded to the presence of my feet on their soil. Whispered with one another, back and forth, hesitant about reaching out to me. But I couldn't see how vines could get me out of this predicament, unless they joined tendrils across the narrows to create a sort of bridge—I shook my head.

No uproot. No offshoot. Not yet.

Instead, I embraced Odilon's exquisite timing. My first portal adventure was nothing compared to the second, which was far simpler than being stranded on a small island in the middle of the night, with only my magic and a sentient dress to get me home.

I could do this.

I stroked the dull gold sequins scattered over the dress. They awakened and warmed to my touch, glowing brighter as I pictured Tanner in the moment we met, the front of his body in shadow, his head haloed by golden flecks of light.

I recalled my initial mistrust. The intensity of those early days and all that I learned about myself and the magical world I had been separated from for so long.

My lips warmed at the memory of our first real kisses, the ones not influenced by the Apple Witch's machinations. I pictured the morning after my Blood Ceremony, when Tanner brought me home, bathed me, and waited for all of my bits and pieces to return. And later that evening, at my party, helping me dress, celebrating the woman I was and the witch I was becoming.

Tanner's wolf, unflinching in his protection.

"I'm here," I whispered. "I'm okay." I wanted Tanner to get the message I was out of danger and as I floated my arms away from my body, I let go of any thought of needing to be rescued.

I reached to the sky, crossed my arms and bent my elbows, positioning my lower arms behind my head. I placed my palms over my tattoos. Lifting my heart beyond the steel gray clouds, to the constellations, I thanked Bear for her protective spirit. Walking my fingertips lower, as much as my shoulder joints would allow, I stroked the wing feathers sewn into the dress.

"Grandfather. I'm okay. You will know if I need you." I held the image from the night before, of Christoph soaring above the trees as he flew to my house. Reaching for the stars again, I spread my arms, imagining my sleeves were wings.

When I finished sending my message to Christoph, I paused. Maritza had stitched a repeating motif along the bottom of the dress, the section that was now soaking wet. Bull kelp, with its long frond and the bulb at one end. Local seal populations floated in masses of it offshore and though I couldn't discern one set of raised stitches from another, I was certain I'd overheard Maritza instructing Leilani to add a seal along the hem.

I bent at the waist and rubbed my hands over cold wet wool and invoked the water elements—the kelp and the seal. "Mama, Papa, I need you."

Standing straight, I ran my hands up and down the center of my torso and whispered to my friends waiting on the far shore, "Ivy wind and ivy bind. I am ready for your help." The vines were a sure bet. Standing on a narrow island, at night, with no means of communicating with humans other than wholly useless yelling, I chose the elements that made the most sense. Denizens of the water and minders of the earth.

Though I had never called on the vines hiding throughout the clusters of trees on this hunk of rock, they already acknowledged my presence. I knew they would answer my call. And when a snake-like thing approached the island from the water and tapped at my ankle, I understood the vines had come up with a solution.

Basket. Throne. Pull.

I lifted my face and laughed along with the stars. Odilon had thought to strand *me*.

The slender bit of vine tapping at my ankle circled up my calf and the front of my thigh and burst into a leafy greeting when it reached my cheek. "Keep your thorns in," I remonstrated gently, stroking the surface of the newly unfurled greenery.

The island's vines conferred in hushed consultation. An eruption of sound had me pivoting at the water's edge. I tried to run, but the vine that had wended its way across the channel wasn't letting me go. Together, we watched the other vines weave themselves into a basket shape big enough to accommodate me and, with a loud series of rips and pops, uproot the base of each section from the soil.

The basket was finished. I was moored in place.

"I think they need your help," I said, sliding a finger between my skin and the possessive little leaves. The vine holding me in place slithered down my body, let go of my leg, and whipped up the beach. Droplets of salt water hit my skin until the vine stopped, wrapped itself once around the basket, and drew the rescue craft past me and into the water.

I picked up the plastic bag holding my belongings and made my way across the glowing white midden to the waiting vessel. In the dark waters beyond, inky black heads broke the surface. My aquatic escorts had arrived. I secured the bag between my teeth, gripped the edge of the basket, and muttered, "Here goes nothing." Flinging one leg over, I felt for the bottom of the basket with my foot and shifted all of my weight.

While trying to not tip the entire thing over, I heard a rippling sound from the water and the basket lifted slightly. With the plastic bag still between my teeth, I glanced over the side to see a massive raft of kelp weaving into a pontoon. I grabbed hold of the vine that had come from the opposite shore. "I'm ready."

I had to drop the plastic bag between my knees. The shoes might get wet and ruined, but I'd never ridden in a custom-made water chariot and I was secretly thrilled. Not only had I called the elements to me using the spells embroidered into my dress, but it looked like I would arrive home intact and with enough time to plan Benôit's rescue.

Rain started to fall at the midway point between the island and the nearest shore. Though the wool offered protection and the basket began to pick up speed, every inch of bared skin was pebbled with goosebumps. Nearing shore, the basket slowed and sank lower in the water. Loud splashes announced the departure of the seals and the smell of low tide greeted my nostrils. My faithful invasives, tugging me and the basket across a short stretch of muck, finished their task with a sudden stop. We'd hit the end of a rotted boat ramp.

I reached for the splintered wood, grabbed the plastic bag, and planted one knee on the closest plank. "Thank you," I said, patting the rim of the basket as I disembarked, unsure what else I should do. The tip of the vine, leaves intact, wrapped itself around my wrist and pulled.

The worn and rickety ramp led from the beach to a cottage. The windows were darkened and there were no cars in the driveway, but once I got to the street I knew exactly where I was. I unwound the vine and set it on the ground.

Ivy tired.

Calliope tired, too, I answered wordlessly, grinning. Not only was I wearing a sentient dress, but my vines were developing a bigger vocabulary and a sense of humor. Waving goodbye, I headed to the road that would take me toward Long Harbor and the ferry terminal. I could call for a ride from there.

TANNER PICKED ME UP IN HIS TRUCK, SCATTERING ROCKS AS HE roared into the deserted parking lot. He'd brought a blanket and wrapped me tight before buckling me in. Eyes gold, mouth pinched, and rocking a fisherman's knit sweater, he asked, "Are you okay?"

I nodded, teeth chattering and shivers coursing through my limbs. "Need heat," I said.

He got me home in near record time. The only way I could have gotten there faster was by ambulance—or if Christoph had flown me in. I stumbled to the house, every step reminding me I had new cuts on my feet. Lights blazed from the kitchen and living rooms. Rowan waited at the door. She followed me down the hall and took over.

"I might be getting a little shocky," I said, unable to keep my teeth from knocking together.

"Tub. Now."

I dropped the blanket and stepped into the tub, still dressed. Ro got the water going, plugged the drain, and stripped me of my clothes. My elbow and shoulder joints were locked from the cold and my held-back fears.

"You can lie down," Rowan said. I nodded and pointed to the cup perched on the edge of the sink.

Water, I mouthed.

"Wes?" Ro kept one hand on my forearm as she opened the door a crack. "Warm up that tea I made, would you please, and put it in the biggest mug you can find along with a tablespoon of honey."

The shakes hit me hard. I couldn't stop, no matter how hot the water. I was home, I was safe, and I had a lot to absorb.

My father was alive.

My father worked for Odilon Vigne.

While under Odilon's employ—or at his direction—my father found a magical rarity and the scion of Clan Vigne was willing to go to any length to secure the one thing that would trigger the next phase of the Melusine's life cycle.

Du Sang blood. *My* blood.

"Calliope." I started at the sound of Rowan's voice and sat up. She rubbed my back with a soapy washcloth.

"Thanks for being here," I said. I drained the glass of water and handed it back to her. "I've missed you."

"Yeah, lots of mamas giving birth in August and it hasn't slowed down yet. I've delivered more babies at home the past six weeks than in the past couple of years, here and on the other islands."

"And has a certain druid been laying claim to your free time?"

"Free time? What's that?" Ro handed the washcloth and soap to me. "You can wash your front."

"Free time is that thing normal people have where they sit on their decks and drink beer and don't worry about magical shit exploding around them," I joked.

Rowan laughed and stood. She lifted my bathrobe off its hook and held it open. "Your friends await news of your adventures. Better hurry it up before the wolf out there gets antsy and blows the door down."

"Can you put something on my feet first?" I asked, folding the front halves of the bathrobe across my breasts and looping the tie once. I sat on the lid of the toilet and lifted my legs.

"Ouch," she said, crouching and assessing the damage. "Where's your first aid kit?"

"In the kitchen. But I think there's more of Belle's salve and another packet of gauze from when they patched me up earlier on the shelf up there."

I MADE IT TO THE LIVING ROOM ON STINGING, BANDAGED FEET AND accepted the spot cleared for me on the couch. Tanner and Christoph moved in from where they must have been pacing and planted themselves on the low table. "Tell us—" and "Start at the —" issued from their mouths in concert with Rowan handing me a mug of tea.

"Odilon has Benôit."

"What?" Christoph stood, fumbling for the glass he'd set between himself and Tanner.

I leaned forward and tugged on Christoph's pant leg. "I should clarify. Odilon says he has *a Benôit* on the yacht. I did not see this person, and it was not clear to me if he was there voluntarily or as a hostage or...or something else, but it is clear to me this Benôit is probably my father."

Christoph wiped at the sides of his face with both hands. "I haven't had a single communication from my son in...in twenty, twenty-five years? I don't even recall at this point." Something told me my grandfather, if pressed, could produce the exact date and time of his last encounter with Benôit. "What do we do now?" he asked.

"Odilon made it clear what he wants." I adjusted the front halves of my bathrobe to cover my bared legs. "He wants the du Sang blood."

"To what end?"

"This Benôit came into possession of a clutch of Melusine eggs. Odilon got his hands on the eggs and says he has kept them in stasis for years, waiting for an heir of Clan du Sang to appear." I set my mug on the side table and spread my arms. "And here she is."

"Melusine?" asked Tanner. He half stood and swung his body so he could sit beside me.

I nodded, curling into his side. "Benôit found the clutch of fertilized eggs in a waterway where fresh and salt water mixed. Odilon said introducing my blood to the ova would begin their awakening process. And there's something else." I raised one hand. "Guess what looks exactly like those glass balls I found at that strange portal?" I pressed my lips together and nodded again. "You guessed it. Melusine ova."

The confusion on the faces of the four adults in the room mirrored my own. "I take it none of you have heard of this phenomenon before?"

"Melusine were thought to have passed into legend early in the twentieth century," said Tanner. "I've met merpeople and selkies and other water-based shifters and Magicals, but never one of the Melusine.

"That I am aware of," he added.

"There's more." I held the mug of tea in both hands, close to my chest, pulling as much warmth into my body as I could. "Odilon wants my answer by five o'clock tomorrow afternoon."

"What answer?"

"If I am willing to exchange my blood in return for him letting go of his pursuit of properties here on this island. If I do not agree, he made it clear I should consider my offspring and their friends fair game in whatever grand scheme he has going."

"All of the properties?"

"He said the notes on three properties come due tomorrow. He did not specify which three they were. I would guess they might be the orchards and farms we suspect have portals and tunnels, maybe more." I knew the Pearmain property was safe from Odilon's grasp, at least for now.

"But what about Benôit?" Christoph asked.

"I think that if we want to confirm *this* Benôit is *our* Benôit, we'll have to remove him from the yacht by force. Or negotiate further exchanges with Odilon." I snuggled closer to Tanner's heat and the solid mass of his body. I was suddenly drop-dead tired.

Rowan spoke up. "I think Calliope needs to get to bed. I'm not sure what I can offer, but please keep me in the loop." She went to stand, then added, "Calli, wait a sec. You said the eggs had been placed in stasis. Did Odilon say how long ago they were found?"

"Thirty-something years ago. Around the time my mother and I moved to the island."

"And he gave you no other details?"

I shook my head. "Nothing, other than he seems to think they require my blood—or the blood of a du Sang—to trigger their growth. I didn't think to ask him any more questions, like are the eggs then implanted into a host body? Or do they develop outside of a body, but still in a cluster, like amphibians? I have so many questions—"

"Female bodies, whether they're magical or human, are my business, Calliope," Rowan said. "There's got to be another way to save these creatures without holding your blood hostage, and I want to help."

We stood and hugged. She and Wes left together, and Ro threw a concerned look at me as she waved goodbye.

Christoph placed a shaking hand on my arm. "Give me your father's rings," he said. "Now. I need to go." The thick bands, wedged on my little fingers, came off with a steady twist. I handed them to Christoph, and he was out the door before either Tanner or I could protest.

"Do you think he's going to the marina?" I asked, even though I knew the answer. I wrapped my arms around Tanner's waist and joined him in staring past the front door into the darkness of the night.

"Yes. That's what I would do if I were in his position. I just hope he doesn't get it in his head to try a one-man rescue mission."

THE RAIN THAT HAD STARTED WHEN I WAS ABOARD MY MAKESHIFT boat switched into high gear, pounding at the roof and decks. Tanner closed all the windows and turned on the electric heat in my bedroom to help take the damp and chill out of the air. We were in my bed, eyelids leaden, when the front door slammed open, then shut, and heavy steps tromped down the hall to my door.

"Calli-lass, I need to talk to you."

Tanner pulled on his sweatpants and opened the door. "Come in."

Christoph's drooping wings dripped water across the wood floor. His face was haggard, lit by a faint spark of hope. Tanner slipped behind him and returned with an armload of towels. He spread an old beach towel with a torn hem and faded stripes onto the floor, told Christoph to stand there, and draped two more over my grandfather's wings.

"What did you find?"

Christoph extended his arm and uncurled his fingers. The outer surfaces of my father's rings were alive with moving shapes. "There is no doubt in my mind that the man on the yacht is my son. The rings confirm it." He fisted them again and pounded his heart. "I must get to him. There's no way he's on that boat willingly. No way."

Rain on the roof. Water on my floor. Sorrow in Christoph's every cell. An idea formed in my head. I explained the bare bones to Tanner and my grandfather and suggested we all get a couple hours of sleep.

CHAPTER 21

In the low gray light of dawn and a thick cloud cover provided by our skilled water witch, a trio of river otters escorted me back to Chocolate Beach along with a motivated wolf with amber eyes. The four of them helped me pull my kayak up the beach and into a wooded copse. They would come out of the hiding spot and intervene if it looked like Odilon would not follow as I predicted. One of them would retrieve my kayak later in the day.

Sliding Christoph's newly acquired cell phone from the waterproof gear bag, I dialed the private number on the card Odilon had tucked into my clutch and said hello.

"Calliope du Sang, to what do I owe the honor of this unexpectedly early phone call?" he asked. The gravelly texture of his voice handed me my first victory of the day. I'd gotten the scion out of bed.

"A passing kayaker took pity on me and loaned me her cell phone," I said. "Come and get me. Bring the yacht. And food and water. I'm right where you last saw me and you have thirty minutes."

After I hung up, I put the phone back in the bag, sealed it

watertight, and placed it carefully in Tanner's mouth. I shooed the wolf and the otters to take up their places. Once I was convinced they couldn't be seen from where I was standing, I walked into the water to soak the bottom of my dress and splash ocean water over my head. For this to work, I had to look as though I'd spent the entire night on this tiny spit of land, in the cold and the wet.

With my legs bare and my skin turning blue, it wasn't all that hard to reach that state. Though I couldn't seem to dampen the cold fire of determination burning in my chest.

Less than a half hour later, the bow of the *Merry Widow* cut through the fog. I stood my ground as Odilon steered the yacht, anchored, and settled himself in the tender. He was alone, clad in shorts, boat shoes, and a hooded, charcoal-gray rain slicker, one of the expensive kinds.

He motored in and I waited, refusing to help when he tossed the bow line toward me. He pulled the rope in, tossed it a second time, landing it within inches of my legs. I deigned to grab it and gave a half-hearted pull.

"What do you expect?" I asked, raising my voice and exaggerating the tremors that knocked my knees together and made it hard to extend my arms. "I'm thirsty and I'm hungry and I might be hypothermic."

Odilon stepped out of the little boat and splashed through the shallow water toward the shore. He walked past me, pulling until the hull was well onto the beach and dropped the line. "I brought you a banana," he said, reaching into one pocket. He extracted a bottle of flavored water from the other and waited while I ate and drank.

"I take it you've made a decision?" he said, pocketing the plastic bottle I had emptied in a few long pulls.

I nodded while I devoured the fruit and motioned for him to come closer, and closer still, until his chest was inches from mine. Dropping the banana peel onto the crushed shell beach I brushed my hands up and down the front of the water-logged dress and whispered to my beloveds,

"Ivy work and ivy play,

"Bind this man and make him stay."

The black stitching lit up in shades of jade green, peeled away from the chest area first, and began to bind Odilon to me. A raft of bull kelp slithered up the beach, covering Odilon's feet and legs. Gaze locked on to mine, he didn't seem to notice what was happening around us. When I took hold of Odilon's wrists and held them tight, the bracelets Malvyn made loosened, snaked off my wrists, and wound themselves around and around the scion's fingers. My "decorative frippery" now prevented him from arming himself as many Fae could.

"I want my father," I said. "Only when I know he's alive, off your boat, in my care, and receiving medical attention will we begin the next stage of our negotiations."

"And what makes you think I will cooperate?"

"I want to help the Melusine on my own terms, Scion."

"You want to willingly help me?"

I shook my head, splattering his front with more droplets. "No. I want to help the Melusine because it is what I am meant to do and because I want to know what really happened to my mother. You've kept the ova all these years. What's a little more time to allow me to satisfy my curiosity?"

The look in Odilon's eyes confirmed what I suspected. He knew much more about Clan du Sang than he wanted to let on. "What if I don't agree?" he asked. "I can easily rid myself of these encumbrances." He tried to lift his arms and couldn't. The vines had made efficient work of binding his limbs to his torso.

I gazed past his shoulders. "Look behind you."

Odilon turned his head as much as he could, given he was rooted in place. Christoph stood on the bow of the *Merry Widow*; a limp body draped across his arms. I steeled myself to not react, especially when my grandfather stepped off the boat, extended his wings, and flew toward the heavily wooded part of the shoreline. Thanks to Airlie, a rolling bank of dense fog kept Christoph's wings from human sight.

At the touch of my hand, the ends of the spelled threads disengaged from the front of the dress, allowing me to step away from Odilon. "I will be in touch," I said.

My four beastie boys ran out of the woods. The basket that had carried me away from Chocolate Beach less than twelve hours ago bumped against Odilon's skiff. My wolf leaped into the water, dragged the basket to me, and held it steady as I climbed in. I tugged the vine connecting my craft to the shore and wished Odilon well.

"You will be released once I've made it home."

Tanner trotted close to Odilon, shook the water off his thick coat, and bounded back to accompany me to the far shore. For one prolonged moment, I tasted victory. I let myself savor the sensation, because Goddess only knew what awaited.

TANNER, RIVER, WES, AND KAZ WERE IN THE PROCESS OF SHIFTING by the time my craft landed. I followed four naked backsides as we ran to where they'd parked the truck and car. Tanner unzipped my dress. I shrugged it off and peeled my underwear down my legs before climbing into the passenger side of his truck and reaching for the waiting stack of sweatpants, sweat-shirt, and heavy wool socks. He climbed in, pants already on, and started the engine at once.

Tanner tapped the glove compartment. "Your cell phone's in there and you've got messages," he said, brushing a cold kiss across my colder lips. He drew on a long-sleeved shirt, caught my chin in one hand, and searched my face. "You did great. I had no idea my girlfriend had acting chops."

"Your girlfriend?" My teeth were chattering. I tucked my frozen fingers under my armpits. "You asking me to go steady?"

"Sure am," he said, adding a bulky knit sweater to his ensemble.

"Cool." I found my cell phone and switched it on. "Maybe we can talk more about this when things have calmed down."

"Do things ever calm down around here?"

"Not since the day I met you," I reminded him with a tremulous, blue-lipped smile. Tanner laughed and wiped the condensation off the inside of the windshield.

Kerry had sent me the selfie I asked her to arrange. Opening the file, I crowed. She'd done a great job of getting a full frontal picture of my replacement's face. I forwarded the image to both Sallie and Azura and added we needed to know whether or not the guy was Fae as soon as possible, as in before they went to work. Then I remembered we had the truck Sallie had been using to get to her job at Brooks Farm.

First things first. "Do you know where Christoph took Benôit?" I asked.

Tanner backed the truck out from where he'd parked nose-in, pulled forward onto the road, and hit the turn signal. "Belle's house. She's got an entire herbal apothecary set up and a couple of treatment rooms she uses for patients who need to stay overnight or longer. Rowan and Airlie are meeting us there. Everyone's as ready as they can be to assist."

The fog was heavy on the roads. Much as I wanted to curl against Tanner and warm my hands on his skin, I stayed to my side of the bench seat. I lifted my feet to the dash and covered the heat vents with my toes. "I feel numb," I admitted.

Tanner shot me a quick look and adjusted the headlights. "Want to talk about it?"

"My father—Benôit—feels more like a figment of my imagination." I closed my eyes and pressed the back of my head against the seat. "I don't have a lot of memories of my mother, but at least I have them. I have nothing for him, not even…an emotion."

"That doesn't make you a bad person, Calli. You know that, right?"

"I do. And I'm still terrified to meet him."

"Try looking at Benôit as someone who needs medical attention, first and foremost." Tanner slowed into the next turn. "We have no idea what his story is. Maybe he's done terrible things or heroic things or both. At the least, we can all give him a chance to explain himself. Plus, Christoph's a wreck."

I nodded. "I noticed. I've been trying to imagine what it would be like if Harper or Thatch just disappeared one day." I sat up straight, tucking my lower legs to one side to face Tanner. "It would break me."

Letting myself reach for my druid, I added, "Which is why I can't cut the boys off from their father completely. At some point, they're going to want to talk to Doug and I'm going to have to let that happen."

"You're good mom, Calliope. And we're here."

Belle's home was one of the island's few Victorians. It was certainly the prettiest. To walk through her front gate was to enter a place where plants reigned and were revered. Lights shone from every ground floor window. Tanner and I followed the trio of druids to the porch. Kazimir knocked lightly before he pushed on the door and let us in. "Shoes off," he said, his voice low.

Rowan appeared and went straight to Wes. He molded his body to hers and kissed her full on the mouth. "What do you need from us?" he asked.

"More of that," she answered, "later, when the patient's stabilized and Christoph's awake." Ro let Wes hold her hand as she included the rest of us in her report. "The primary patient—Benôit Courant—is in pretty rough shape. He's dehydrated, malnourished, and has sustained traumatic injuries. Belle and Airlie and I are working on him. Christoph's asleep in one of the other rooms. He was having a hard time staying out of our way and agreed to let Belle treat him for stress. He's been out about ten minutes.

"Calli, Christoph confirmed Benôit is his son, and therefore your father. Do you want to see him?"

My response stuck in my throat.

Rowan let go of Wes and took me into her embrace. "If it's any help, we have Benôit sedated. Right now we're working on getting his core temperature up and getting fluids into him."

"I'll come," I said.

"Help yourself to anything you find in the kitchen. Belle brewed a special tea for all of you." Rowan waved Tanner toward the kitchen, drew me to her side, and guided me down the hall. "Benôit's body has been altered, Calli. I want you to prepare yourself."

She opened the door. In the dim light, I noticed Belle and Airlie first, standing on either side of the hospital bed in the center of the heated room. A fire crackled in the woodstove and a kettle added steam to the air.

The body—Benôit—was lying on his side, facing away from the door, with a pillow cushioning his head and a blanket covering his lower half. Airlie had her hands on his head and his hip. Belle dipped her fingers into a container on the bedside table and rubbed something over his bared back. "You can stand near me," she said.

I stepped to Belle's side. Smelled her gentle, floral presence. Traced my glance from her shoulder, down her arm to her small, but strong and capable, hands. Underneath the thick salve coating the man's back was a web of scar tissue and newer cuts. Near the shoulder blades, the scars gave way to broken bones. Wing bones. The big ones that would have connected his wings to his underlying human bones. Above the bones and across his shoulders grew small bits of seaweed and clusters of barnacles.

Unshed tears ran down my throat. I went to touch him. Belle

grabbed my wrist. "Wait, dear one. Your touch could startle him out of his healing process."

I nodded my understanding, and asked, "Is he in pain?"

"Benôit is in many kinds of pain. I'm treating the physical. Airlie is reading his emotional condition." Belle reached for more salve. "She's the perfect ally for him right now. She may not know the sacrifice he's made—or that was forced upon him—but she understands beings who are called to the waters. She can soothe him as well as any herbs and topicals I have to offer."

"Do you know what she's doing?"

"Singing the songs of the many seas and riverways in this hemisphere of the world. With her hands, she feels when he reacts to any one verse or song in particular. That allows her to go deeper. When she's done, we'll know where he calls home."

"May I see his face?" I asked. I reached for the apron strings tied in a loose bow at the back of Belle's waist. She reached behind, found my hand, and drew me forward.

She pressed a finger to her lips and nodded.

I held my breath. Took a step closer to the bed. Benôit's left arm had been amputated below the elbow. Hanks of his hair fell over the side of his face, leaving only his jaw and mouth visible. There were bald spots on his scalp where hair had been ripped out.

He opened and closed his mouth, over and over again, like a stranded fish, then stopped, his lips parted. Airlie stifled a sob. The tears streaming down her face dripped onto his head.

"Did you get what we need?" Belle whispered to her. Airlie nodded. Moving with what looked like a preplanned sequence of steps, Belle pivoted to the tray table beside her, picked up a large syringe, whipped down the sheet and plunged the needle into the flesh near where I expected to see a man's buttocks.

There were no buttocks, no legs. Only the bottom half of an aquatic creature. Underneath the blanket, the lowest section of the creature slapped the mattress twice, violently, then stopped.

"Done." Belle stepped back. Airlie cautiously lifted her hands off Benôit. The two witches looked at each other across the now-still form. "He should be out for at least six hours," Belle whispered, "Goddess willing."

"Thank you, Belle. For everything."

"You are welcome. I want to keep him here for a few days. Christoph knows he is welcome to stay in one of the guest rooms. I wouldn't even try to send him home. Kazimir has volunteered to be his caregiver." Belle looked over her shoulder and spoke to the druid, "We're going to need at least three buckets of fresh seaweed, as soon as you can get it here."

Kaz nodded and left the room. I heard the sound of a zipper, then the front door open and close, and took that as my signal to have one more look at the mangled wing joints on the patient's back before I left.

"I don't think there's much of anything I can do here," I said to Tanner and River when I encountered them standing in the hall. "I may as well go home."

SALLIE AND AZURA WERE SEATED AT THE DINING TABLE, THEIR phones at their elbows and the Fae directory they'd procured on their trip to Victoria between of them. Two plates of decimated pancakes and orange peels sat in the center of the table. Harper and Thatch were in the kitchen, along with Leilani. All conversation stopped when Tanner and I walked in the front door.

"Hey," Thatcher said. "How'd it go?"

"Christoph rescued Benôit and we have about six hours to figure out how to make Odilon an offer he can't refuse." I leaned my weight against the center island. "Can you guys make breakfast for us?"

"Thatch, beat two more egg whites, please. Harper, see if there's another jug of maple syrup and cut up more oranges." Lei-li pivoted and stared at me and Tanner for a moment. "You guys look like you need my power pancakes."

I waved a tired hand. "A short stack for me, please, for starters."

Tanner said, "Put me down for a dozen."

Harper had his back to me. "So, what's he like?" he asked. Thatcher stopped whisking and Leilani elbowed Harper. My breathing suspended. Beneath my wool-clad feet, House's wooden bones and boards went quiet, too.

"My father is not doing well," I said, delivering my words slowly and with care. "He's heavily sedated and his wings are gone."

"How's Gramps holding up?"

I shook my head. "Belle had to dose him with herbs to get him to settle down. He and Benôit will be staying with her."

Leilani continued to give out orders. "You two go sit. We'll bring your food over."

Sallie and Azura greeted us with shy smiles that couldn't mask their excitement. "Aunt Calli, we found him, the guy who's working at your old job."

"That's awesome," I said. "Were you able to get his address? And does his Fae name match the one he gave to Kerry?"

They looked at each other, then at me. "His name is Hosea," said Sallie. "Hosea Brooks. As in brother to Lolly Brooks, owner of Brooks Family Farm."

My jaw almost hit the table. "Tanner, did any of those complaint letters going out from the Agricultural Commission's office get sent to Brooks Farm?"

Tanner searched his laptop. "No. But the orchard nearby, the one Adelaide put a bid on, they're one of the properties due to go into receivership at five-oh-one today if their note's not paid."

"Calliope, there's more," said Azura. She tapped the heavy volume, tilted her head, and ran her thumb over pages marked by sticky notes. Finding what she was searching for, she slid her thumbs between two pages, opened the tome, and motioned me to come closer. "Guess who's first cousins with Lolly Brooks?"

I almost didn't want to know. "Surprise me," I said, looking over their shoulders.

She pointed to two names I knew all too well. My ex-husband, Douglas Flechette, and his twin brother, Roger. "Crap. So, either Odilon is in cahoots with all of them, or Roger and Hosea and Lolly are trying to pull something over on Clan Vigne. Or at least on Odilon."

"Zura and I have been discussing this, Aunt Calliope, and this is what we think is going down." Sallie cleared her throat and motioned me to take the seat across the table from her and her girlfriend. "Odilon jilted Meribah and Adelaide after they pulled that shit on you this summer, and then he turned around and bought their realty and land development business from them."

I added, "He did mention that having the owners of the business in jail was not a good financial move and that he stepped in to save the business. But last night, when I got to the marina and saw Roger, Odilon introduced him as his head of security."

"Which would mean Roger has access to at least some of Odilon's private information."

"While his mother and aunt are under house arrest, and his brother's under psychiatric care, Roger's making a play for...for what? Getting the business back?"

I shook my head. "He knows Odilon wants the properties that are critical to the transportation routes used by Magicals." I kept to myself my fears that he might have knowledge of the special apple trees or that he suspected trees like my crabapple might be hiding important secrets.

"Mom?" Thatcher placed two plates of pancakes on the table and motioned for Tanner to sit next to me. "Harper and I have a confession to make."

"I'm listening." I was also starving. I slid thin pats of butter between each pancake and poured a generous stream of warmed maple syrup over the top. Tanner repeated my movements on his much taller stack. Pressing the edge of my fork into the fluffy goodness, I speared a piece and put it in my mouth.

Leilani joined Harper and Thatcher behind Sallie and Azura's chairs. "While you all were away this morning, the five of us went to the property across the street. We broke into the house from the back, where you said you'd seen the plywood. And you were right, it's covering an entrance."

Harper picked up the story. "There's a metal door and it was locked."

"*Was* locked," I said, using my fork to section off another bite, "as in the lock is now broken?"

"That's correct. It wasn't a very good lock. The electricity works, but the place doesn't look like it's been used in a really long time."

The five of them got very still and quiet. Leilani spoke next. "There are aquariums in there, Calliope. Four of them, and they're huge, probably twelve by six feet, and at least four feet deep."

"It gave us the creeps," Sallie said, adding, "especially the rocking chair."

I took my time absorbing their story while eating my breakfast and sorting through all the possibilities in my head. "We've been told that property and the one to the east are in a blind trust."

One of the kids coughed. I glanced up to see Thatch's cheeks had gone bright red. "Mom," he said, "I have another confession to make." He looked to the ceiling, then to his brother. "Bear used to take me walking on that property, the one across the street. Always the same route, around the marsh, around the house, and back here. Then Bear would disappear again."

The tattoos across my back tingled in response. I rested the tines of my fork on the rim of my plate and rubbed my forehead. Things were so much easier when the boys were little. "And?"

"And I think Bear's job was to watch over the property. I think we should ask your cousin Clyde if he knows anything about that land and that house."

"Can you get my phone for me? It's in the pocket of my sweatshirt." The three standing teens turned as one and practically ran to the coat hooks. Harper handed the phone to me. I scrolled through my messages until I got to the one Clyde had sent days ago. He'd wanted to know when we could get together and go over his mother's will.

"Clyde," I said, when my cousin picked up on the second ring.

"Hey, Calliope, thanks for getting back to me."

"I'm sorry it took me this long. How're you doing?" I asked, accepting the wave of guilt I'd been holding at bay. And the tears filling my eyes. I regretted I hadn't been more available to my cousin or his sister in Aunt Noémi's last weeks, especially given how her moments of lucidity had given me insight into Bear, and so much more.

"We're okay. In many ways, it felt like Mom left us a long time ago but having her gone is still hard."

"I'm sorry to spring this on you right now," I said, pressing the outer corners of my eyes and trying in vain to swallow my tears, "but you mentioned her will in your message. Is there anything in there about the properties neighboring her old house? Or do you personally know anything about the place across the street?"

"That's exactly why I texted you, cousin. Give me a sec to get the papers."

I blew my nose on a paper towel while I waited. Clyde returned and picked up his phone. "Okay, here we go. I took notes when I was at the lawyer's and put the legalese into plain English. Basically, what it says here is that Mom was asked to keep the ownership of the property a secret from you until you came of age. And for whatever reason—maybe her dementia, I don't know—she forgot to tell you that it was a Benôit Courant who purchased those properties and made Mom the, I don't know, like the property manager.

"The estate lawyer said all you have to do is make an appointment to meet with them at their office, sign a bunch of papers, and the property is yours. Oh, and all the taxes and stuff have been paid."

Clyde provided a few more details and promised to let me know if he found anything relevant in the rest of his mother's papers, as he and his sister were in the process of sorting everything out, including what was left of her physical belongings. I promised I would call the lawyer and would also make a date to see Clyde when I was next in Victoria.

I set the phone next to my plate and rubbed my stomach. I was afraid my breakfast was going to come back up, and after last night and this morning I needed the calories to stay inside my body. "I'm proud of all of you for being brave and going to that house and going farther than Airlie and I were able to," I said at last. "And I'm upset with all of you for—"

"Mom, we're not normal teenagers," said Thatcher. He gripped the nobs on either side of Sallie's ladderback chair and rubbed the wood with his thumbs. "And we have another idea."

"What is that?"

Thatcher moved his hand to his cousin's shoulder. Sallie looked up at him before engaging with me.

"We want to come with you when you talk to Odilon."

CHAPTER 22

I showered and dressed in silence. Tanner returned to the stack of papers we'd liberated from the Agricultural Commission's office. He wanted to be sure I had as many details as possible at my fingertips when I walked into Odilon's office.

Amend that. When *my* retinue—Harper, Thatcher, Leilani, Sallie, and Azura—walked into Odilon's office with me. "It's three thirty," I said. "Is everyone ready?"

A chorus of yeses sounded from the living room. I glanced at Tanner. "Are you driving or is Wolf coming along for the ride?"

"Do you have a preference?"

The unanimous opinion from the peanut gallery was, "Wolf!"

Tanner blushed and shrugged his shoulders. "What can I say? Wolf has his mojo back."

"I'll drive your truck and take Sallie and Azura with me. The boys and Leilani can take the Jeep." I spun on the kitchen stool. "We leave in five minutes."

Earlier, Maritza had gifted me a pair of black wool dress slacks. Bas chimed in with the suggestion I wear them with black ankle boots and a white shirt and then handed me a garment bag and a shoe box and wished me a happy birthday. I told him my birthday was months away. He ignored me and promised to take me to his aesthetician in Toronto "when all this calms down and things are back to normal."

I laughed, then agreed I'd earned a spa day.

Tanner loaned me his laptop bag for the papers and whatever else I needed and shortened the shoulder strap so it became a handle. I felt very professional. "I'm going to the side yard to shift," he said, holding my face and kissing my forehead. "I'll ride in the back of the truck."

The girls and I were buckling in when the truck rocked with the weight of a large silvery white wolf. He yipped twice, turned in a circle, and settled onto the old blanket Harper had tossed in.

"You two doing okay?" I asked, pulling out after the Jeep. Leilani blew us kisses from the back seat. Sallie was beside me, Azura's hand clutched on her lap.

"I feel better now with a collar." Malvyn had surprised Sallie with a simple choker of chrysalis shapes linked horizontally, each inscribed with a slightly different design.

"Mal did a beautiful job."

Sallie beamed one of her rare smiles and sat up taller. Azura had insisted they both dress up a little and was wearing another of her vintage 1950s-style dresses with a full skirt. Sallie had reverted to wearing all black, but nothing was ripped and she had even polished and strung new laces through her favorite Fluevog boots.

We didn't speak again until we pulled into the parking lot and disembarked. Wolf thumped his tail and I rubbed him behind the ears. "I have my pin," I said. I showed him where I'd placed it, right over my heart. He thumped his tail again and lowered his snout to his paws. "You be good."

Sallie and Azura stood to my front. Harper and Thatcher positioned themselves behind me, with Lei-li between them. I couldn't resist joking, "Champagne's on me if we come out of this alive."

The Fae girls pulled the big glass door open and Thatcher held it until everyone was inside. We walked up the carpeted stairs in formation and repeated the door opening again at the landing. The same man as before was behind the reception counter. He stood as we entered.

"Calliope Viridis du Sang to see Odilon Vigne, scion of Clan Vigne."

"And who is—?" he asked, waving his tablet at the teenagers. "Who are all these people with you?"

I stepped aside. Leilani came forward and offered her hand. "Leilani Margarita Brodeur, daughter of Malvyn Brodeur, Enforcer for the Board of Magical Governance, and James Brodeur, Botanist."

The others followed her lead. "Harper Jones, first son of Calliope du Sang."

"Thatcher Flechette du Sang, second son of Calliope du Sang."

"Sallie Flechette, favorite niece of Calliope du Sang."

"Azura Isadora, future ice mage and houseguest of Calliope du Sang."

The man's eyes widened with each teen's introduction. "I shall let the scion know you are here."

"Help yourselves to water," I said, pointing to the waiting area.

"We're good." Thatcher moved to my side, and Harper and Leilani joined hands.

Inside, I was calm. I kept remembering what I had experienced during the Joining, the cellular connection to my land. I had a notion to try to do that with water, next time I had a free day and an ocean or a lake to float in. Nothing was going to be taken from me that I wasn't willing to give.

Or negotiate away.

"Come with me." We followed the man down the hall to Odilon's office. The scion stood as we entered, papers stacked in three piles in front of him. He came around his desk, kissed both my cheeks, and introduced himself to my five cohorts. After, he indicated everyone could take one of the seats his assistant had brought in while introductions were being made.

"I wasn't expecting anyone else at our meeting, Calliope."

"They insisted on joining me."

"And why is that?"

Harper stood and took the lead. "We heard you had professed an interest in our well-being, Mr. Vigne, and we came to let you know we are doing fine. I only recently discovered that not only do I have wings—a gift from my mother's side of the family—but I have Fae-born talents, as well." Facing me and Odilon, Harper demonstrated an ability he hadn't yet shown me. In under a minute his facial features began to resemble those of the gyrfalcon he had chosen to emulate.

"Impressive," said Odilon. Harper grinned and sat down. The scion turned to Thatcher. "And what about you?"

Thatch leaned forward, elbows on his knees and fingers interlaced and studied Odilon before speaking. "I know that you were caught off guard, seeing all of us arrive with my mom, and that you fully expected her to give in to everything you want from her, including your offer of a romantic partnership. I also know that you become deeply embarrassed when you misjudge people." Thatcher paused, then added, "You rarely miss the mark in your assessment of their strengths and weaknesses."

Odilon placed his hands on his hips. "I could use someone like you on my staff," he said. "If you're ever looking to go beyond farm work."

"I will keep your offer in mind."

After a protracted silence, Azura and Sallie looked at each other. Sallie nodded, and Azura stood, fluffing at her skirt. "My family sits low in the Fae's clan rankings. I, however, think I have magic worth cultivating and a great deal of experience in the food service industry."

"I would wager your talents lie more in the fields of marketing and communications, Ms. Isadora. Please leave your contact information with Raul before you go. I can't promise anything, but once this current mess is sorted—and if I decide to make Salt Spring Island one of my bases—I could use a few younger people on staff for projects that are still on the drawing board."

"I shall do that, Scion. Thank you."

Sallie went to touch her throat and instead stuck her hand out to shake Odilon's. He held on an extra beat before letting her go. "Ms. Flechette."

"Mr. Vigne. My parents throttled my magic and I will not live that way ever again. I want you to know that not all Flechettes have evil intentions."

"And what are your intentions? I take it you have something in mind?"

"I do." Sallie sucked in a deep breath. "I have been offered an apprenticeship with the sorcerer, Malvyn Brodeur."

Odilon looked startled. "Aren't you rather young for entering the Enforcement's Academy?"

It was Sallie's turn to look confused. Then she grinned. "He's going to teach me how to make jewelry," she said, lifting her new collar away from her throat, "like this." Odilon bent from the waist for a closer look at the cast pieces and their mirrorlike sheen. He went to touch the metal and jerked his hand away.

"Your necklace has been spelled."

"Yes, it has. At my request. Until I'm ready to embrace the Fae magic I inherited."

"You're afraid there's a chance you might follow your parents' example," Odilon stated, nodding his head when Sallie answered with her silence. "I carry that same fear."

He gripped the side of my niece's shoulder. "Thank you for updating me on your circumstances, Ms. Flechette. Perhaps I should have told you earlier that a fund has been created to assist you with living expenses, should you need the help."

Leilani was the last of the teens to speak. "Last weekend was the first meeting of the mentoring program for magical youth." She pointed to Sallie and Azura. "These two girls were the only Fae there—unless the being who took the pictures you showed to Calliope is also Fae with a really good disguise."

Odilon crossed his arms. His face remained impassive. "Go on," he said.

"We five would like to propose that more Fae teenagers be allowed to join us every month. This program could go a long way toward improving relations among different factions of Magicals." She mimicked his pose. "You know, like not having to live under the weight of our parents' biases and misguided notions of who should come in contact with whom."

"I will think about it. In the meantime, I will also inform a certain being on my payroll that their services are no longer needed. That will have to do for now."

"That's a start," Leilani said, before returning to her seat.

Odilon turned to me. "Calliope, do you think we might have a few minutes alone?"

"Are you okay waiting for me in the lobby?" Thatcher gave me the signal we'd worked out. Odilon stood by the door and shook hands with each of the five teenagers as they left the room.

"That was unexpected." Odilon closed his door and took a breath before he turned to face me. He gestured to one of the leather chairs. "Please, sit."

I nudged the chair with my knee—I wanted to face the door—and placed Tanner's bag on my lap. I extracted the papers I'd brought while Odilon took his seat behind the desk. "I have some information you might be interested in," I said, showing him the enlarged image of my replacement at the Agricultural Commission's office. I had cropped out Kerry's face. "Do you know this man?"

Odilon studied the page. "I believe I have seen him before, but I don't think I know his name."

"His name is Hosea Brooks. He is related to Lolly Brooks,

who owns Brooks Family Farm. Hosea and Lolly are cousins to my ex-husband, Douglas Flechette—whom I assume you know—and his twin brother, Roger."

"And why should I care about this?"

"Because Hosea used deceptive tactics to finagle his way into being appointed my replacement at the Agricultural Commission's office. Using his new authority, he has been harassing local farm and orchard owners to the point where some of them are considering selling off their properties because they cannot fix what Hosea says they must or pay the fines he professes to have the authority to levy."

"I take it these farms and orchards are in fine working order and this Hosea has manufactured false claims in order to—"

"In order to make a land grab for places that are suspected of having, or are known to have, magical beings tending to the land or to possible portals, or any number of things." I took a deep breath and continued. "There's more. A lot more. The owners of Brooks Family Farm began an aquaculture project last month. They've begun to dig two ponds on a section of the property that is now fenced off, electrified, and guarded."

Odilon's jawline tightened. "Roger planned to take the Melusine from me."

"That would be my guess. We also uncovered further evidence of collusion between him and Hosea. Roger sees this as a perfect time to take over his family's business."

"But I already purchased the family business."

"Did you read the fine print?"

"Roger assured me—"

"Wait, you had *Roger* broker the deal for you? Odilon, pardon my disbelief, but didn't you take a hard look at the fine print before you took over?"

Odilon glared at me. "I was blinded by lust," he said.

I tried not to laugh. "I would make you a different offer."

"And what is that?"

"Let me have the Melusine ova. They are *my* inheritance, though I can see how you could make a case that possession is nine-tenths of the law, even for Magicals."

He lifted his chin. "Convince me."

"I think you can understand when I would also point out that sometimes the sins of the fathers must be rectified by the actions of their offspring."

"Are you referring to my father, or yours?"

"Perhaps both," I said. "I've seen Benôit, but I have yet to speak with him. He needs medical care. And time to heal."

"I want you to know he was like that when I hired him, Calliope. Very rough around the edges—and damaged. Physically, mentally, and emotionally."

"Then why did you hire him?" I asked.

"Because of your mother." Odilon cast his gaze to his lap. "My father can be a cruel and unforgiving man. Your mother's best friend was one of the few—if not the last—Melusine known to be left in France. Her name was Agnès. She spurned my father's amorous advances. He retaliated by banishing her from the land." He sighed and continued. "It was your mother's friendship, and her proximity to water, that gave Agnès the strength to imagine she could establish a new home in Maine."

"Agnès was pregnant," I guessed.

"Yes."

"And do you know by whom?"

"I have my suspicions. But I have no proof. That will come when we see if any of the ova are viable after so long in stasis."

"Does this mean you will turn the aquarium and its contents over to me?" My heart thundered in my chest as the long-term implications of this discussion began to sink in. Odilon nodded, his expression grave. I wished Thatcher had stayed and could assess the veracity of the scion's words and actions.

"You and I would make a formidable couple, Calliope Viridis du Sang."

"You have my gratitude," I said, ignoring his offer and coming to my feet, "pending forgiveness of these notes, your promise there will be no retaliatory measures taken against these farmers, and safe delivery of the Melusine. I am confident you will deal with Roger and with Hosea. And I think Brooks Family Farm and the adjacent property Adelaide sought to purchase will be delighted to know you're their new owner."

Odilon smirked. "I doubt that," he said, "but I will accept the modicum of joy that will come with those acquisitions." He grasped the door handle. "You will have the Melusine ova as soon as you are ready to receive them, and you have my promise that no harm will come to them in the interim."

I walked down the hall, waved to the cluster of teenagers seated in the waiting area, and paused at the bottom of the wide stairs. I didn't trust my arms had strength enough to open the heavy glass and metal door.

Wolf yelped when he saw us and lathered my face with his tongue. "I'll tell you all about it when we get home," I promised. "Right now, I need a drink." He yelped again, then settled in the back of the truck. I asked Sallie to drive. On the way home, we picked up the platter of sushi Azura had the forethought to order and stopped at the liquor store for bottles of chilled champagne and sparkling apple cider.

James and Malvyn met us at the front door with the news that Kaz and Wes had spent the day with Christoph and would stay at Belle's another night. Rowan had left a message that she planned to join Belle once she finished with patients.

"I really want to see you, Calli," her voicemail continued, "but Wes let me know he's leaving on Monday for his next three-month commitment. I think you know the project he's talking about, the one about the secret place. Anyway, he and I have lots to talk about. Cross your fingers we can figure out this long-distance relationship stuff. I'll see you soon. Promise."

CHAPTER 23

After dinner, exhausted to the marrow in my bones, I couldn't sleep. I had to do something to keep my hands busy.

"Can you bring in the basket of crabapples we picked?" I asked Tanner. "I left them on the back deck."

He did and poured them into the sink full of water I had run while waiting for him to say goodbye to Mal and James. "Anything else you need?"

"You could help me wash these. If you don't have anything better to do."

"If scrubbing crabapples means I can hang out with you, it'd be my pleasure."

We worked side by side at the sink in companionable silence. Tanner washed and towel-dried the apples while I twisted off the stems and quartered each piece of fruit. After, I pulled my twenty-quart stock pot out of the closet, rinsed it, added the chopped apples, and filled the pot with enough water to cover the fruit.

"How long will this take?" Tanner asked, stifling a yawn.

I glanced at the pot, the kitchen clock, then back at him and laughed. "All night?"

"Do you want me to stay up with you?"

"You can go to bed and be useful in the morning. This won't really take all night. I have to bring the water to a boil, let the apples simmer for about thirty minutes, then pour the pulp into jelly bags and let them drain overnight.

"It's labor intensive but my aunt did this every year and since I moved back into House, I've made the effort to, as well. Kind of a sentimental gesture." I shrugged. "You seemed to like it on your toast."

"I sure did and I look forward to more." Tanner kissed my forehead. "I'll warm up the bed. Come get me if you decide you want the company. You've had a big day."

I corrected him. "A very big couple of days."

I TIED CHEESECLOTH BAGS OF APPLE PULP TO THE HANDLES OF wooden spoons and hung them over two big pots set on the kitchen counter. The constant stream of juice soon slowed to drips as I put dishes back into cupboards and washed what was left in the sink from earlier meals. After tossing my apron into the laundry closet, I scooped my customary spoonful of the sour, soupy mash and shuddered as I swallowed it down.

I followed that with two more spoonfuls and a leftover cookie and still I wasn't ready for bed. I picked up the leather Mary Janes. The bottoms needed to be resoled. I wiggled my feet into my faithful Blundstones, tugged my sweatshirt over my head, and turned off the last of the lights inside the house.

At the foot of the porch steps, I paused. It was well after midnight, closer to two, and though the night was peaceful, my insides were as jellylike as the contents of those cheesecloth bags.

What the heck have you done, Calliope Viridis du Sang?

You said yes, I reminded myself.

I said yes to a dream, I said, playing the Devil's advocate to myself as I meandered to the end of the driveway, crossed Fortune's Folly Road, and leaped over the ditch by the side of the road.

My feet continued to propel me forward, step after step, as I bushwhacked through the brush, up the rise, and into the wooded area on what was soon to be—legally—my property. I wasn't done talking to myself, and continued on until the broad, eternally reaching limbs of a bigleaf maple split the sky in front of me, blocking out the stars.

I'd made it to the abandoned house, with its never-used aquariums and ghostly rocking chair. I walked around the side of the decrepit house, still arguing with myself in my head, until my booted feet met the trammeled path between the back of the house and the marsh.

Calli.

Mama?

I shot the hood of my sweatshirt off my head and quickened my pace, sure my mother's voice was coming from the marsh.

I'm coming. Wait for me.

By the time I was splashing through the mud in the shallow area nearest the house, I had shed my sweatshirt. The muck helped me to pull off my boots. I waded in farther, still calling, both in my head and out loud.

I tried to get my stretchy bra over my breasts but by then it was soaked and uncooperative. For some reason, I'd pinned the enameled wolf to the strap. It poked my collarbone when I landed chest-down on a submerged rock and got dislodged as I scrambled to disentangle my arms from a thick mat of weeds.

I'm coming. Wait for me, Mama.

Please.

All those dreams where I followed my mother's feet flashed in front of my eyes. I couldn't see through the mud and the stalks of cattails, much less move.

I stopped talking to myself. Embraced the silence. Gave in to the growing cold of my muscles and the taste of rotting plant matter on my tongue.

You smell like the in-between.

Maybe this marsh was the in-between. I'd ask Wes the next time I saw him.

You smell like death.

Maybe this was.

"Does anyone know if she ate the apples?"

"Yes. Well, I never actually *saw* her eat the apples, but she was making apple jelly when I went to bed."

I nodded.

Of course, I ate the apples. Though my aunt had warned me, every year and with every batch, to never eat the apple jelly until after the sugar had been added and the jars had been filled and processed and left to sit on the shelves in the cellar for a full three months.

Then, I could have the jelly. As much as I wanted.

While Aunt Noémi was washing, cutting, and boiling the Old One's annual offering, every wooden spoon in the kitchen was off-limits.

I could wash jars and lids and sterilize them.

I could melt the wax to pour on top of the jelly once it had been ladled into the jars. But I could not taste the thick, sour pulp Auntie Noé carefully—religiously—poured into cloth sacks and set to dripping overnight.

But I had.

I'd snuck out of my bedroom and down the stairs and skimmed off enough unsweetened crabapple mash to fill a small glass. I'd snuck it back up to my room, savored each thick sip under the patched and repatched quilt. Then, I'd washed and dried the glass and returned it to its shelf in the kitchen cupboard.

"Of course I ate the apples."

Alabastair's face was inches from mine. He jerked back when I unstuck my eyelids and tried again to speak. The dried mud in my mouth made articulation next to impossible. Bas rolled me onto my side, stuck a finger into the side of my mouth, and forced a stream of water over my tongue.

I tried not to throw up, I really did.

"I'm glad you weren't wearing your nice shoes," I said, when my mouth was free of debris.

Chaos erupted. Harper and Thatcher. Alabastair, Maritza, Christoph, and Rowan. Belle's trill. Which meant Kaz was somewhere in the mix, along with Wes.

"What's all the fuss?"

"Mom, you were *dead*."

Oh.

"I was?" My big, beautiful sons hauled me to sitting and sandwiched me between their chests. "I'm sorry."

Christoph took my face in his hands and squeezed until my cheeks and lips and nose were smashed together. "Don't you ever, ever, *ever* do that again, Calli-lass."

"What did I do?"

Maritza peered around my grandfather's shoulder. "You ate a strain of apples related to the Apples of Immortality, you smart little witch, and managed to not die a complete death, thanks to your wolf being a very light sleeper."

Oh.

"Tell me," the needle witch said, "did you have to sneak the pulp when you were little or did your aunt give it to you?"

"I snuck it," I admitted, still wedged between my sons and Christoph. The three of them were quietly crying. I wasn't entirely clear on what all the fuss was about.

Maritza beamed at me, raised her gaze to the ceiling and crossed her hands over her chest, and laughed. Wolf howled and jumped up on the exam table.

"Where am I?"

"Belle's," Rowan said. "She was already set up to treat Benôit.

Another five minutes and we were going to call Jack to meet us at the hospital and fire up the Medivac helicopter."

Wolf nuzzled the back of my neck and jumped back down.

"Can I go home?"

"Calliope Viridis du Sang, no you may not," said Belle. "There's room enough for everyone right here." She harrumphed for good measure and muttered under her breath.

"Can I have something to drink? I'm so thirsty."

"That you may. Kazimir, the elixir?"

Harper and Thatcher stepped away enough to give Kaz room to deliver a shot glass filled with a whisky-colored liquid and a steaming mug of apple cider. I swallowed the elixir first. It went down like a handful of sand.

"Thank you," I whispered, bringing the rim of the mug to my mouth and blowing for good measure. The warm fluid, laced with spices whose names broke apart in the fog hovering at the periphery of my awareness, soothed the inside of my battered throat.

Belle and Rowan began to shoo everyone out of the room. I'd never seen so many worried gazes directed at me. I tried to absorb what I'd done, but it was too soon and I was too tired for much of it to make sense. "I'd like to go to sleep now."

I finished the cider and handed the mug to Rowan. She cradled it in her hand and spoke. "He wants to see you."

"Tanner?" I asked. I was ready to see him, too, and ask him to rub my back, spoon me into sleep, and promise to make sure there were no more night walks in my immediate future.

"Your father. Benôit. He's awake."

Tears flooded my eyes and poured down my cheeks. "I'm not ready," I said. "I'm not. I don't even understand what just happened."

"Belle added herbs to the elixir and to the cider that will help you get the sleep you need," she said. "And now that Benôit is here, you have all the time you need to figure out when you want to see him and what you want to say."

The healer released me into Tanner's care. I knew it was him. I knew his skin and I knew his scent and I knew the emotion radiating from the center of his chest.

BELLE SENT ME HOME ON SATURDAY. CHRISTOPH, HARPER, AND Thatcher treated me like I was breakable. I tried to tell them I was already broken, split in two widthwise in some weird way that Tanner said he understood.

Airlie understood, too. The following Monday, when my sons were at school and Sallie and Azura were helping Christoph install the outdoor shower in the bunkhouse, Airlie offered to come over and treat the sadness turning my muscles to sponge. Tanner showed her in to my bedroom, brushed my hair at my request, and let me know he'd be in the kitchen baking sourdough bread in case I needed anything.

Airlie laid her hands on my forehead and my belly and sang me the songs of water, the same ones she'd sung to Benôit. When she finished, tears soaked my pillow. "It is time for you to remember," she said. "Remember your mother, remember your first home in Maine. Swim in the Atlantic. Remember the waterways your mother and her sister swam in when they were girls, and their mother, too."

My chin trembled. All I could do was nod and agree. "I'm so torn," I said, unable to raise my voice above a ragged whisper.

"About the Melusine?" Airlie asked.

I couldn't answer. Before leaving to spend a week with Wes at his latest assignment, Rowan and I had time for one short conversation about the ova. She recommended I take possession of the stasis tank and do nothing other than make sure the tank's motor was never unplugged. For now. Until I was stronger in my body and surer of my commitment to the undertaking.

"Do you feel up to a walk?"

"Where to?"

Airlie slid her forearm under my shoulders. "Sit up," she said. "If you can manage that, put your feet on the floor and stand. After that, try walking to your bedroom door. I'll be right beside you."

I managed two trips from my bed to the door and back. "I can do more. Are we going outside?"

"Yes. Let's get some clothes on you."

I waved to Tanner as we passed the kitchen island. He helped get my feet into a new pair of Blundstone boots and my arms into his zip-up sweater. I pulled a toque over my head.

Airlie held my hand, led me across the street and onto the deer path my sons were widening. We walked in silence until we stood at the edge of the marsh.

"Here's where you walked in," Airlie said. "And over there is where your wolf hauled you out." She pointed to the left, still holding my hand. "This marsh almost took you, Calliope. These waters are in need of reclaiming. I believe you have it within you to make these waters yours."

A swirling sensation from the depths of my belly agreed.

"Come. There is one more thing I have to show you." Airlie tightened her grip on my hand and led me to the old house. The plywood had been removed and a new door put in. She slid her finger along her neck, lifted a silver chain, and showed me a hefty, enchanted key. "A trusted few of us were given copies. Yours is at your house, to use when you are ready."

Airlie inserted the key and pressed her palm to a keypad. Something clicked inside the door. She pushed it open, closed it behind us, and led me into the room with the aquariums. Efforts had been made to lessen the creepiness factor. "Lastly, your father wants a chance to redeem himself."

I wiggled my hand from Airlie's hold and stepped to the

closest tank. Pressing my palms and forehead to the glass, I tried to picture the tank filled with water.

"Benôit knows what the Melusine require, Calliope. He knows, and your aunt knew."

MEETING WITH NOÉMI'S CAPABLE AND PERFUNCTORY LAWYER WAS anticlimactic. She reviewed the terms of the will, I signed a mountain of paperwork, and we were done. Afterward, I joined my cousin Clyde for lunch at his favorite noodle place. He gave me possession of the battered piece of carry-on luggage parked by his side and informed me it was filled with everything he could find that pertained to his mother, my mother, and their side of the family.

"Some of it is journals," he said. "I didn't read those because, you know—I don't know, there's something weird about reading your mother's journals." He looked over at me. "But I'm fine with you reading them, Calli. And if she left any clues to the location of the family fortune, just make sure you split it with me and my sister, okay?"

I laughed and agreed, paid for lunch, and promised I would be in more regular touch.

Clyde walked me to my car. We hugged, he got into his sedan and waved, and he left. I strapped the suitcase into the passenger's seat and kept my hand on it the entire drive to the ferry terminal.

During the thirty-five-minute crossing from Swartz Bay to Fulford Harbor, I fiddled with the carry-on's heavy-duty zipper pulls. At one point I even unstrapped my inanimate companion and undid its zipper all the way. Lifting the suitcase's cover, I rested a hand on a stack of manila envelopes. No tingles, no pinpricks, punctures or bites. Just the smooth surface under my palm and the smell of old paper.

I found Aunt Noémi's journals underneath the envelopes and

official-looking papers. At first, I thought they were accounting ledgers. Pebbled black on the outside, pale-green paper on the inside, held closed by a loop of black elastic. I lifted the top ledger. The elastic would not budge.

I grinned, felt for the dagger I now carried everywhere with me, and pressed the tip to my finger. I offered the ledger a taste of my blood. The elastic released, allowing me to slip the loop off and open the book.

Every page was filled with my aunt's writing. Neat in some entries, scrawled in others. These were not records of financial transactions.

Noémi Virginie du Sang's grimoires were deceptively mundane on the outside and filled with knowledge on the inside. I closed the cover, slipped the loop back in place, and returned the ledger to the suitcase.

When I pulled onto Fortune's Folly Road, a big aluminum Airstream trailer was parked half on the road, half off, a few yards past my driveway. The driver's-side door opened, and a long leg clad in denim came out first, followed quickly by the other leg and the rest of a very handsome druid.

Tanner shut the door and jogged over to where I was parking my little electric car. I shouldered my purse and extended the suitcase's handle. I wasn't going to let the innocuous piece of luggage out of my sight.

"What's that?" I asked, accepting the warm hands cupping my face and Tanner's delicious, drawn-out kiss.

"*That* is the Blood Mobile," he said.

"The *what?*"

"I remembered you once telling me you had a thing for Airstream campers, and I saw this for sale over near Nanaimo. I went over last week and checked it out, and—"

"And you bought it and named it the *Blood Mobile?*" I looked up at him, the sunset turning his entire face and body golden. "And where do you think you're going to park it?"

"Well, that's where you come in."

"Go on." I pulled him toward the camper, suitcase in tow, unable to hide how eager I was to see the inside. "I'm listening."

"Your expanded empire needs an on-site caretaker. And I need a place to live." He opened the little door to the sleeping area, where flowers, champagne, and chocolate truffles waited by a very comfortable looking, fully decked out, queen-sized bed. "And—you and I need a love nest."

"A love nest? Hmm." I set my purse and the suitcase under the tiny table next to the kitchenette, kicked off my shoes, and crawled across the bed. I plumped one of the pillows and tucked it under my head.

Tanner stayed where he was, still bathed in the evening light now coming in through the space between the little curtains. "Yes, Calliope Viridis du Sang, a love nest."

I curled onto my side and patted the mattress. Tanner shook off his flip-flops and crawled to me. "You know the boys are going to want to hang out in here," I teased.

Tanner raised one eyebrow. "I can cloak the entire Airstream and soundproof it, too. No one's allowed in here but you—" he kissed me "—and me."

He kissed me again for good measure and stroked the side of my face. "You scared me, Calli. More than I've ever been before."

I nodded. "I scared myself. More than I've ever been scared before. I've been feeling so tired, so…strange. I'm sorry I didn't tell you."

Tanner moved his hand over my shoulder and breast and stopped at the curve of my hip. "Will you see Belle regularly? I know she's worried."

"Everyone's worried," I interjected, "and, yes, I'll see Belle and Rowan and whomever else I need to see until I'm—until I'm better." I tucked the pillow more firmly under my neck and traced the top of Tanner's nose and the outline of his upper lip. "I thought everything that was happening to me happened to all Magicals."

"Turns out, you're special," my eager druid said, pulling me toward him and sliding his hand between my shirt and my back. "Very, very, *very* special."

"Special enough to love?" I asked, snugging my knee between Tanner's thighs.

"Special enough to love for a very, very, *very* long time."

THE END

ABOUT THE AUTHOR

Author Coralie Moss likes to start her Urban Fantasy stories with witches and other Magicals, and plunk a surprise or five into their seemingly normal lives. She lives on Salt Spring Island in British Columbia—the site of much magical inspiration—with her husband and two rescue cats.

Join Coralie's mailing list for book news, giveaways, and the occasional homage to apples.

facebook.com/CoralieMossWrites
bookbub.com/authors/coralie-moss

ALL OF CORALIE'S BOOKS

Join Coralie's mailing list
for news & ongoing short stories (www.coraliemoss.com).

Many of Coralie's stories are also available in "closed door" editions (meaning there is no adult content).
Visit her website for more information.

The Goddessverse Fantasy series includes:

- **The Goddess & the Woodsman** (book 1)
- **Persephone Lost & Found** (book 2)
- **Demon Healer**, a paranormal romance novelette (book 3)
- **Medusa's Proxy**, a paranormal romance novelette (book 4)

The Shifters in the Underlands series includes:

- **Paper Dragon** (book 1)
- **Blood Dragon** (book 2)

- **Moon Dragon** (book 3)

The Sister Witches Urban Fantasy includes:

- **Once Blessed, Thrice Cursed** (book 1) Set in Northampton, Massachusetts, and introducing Clementine, Beryl, and Alderose Brodeur.
- **Demon Lines** (book 2) is the continuation of Clementine's story.
- **The Scarab Eater's Daughter** (book 3) gives us the sisters' continuing adventures from Alderose's point of view.
- **Beguiled, Bewitched, & Broken** (book 4) features the middle sister, Beryl.
- **The Sister Witches Urban Fantasy Series: Box Set 1** (includes book 1-4)
- **Witches Everbound** (book 5) completes the Sister Witches Urban Fantasy series.

The Calliope Jones series of novels includes:

- **Magic Remembered** (book 1)
- **Magic Reclaimed** (book 2)
- **Magic Redeemed** (book 3)
- **Magic Restrained, a novelette** (book 3.5)
- **The Magic Series Box Set #1**

Join Coralie's mailing list for news & ongoing short stories.